Gail Hulnick

Red Herrings Radio

Red Herrings Radio

Red Herrings Radio

by
Gail Hulnick

WINDWORD GROUP
PUBLISHING & MEDIA

Red Herrings Radio

Also by Gail Hulnick

Fiction:
MEDIA MYSTERIES
The Lion's Share of the Air Time
A Bird in the Sand
Sleeping Dogs Lie
Kangaroo Court
Monkey Me Monkey You

RESORTING
Resorting to Murder
Resorting to Larceny
Resorting to Fraud
Resorting to Short Stories
Resorting to Arson

Nonfiction:
RUMBLE STRIP
Rumble Strip Canada 150
Rumble Strip USA Off the Interstate
Rumble Strip Europe Could We Live Here?
Rumble Strip Benelux and a Boat
Rumble Strip International World Voices

YOU'RE ON!
100 Ways to Shine in the Media Spotlight
100 Ways to Win NaNoWriMo

Gail Hulnick

Gail Hulnick

To my friends from radio days

Red Herrings Radio

Gail Hulnick

Table of Contents

Chapter 1

September 7
1964

On some distant street, a siren screamed. One naked light bulb glowed just above the back entrance to the Toronto radio station, and Lillian kept her eyes on it as she darted toward it from the spot where she parked her Volkswagen Beetle. She unlocked the door, then slid inside as quickly as she could. At 4 in the morning, it was deep dark everywhere, especially in this parking lot. If there were any crazies around, she didn't want to see them. She just wanted to get inside. She pulled the door closed behind her and heard the metallic click as the bolt shot into place.

The hallway outside the studio was also spooky at this time of morning. Lillian was one of the first into the building every day. The lights were off almost everywhere until she turned them on. The exception was Master Control, the room where all the radio technical equipment came to the hub that sent the signals out across the city and beyond.

At the far end of the hall, she could see light filtering under the door from Master Control. Pulling the heavy door partway open, she heard a Beatles tune. Lillian called out, "Raymond? Good morning?"

There was no reply. Usually, Raymond (or whichever technician was on shift overnight) sat in a high-backed chair on wheels, facing a console covered in sliders, switches, faders, pots, dials, meters and all the other parts that work together to allow radio to somehow magically be made.

Tape spooled around the heads of a machine at the left end of the control panel. In these early morning hours at CUBR, things were a lot more laid back than they would be very soon, during the super-important morning drive slot. By 7 a.m., the station would be bustling with DJs, news reporters, the sports guy, the weather guy, and even a few of the managers.

But for now, it was as quiet as a graveyard. Raymond must be off taking a short break. Lillian took a few seconds to look around and just be there: she really loved this radio station and she loved her job. More than any other job she'd done so far—although there hadn't been many of them.

Raymond's break had to be a very short one since he was the person responsible for making sure they stayed on the air. Many things ran automatically, but there still had to be a person there to solve the problem if they suddenly went to dead air. Master Control was staffed twenty-four hours a day, seven days a week. The overnight shift ended at 6 a.m., when the *Dawn Patrol with Josh and Eddie* signed on, although sometimes Raymond stayed on a bit longer to cover, if the tech coming in at 6 was running late.

Lillian would be the one turning on the lights in the newsroom at 4 a.m. Just around the corner from Master and the studio where the morning DJs did their thing, the newsroom would be a hive of activity by 5 o'clock. Lillian's job as researcher was to pitch in wherever she was needed: an extra pair of hands in the editing booth, an extra dialing finger if someone needed a phone call made, sometimes a running pair of feet, if something had to be delivered to the studio in a hurry. The producer and the rest of the crew usually arrived by 5:30 and the half hour before the first newscast was often a mad scramble, (if anyone could be said to be scrambling so early in the morning, half asleep, with not nearly enough caffeine in their systems yet).

Lillian had been on this job for six months and she adored it. She had no intention of screwing it up by being late or too slow at getting the prep jobs done. She had been working at the radio station for all of half an hour that first day when she figured out that it was no different from any other place. Don't speak unless spoken to, better seen and not heard, better to stay silent and be thought silly, than to open your mouth and remove all doubt.

That last one came from her grandmother. She'd never had the nerve to challenge her and ask why the old woman assumed that whatever came out of her mouth would be judged to be less than intelligent. She was used to accepting the things she'd been taught without question.

Lillian also knew within the first half hour that this was a job she wanted to keep, so she'd kept her head down and agreed to every request as eagerly as she could. This 4 a.m. assignment was tough to live with, but she'd found ways to make it acceptable.

First things first: coffee. The pots and the mugs were on a table under the newsroom window. Lillian dropped her coat over the back of her chair, then went to the sink to fill up the coffeepot. While the water ran through the grounds, she watched the reports coming in over the Teletype machine. Nothing very interesting, just the usual clattering noise and scrolling paper. It would ring five bells if there was a bulletin, ten bells if there was a flash. Lillian had never been there when a news flash came in, but Raymond had told her that nine and a half months ago, when Kennedy was shot, the news wire machine erupted with fifteen bells—five for the bulletin and ten for the flash.

This morning, the copy was full of stories about the Beatles' first tour of North America. The Beatles. Lillian felt a smile lift her face just at the thought of their name. The melody and words of her favorite Beatles song ran through her mind. Paul, John, George, and Ringo had been to L.A., they'd been to New York, and they'd brought glamor to Canada, with their stop in Vancouver. Today, they'd be coming here to Toronto.

The entire city was vibrating.

"Good morning, Lill." It was Chuck, the morning newsman. He threw his coat toward his chair, then came over to the wire machine to watch the stories scroll by. He spotted the summary, pulled the paper toward himself and ripped it cleanly just below the last of the highlights. Rolling the paper around his hands, he grinned at Lillian, then carried the morning news off toward his desk. Some of it would be rewritten and some would be read just as it had been ripped off the wire. "Thanks for making the coffee."

"I'm just going to take some to Master and to the overnight jock," she said, lifting a mug. "Do you have anything you need me to do right away?"

Chuck shook his head. He was one of the old-timers and he could probably do the entire news run, report half a dozen stories, and run the board all on his own, while presenting the news in a dynamite deep baritone that was amazing, coming from such a short, slight, average-looking guy. Lillian hoped she was earning her keep around here, but sometimes she felt unnecessary.

When she got to the heavy Master Control door, she decided not to navigate her way in while holding two mugs of fresh coffee. She'd tried that once before and had drenched herself in a hot, dark roast from Colombia. At twenty-one, you'd think she'd know how to juggle a couple mugs of coffee, but neither waitressing nor juggling had shown up in her work history yet. The door to Studio M down the hall, where Gerry, the overnight guy, was playing Top 40 tunes, was a lot lighter to push; it was easy to use her hip to get in and wave her mugs in Gerry's direction.

There was not much to look at, she'd been surprised to see, when she first started working here six months ago. A small table, covered in a soft cloth meant to absorb sound, a serious-looking microphone, two chairs, one for the DJ and one for a news or a sports guy or a guest, and a wall dominated by a glass that looked through to the control room, where a producer or technician sat to do their jobs.

Lillian set Gerry's coffee down on a side table, backed out of the booth, and went down the hall to Master. With her free hand, she pulled open the heavy door. Still no sign of Raymond.

But what was that? On the floor?

She saw a heap of some kind, just to the left of the two chairs that sat in front of the board and just a few feet under the clock. It looked to Lillian as though it could be a woman's leg.

She felt sick to her stomach.

Moving slowly toward the object, she set the coffee down on the floor. Never, never, put it near the equipment, she remembered Chuck telling her. Staring as hard as she could, she tried to decide: was that a foot? Not that easy to see in the gloom of the control room. It was probably something she was imagining. What *was* she imagining? It looked as though it might be a foot in a boot.

Lillian tapped the light panel with the side of her hand. The room burst into the bright, 'it's daytime-let's get down to business' state it usually had at 4:15 every morning. There *was* a foot. In a boot. And there was a woman's body, lying there on the floor.

She thought she recognized that boot.

For what seemed like an hour, Lillian was frozen. Then she backed toward the door, pushing it partway open. She felt something rise in her throat and she swallowed, hard. Her next instinct was to scream.

The door opened the rest of the way.

"Lillian! What is it?" Raymond asked.

She tried to calm herself down, taking deep breaths. "There's someone in there. On the floor."

Raymond pushed past her, then she followed him back into the control room.

The young woman on the floor was face down. Long, black hair sprayed out over what looked like a peasant blouse, tucked into blue jeans belted with woven leather. She was wearing dark brown desert boots.

Lillian did know those boots.

"It's my friend Susan," she said to Raymond, grabbing the receiver from the telephone on the board and dialing zero.

Raymond seemed to be in a trance.

"I need an ambulance!" Lillian shouted into the phone.

The technician stared at the mixing board, fiddled with one of the pots, gazed at his own knuckles, and then reached up to run his hand through the sandy-colored hair he hadn't combed in hours and bring it to a halt behind his right ear, somewhere a couple of inches above his plaid shirt collar.

Lillian dropped to her knees. "Susan! Susan, what's wrong?"

Susan's eyes were closed and she didn't reply. Lillian tried to see whether she was breathing, but it was hard to tell. She picked up her friend's wrist and put her fingers against it, the way she'd seen it done on television. Was that a pulse? She wasn't sure.

"Raymond, what do we do?"

But there was no help from that direction. Raymond shook his head, then gripped the back of the control room chair.

What could this be? Had she fainted? Had a heart attack? But who did that, at age twenty-one? Lillian inched forward so that she could put her arms around Susan's shoulders. She did seem cold.

"Find a blanket, Raymond! No, wait—go meet the ambulance at the front door and show them where we are. No, go to the newsroom and get Chuck to meet the ambulance. Then, you go get the blanket!"

After taking one more look at Susan, lying there on the floor, Raymond skittered out through the door, leaving Lillian alone with her friend. She spoke to her a few times, but got no response. Dear God, what was happening? Was she sick? Passed out from something?

Or worse?

She had no idea how much time had passed when the door opened and two men rushed in, carrying medical equipment, with Chuck right behind them.

"Stand aside, miss, and let us do our job," one of them said, and Lillian reluctantly released Susan and stepped back to let them care for her.

The door opened again and a man in a navy blazer and tan slacks flashed something in his hand toward Chuck. Behind him, two police officers came in. Just past the door, each time it opened, Lillian could see the radio studio hallway filled with people in uniforms.

Lillian sat shivering and clutching a blanket that the ambulance driver had been kind enough to put over her shoulders. Raymond had not returned, but Chuck was still standing at her side.

"Excuse me, miss?" The man who spoke to her was the one not wearing the uniform. His manner telegraphed that he was in charge. "I'm Detective Sinclair. When you're ready, I have a few questions I want to ask you."

Lillian looked up at him. Could he *be* any taller? She made a move to stand up, to try to get a little closer to making eye contact with him, but her knees wobbled and she sat right back down.

"My partner, Detective Deborah Kincaid, was delayed in getting here, and I don't want to wait for her to arrive to find out what I need to know from you. Do you mind?"

Lillian shook her head.

"First question," he said. "Who found her?"

"I did," Lillian said.

"And you are?"

"Lillian Clarkson. I'm a researcher for the newsroom."

"Any idea who she was? Did she work here, too?"

Lillian looked around, wishing she had one of the coffees she'd made earlier. Or a cigarette. "No, she is a scientist."

"A scientist?"

"A computer scientist." Lillian took a deep breath. "She is Susan Taylor. She's a grad student at the University of Toronto." She stopped to swallow. "She's my friend, too. We moved here together from upstate New York and we used to be in a band together."

The detective started to ask another question, then seemed to get an understanding of how close Lillian was to going over the edge.

"Is she . . ." Lillian couldn't get the words out.

"Yes. She's gone."

Lillian had never seen a dead person before this. She gazed at Susan's form, trying to memorize it, then fought back a ridiculous urge to grab her by the arm and try to shake her awake. She watched the police officers move back and forth around the control room, measuring, taking photographs, making notes. The paramedics did what they had to, and then Susan was carefully lifted into a bag, a zipper pulled over her face. Lillian felt a loud moan come from somewhere deep inside herself, but when she looked around, it seemed that no one had heard anything. She stared at the bag and at her friend. She was not Susan anymore; she was not even a woman. She was just a body.

Lillian turned to Detective Sinclair. "What happened to her?"

"We don't know, at this point. We'll sort all that out, but I have a few more questions, if I may. Any idea why she might have been here, if she didn't work here?"

"She might have come here looking for me," Lillian said. "It's a weird time of day, I know, but she knows I work the early shift and she's been with me to the station before."

"At 4 a.m.?"

Lillian shook her head. "It seems unlikely, yeah. But ... maybe she had something on her mind. Maybe she wanted to see me right away—"

"She was here for an interview," Chuck said.

Lillian looked at him, blinking involuntarily. This was news to her.

"She came in about 3:30 with Josh," Chuck went on. "She was supposed to do an interview with Maggie MacRae for her show later on, about some special thing she's doing in the U.S."

"And Josh is?" Sinclair asked.

"Josh is the morning DJ," Lillian answered. "*The Dawn Patrol with Josh and Eddie*. Have you ever heard it?" Not waiting for the detective's reply, she went on. "Josh is an old friend of ours. From Albany. His younger brother, Des, was in the band with Susan and me, when we all first tried our luck in Toronto."

"Then she went into grad school?"

"We lasted about a year, then all of us wanted to do something else," Lillian said. "Susan went back to school, and I came to this radio station."

Chuck squeezed Lillian's shoulder. "Raymond set Susan up in Studio V, to listen to Josh's show and wait for Maggie to come in to do the interview. Josh was going to hang out with her there until it was time for him to go prep," Chuck said.

"Where is this Josh now?" Detective Sinclair asked.

"He's getting ready to go on the air," Lillian said. "He doesn't know about any of this."

"So, he would have been the last one to see her," Sinclair said, almost as if he were talking to himself. "I wonder why she left that studio and came in here?" He looked at Lillian and Chuck, but neither had anything to say. "Fine, I'll catch up with Mr. —?"

"Marshall," Lillian supplied.

"Mr. Josh Marshall, later," the detective said. "I'll probably have more questions for you both, too. Detective Santelli will take your phone numbers and addresses," he said, pointing to a small, dark-haired woman wearing a navy-blue blazer, grey pants, and a blouse buttoned up all the way to the top. Lillian nodded at her, but got no response.

"Detective Sinclair?" she said. "What caused it?"

"We don't know yet, Miss Clarkson. There's nothing obvious, as you can see. We'll know, from the coroner, soon enough."

***

Lillian wasn't sure what Josh would do as soon as he heard about what was going on. Putting herself in his shoes, she didn't think she would want to speak so much as a single syllable on air. She probably wouldn't be able to. But Josh was a pro with twenty years in the business and maybe he would insist on taking his usual chair.

As it turned out, he didn't have to show anybody how much professionalism he could muster just hours after having a friend die at the station. Oscar, the *Dawn Patrol* producer, took over when he arrived. "Find Eddie and tell him he'll be flying solo this morning," he said. "I'm sending Josh home."

Lillian bent her head over the papers on her desk and tried to avoid Oscar's notice. Didn't work.

"What about you?" he said. "Maybe you should go home, too? What does Chuck say? How are you feeling?"

"I don't want to be at my place all by myself," Lillian said. "I can work."

Oscar cocked his head to one side and stared into her eyes. "All right," he said, making up his mind. "Do the phone-around and get the morning traffic."

Lillian felt better here, in the busy newsroom, than she would have at home, but her mind was still numb, and she couldn't understand any of it. Why was Susan dead?

It was a busy morning, even though it was a statutory holiday Monday and many people had the day off work. The news run was dominated by items about the debate in Ottawa over the new flag and the Beatles' arrival in Toronto for a concert that night at Maple Leaf Gardens. Josh and Eddie had programmed Beatles music throughout the show.

About 8:15, Chuck raced past her desk, heading for the news booth, a sheaf of paper in his left hand, a cup of coffee and a cigarette in his right. "You okay?"

"I'm fine, Chuck, thanks. Just a little sad, with all the Beatles music," Lillian said. "Susan and I were going to go, tonight."

"No way. I'm sorry."

Neither one spoke for a few seconds. "Will you go anyway?"

"I don't know. Some shows go on and some don't."

The Dawn Patrol certainly did, and those listening at home would have no idea anything had changed.

At 9 o'clock when the show was over, Eddie wandered into the newsroom. "Didn't feel right, doing it without Josh," he said. "Like talking to myself all morning. Or to a wall. How is he? Is he okay?"

"Yeah, he went home, said he'd be fine," Chuck said. "I'll check on him in a couple of hours."

"Anybody know why Susan Taylor was in the station this morning, anyway?"

"She was scheduled to tape an interview. Couldn't do it live, after nine, because she had classes at the university."

"Something about the Beatles' show tonight?"

"Why about the Beatles?" Chuck asked.

"Because everything today seems to be about the Beatles," Eddie said. "And she's about the right age."

"No, something about the work she does with computers."

"Anybody get any details about what happened to her?"

Chuck shook his head. "Cops aren't saying a word. Raymond, the tech, he said she looked peaceful. Not messed up at all. He's gone home, by the way."

"Same as Josh." Eddie helped himself to another cup of coffee from the office pot. "I guess Josh has known her for a long time."

"He helped her get started when she first moved here," Chuck said. "She was a high-school friend of his younger brother, Des. Was in a band with him—a bunch of you were, weren't you, Lill? You and Susan and Des? And Susan's boyfriend?"

Lillian wished she were invisible; she really didn't feel like talking to them. But now that they'd brought her into the conversation, she couldn't be rude. "We were all in a band. Mountain Sky."

Chuck and Eddie both looked down into the depths of their coffee mugs. "Has anybody called her family?" Eddie asked.

"Somebody should, I guess," Chuck said.

"Does she have anybody here in the city, Lillian?"

She shook her head. "Her mother and father still live near Albany. Her brother, Norman, was here for a while, but I heard he moved back." She pulled a copy of *The New York Times* across the desk toward her. She wanted just to lose herself in some other subject, somewhere else.

"The police will probably contact the family," Chuck said. "I don't know if they'd know about the boyfriend, though."

"Ex-boyfriend," Lillian said, with such emphasis that both Eddie and Chuck shot a sharp look at her.

The daytime show, *Mornings with Maggie MacRae*, was about to start. Lillian tuned her desk top radio to their competition, *Toast and Jamboree*, and got ready to make notes. Maggie always wanted to know, at the end of her show, what the competition did.

Lillian looked over the news lineup and the stories the reporters would chase for the rest of the day. She also had a copy of Maggie's show lineup. There was Doctor Arnold who was in regularly on Mondays: his topic today was another discussion of the U.S. Surgeon General's finding, last winter, that smoking caused lung cancer. Maggie also had a panel of Beatles fans, a psychologist on suicide statistics, and a gardener on fall flowers.

As Lillian made her way home after her nine-hour shift, she couldn't shake the feeling that the morning had been a dream. A nightmare. That it was all untrue. It just wasn't real. Her memory of the way Susan had looked was as vivid as anything she'd ever seen and she couldn't recall seeing any reason, on Susan's body, for her to die.

Lillian had taken a good look, even though she felt a little embarrassed about her curiosity. But that's the way journalists are made, right? They're curious and they take a look. There was no blood anywhere on or around Susan, no sign of a struggle or a beating. No wound of any kind, on her head, say, as if she'd fallen over and hit it on a desk or something. No sign of bruises or anybody hitting her.

Lillian thought about all the people listening to the radio, in their cars or at home, at the same hour when this was happening. Or many somebodies. In their cars on the QEW, commuting to work downtown from the new suburbs of Mississauga to the west and Scarborough to the east. Standing in bus shelters, listening to a transistor radio, pressed up against their ears while they stood, waiting for the streetcar. Making breakfast in kitchens, listening to a counter-top radio, beside the toaster, under the covers in kids' bedrooms or in the teenagers' bedrooms where it was late-night FM stations, coming in over the quiet waves from Detroit and Buffalo.

Once she had dreamed of hearing her own voice on those airwaves. She and Susan and Des were together every day after school, practicing their harmonies and their instruments. They'd played a few coffeehouses around Albany and when a local music teacher told them they should go to the city, take their shot, they decided to do a test run in Toronto first. The clubs in Yorkville had a reputation as a launching pad for young performers, and Toronto was said to be a lot safer than New York. Her parents and Susan's parents would give approval for a stay in Toronto, and that clinched it.

Lillian and Susan were part of a tight gang of friends that all left Albany about the same time. Penny had an uncle who worked in public radio in Toronto and offered to get her a job. Joyce, the brain of their crowd, was going to university right away, and going to get through it as fast as she could. True to her plan, she'd picked up her B.A. in record time.

Glenda couldn't stand the idea of being left behind, living in her parents' basement, so she moved to Toronto, too, and in six months had a good job working in a doctor's office.

Lillian walked along Queen Street, trying to bend her mind around the idea that Susan would never see this view, this corner, again. Lillian felt the exhaustion that strong emotion brought with it, like dark clouds with an electrical storm.

When she got home, letting herself into her small apartment at the back of an old house with a key that looked like something out of an ancient movie, her phone was ringing.

It was Detective Sinclair. He got right to his point. "Did you ever see Susan do drugs?"

Lillian was shocked. "No! What do you mean? Why do you ask?"

"When we finished our search of your master control room, something turned up. Something unexpected."

Lillian waited. Sometimes silence is absolutely the best response.

"It was a syringe. You know, a hypodermic needle? Is there any reason that Susan might have one of those? Was she diabetic, for example?"

"Not that I know of." Lillian had a sense that Susan's reputation was in her hands and she had to make sure she didn't drop it in the mud. "What makes you think it was hers? Somebody else might have dropped it in there. It's a high-traffic area."

"I know that," Sinclair said. "We're talking to everyone who was in there any time over the past two days. But we figure the cleaners or the overnight technician would have seen it earlier if it hadn't come from Susan." Sinclair cleared his throat. "Miss Clarkson, how well did you really know Susan Taylor?"

Chapter 2

After Sinclair rang off, Lillian stared at her telephone for quite a while, then got up and went into the kitchen to make tea. She knew she had phone calls to make, people to inform about Susan's passing, but she wanted to put it off for as long as possible. She wasn't sure she'd be able to hold it together long enough to finish a call.

She made her tea, then opened the refrigerator and looked at the limited selection. She'd been up since three and usually at this time in the afternoon she was putting together the main meal of her day. Almost anything edible looked like a Parisian delicacy to her, and she was usually ravenous by now.

Not today.

The phone rang in the other room.

"Hi, Lill. Do you know where Susan is? I've been calling her for the last hour," Penny said.

"Are you sitting down, Penn?" Lillian sat down herself. "I've got some bad news."

"What is it?" Penny's voice instantly lost its lilt.

Lillian felt she had to back into it. "This morning I went to work at 4, just like normal—"

"Yeah, I wondered if you were doing that," Penny interrupted. "I thought you might decide to take the day off, since you have Beatles tickets for tonight. I think Susan mentioned she was going to skip a couple of classes to get ready."

"Well, you and I both know that skipping classes isn't quite the same as ditching work," Lillian said. "And going to class isn't quite the same as working."

"True," Penny said. "Anyway, did you at least leave a bit early? Are you ready to go? What are you wearing?"

"I'm not going, Penny. We're not going." Lillian cleared her throat. "Susan and I are not going to see the Beatles."

There was a long silence while Penny took this in. "But why, Lill? Did you have a fight?"

"No, we didn't have a fight," Lillian said. The ache had climbed from her chest up to her head. Her entire mouth and face felt as if they were ripped apart. "Susan died this morning, Penn."

From the silence, it was obvious that Penny was in shock. It wasn't often there was a noticeable break in her conversation like this one. When she spoke again, she whispered. "She died?"

"At the station. Nobody knows exactly when or what caused it, but I found her. On the floor. In a radio studio."

"You found her?"

Lillian was nodding, even though she knew she couldn't be seen.

"That must have been absolutely awful for you," Penny said. "Should I come over?"

"Oh, Penny, that's really sweet, but it's a long way. You were just here last night. We all were—" Including Susan. Lillian felt herself getting choked up again.

"Never mind all that. I'll be right there." And there was a click on the line.

Lillian replaced the phone on its cradle, then picked it up again and listened for the dial tone. As soon as she heard a few seconds of it, she started in on Joyce's number, putting her pointer finger into the holes from memory.

"Hello?"

She could hear the hum of Joyce's Ottawa government office in the background. Phones ringing, people talking. She wasn't quite sure what it was that Joyce did all day, but Joyce had had that job since she'd graduated from university a year and a half ago, and she told them over and over again that she loved it. "Joyce, it's Lill."

"Hi! What's happening?"

"I'm calling with some bad news."

"Alright." The bounce disappeared from Joyce's voice immediately.

Lillian swallowed the hockey-puck sized lump in her throat. "It's Susan."

"What about Susan?"

"She's . . . she's passed away."

"What do you mean, she's passed away?"

Lillian couldn't answer.

Joyce repeated the question. "What do you mean, she's passed away? Do you mean she died?"

Lillian nodded, then realized she couldn't be seen. "Yes." The syllable came out like the bleat of a lamb.

"I'll catch the train."

"Oh, Joyce. That's a long way for you to go. That's five hours, again for you, and you just did it, getting home yesterday."

"Never mind that. I'm on my way."

"No, really, it's too far. You wouldn't be here until late and I have to go to work at 4. Penny and Glenda are coming over. We'll get you and Rhonda on the phone."

"Alright, Lill, you're right. But you know I'm here for you."

"I know."

Two down, and two to go. Lillian dialed Glenda's number. She didn't think she'd find Glenda at home, but she wasn't sure what her schedule was at the doctor's office. After letting it ring a dozen times, she disconnected and tried the work number. Glenda's boss wasn't pleased about calling her over to the phone, but Lillian couldn't help that. Now that she had this underway, she wouldn't stop making her calls and letting Susan's friends know until everyone had been called.

"Glenda? Sorry to bother you at work but I have some important news to tell you. I've called Penny and Joyce . . . it's about Susan."

"What about Susan? Yeah, Marcia, I'll be right there," she said to her coworker. "There's one patient in number four but we still have to find the chart." Glenda was waiting. "What about Susan?"

"She's . . . gone," Lillian said.

"Gone where? Yeah, ask Dina to put Mrs. Williams into number seven."

"Glenda, she's dead."

"What? Are you serious?"

"I am. She died this morning."

The silence went on so long that Lillian thought perhaps Glenda had walked away from the phone.

"But she was just here! Last night! We were all together, at your place!"

"I know."

"I'm going to ask if I can leave. Can I come over?"

"Yes, of course," Lillian said.

The last call, to Rhonda, was long-distance. Usually, when Lillian phoned her family long-distance, she waited until Sunday night when the rates were much cheaper. Daytime calls were limited to important news.

This certainly qualified.

"Rhonda, I'm calling to tell you some bad news." She had no idea how her friend would take this, but Rhonda had a big group of friends in New York, and if she was upset, she would have somewhere to go and someone to talk to.

"Shoot."

"Susan died this morning."

And that was four out of four, she thought. Every one of us absolutely speechless after hearing this news.

"You're kidding."

Lillian could tell that Rhonda didn't mean that literally, and she refrained from answering.

"When did it happen? What was it? How are you? Are you okay? You have to tell me more," Rhonda said.

"I will, but later. Right now, I'm just too upset," Lillian said.

"Yes, I understand. Are you alone? Is somebody coming over?"

"Yeah, Penny and Glenda."

"Did you talk to Joyce?"

"I did. Let's all get on the phone tonight."

"I'd be with you, if I could. You know that," Rhonda said.

"Thank you, yes, of course, I do know that."

"Phone me when you're all together. Maybe we can all get on the line. Do you have an extension?"

"No, but we'll figure it out." Lillian could hear Rhonda starting to cry. It would be hard for her. She had known Susan since they were five years old.

After she hung up and thought about her next, and last, phone call, Lillian knew the news wouldn't hit hardest for Rhonda. It would be devastating for Susan's mother.

The police had already called to inform her, Lillian was sure, and she had Susan's dad and her own friends to support her, but Lillian still thought she'd appreciate hearing from one of Susan's friends.

"Mrs. Taylor? This is Lillian Clarkson."

"Lillian."

It was as if Mrs. Taylor wasn't sure who she was and yet knew her, deep down and for all time.

"I'm so sorry about Susan," Lillian said.

"Thank you, Lillian. Thank you for calling."

There was a silence, and neither of them seemed to know what to say next. They didn't know what to say, and yet Lillian felt that they each knew the other's feelings. Words and conversation weren't necessary.

"I will call you whenever I hear anything more," Lillian said.

"And if you need to talk to me about her," Mrs. Taylor added.

"And please call me, if you want to talk. Or for any reason."

"Thank you, dear," Mrs. Taylor said. "Her father and I are leaving for Toronto this afternoon. The police called and said they want to see us. And we'll have to do something about her apartment, I guess—"

Lillian heard Mrs. Taylor break down into heaving, gulping sobs. The phone handset clattered to a desk or a counter and then Mr. Taylor came on the line.

"We have to go now, Lill," he said.

"Of course, Mr. Taylor," she said.

The death of a friend or a loved one, any friend, is hard; but Lillian couldn't even begin to imagine how it felt to have a child die. It was against the natural order of things. Grown children are supposed to help their elderly parents off to the next world and then mourn; parents were not supposed to remain behind while their children died.

Lillian gave in to the next storm of tears. It was the eighth . . . no, the ninth? She'd lost count.

***

That night, three of the five girlfriends got together, squeezed into Lillian's tiny apartment. They cried together and swapped memories. Rhonda phoned in from New York, then Joyce from Ottawa.

"We should think about who else should know," Joyce said.

"Good idea," Glenda said. "Do you have her address book?" she asked Lillian.

Lillian shook her head. "The police took her purse, I think. I didn't see it anywhere afterward. That's where she kept her address book."

Penny took a sip of her tea, then pulled a notepad and pen out of her own purse. "Let's make a list, then. Des, Joe her landlord, her boss at the university . . . you know, that prof she TAs for."

"I think Josh will tell Des," Lillian said.

"What about Corey?" Penny asked.

Lillian made a face. "Yeah, I guess somebody should tell him. Even though she broke it off. I don't think they've seen each other for a few weeks now."

"Why the face?"

"I'm not his biggest fan," Lillian said.

"Me neither," Penny said.

"He definitely was a jerk," Glenda said. "But I agree we should let him know," Glenda added. "Does anybody have his phone number?"

"Susan told me a week or two ago his phone was cut off," Lillian said. "He's between jobs, apparently." She poured herself another cup. "I'll go over to his place. I've been there before."

"Oh, Lillian, could you?" Penny said.

"Yeah. I'm going to work a short day tomorrow anyway, just be there for the show. I'll go by Corey's place on my way home."

Having their company felt better than being alone, but when they left, the sadness hit again. The ache in Lillian's throat intensified and her head started to throb. Each time she thought of Susan lying there on the studio floor, she tried to force herself to accept the fact that she was gone. But now, it just seemed like it had all happened in a dream.

She watched the hands of the clock tick past 1 a.m., 2 a.m., then 3. At 7, she dragged herself off the couch where she'd fallen asleep after they all left. She was scheduled for the late shift today and it was time to get up and go to work.

Even though she felt as if she'd been hit by a truck.

Chapter 3

September 8
1964

The Queen Street car clattered on its way into view and Lillian got ready to hop on board. She needed to get to work, but she'd told the others that she would take the news to Corey Lang and it wouldn't take long to stop in.

She remembered the last time she'd seen him. She, Susan, and Des had gone to the Colonial Tavern to hear some live music. The lights were low and the cigarette smoke hung in a haze that added to what some thought of as a cozy feeling and others thought of as decadent. They sat at a tiny table that was only half a dozen feet away from a stage raised about eight inches from the floor.

Des had to duck to avoid one of the hanging lamps as they sat down. Susan was so excited she could barely stop jiggling in her seat. Lillian reached over and fondly tucked her hair behind her ear. She was almost as happy to be here as Susan was, although music wasn't as important to her life these days. Radio had moved in to claim a big part of it now.

When she, Susan, and Des left Albany two years ago, they all had stars in their eyes. Their band, Mountain Sky, was going to make it big. That was the plan. Lillian and Des quickly ran out of dough and had to look for other jobs. Susan had enough backing from her parents at home to budget for a year of chasing her dream full time, as long as she toed the family line by enrolling at the university full time, too. Science was her subject—an unusual combination with the folk singing, but Susan was full of contradictions. Always had been.

She blended the two passions, folk singing and computers, elegantly and inevitably. She aced every course she took and didn't surprise anyone when she announced she would receive her undergrad degree in record time. This past summer, she had applied and was accepted for graduate work and Lillian expected that the guitar would spend more time propped up in the corner of her room, once the school year kicked off this month.

Des found work delivering internal mail at one of the downtown banks. His older brother, Josh, who was a big noise at the third most-listened-to private radio station in Toronto, opened up a place for Lillian in the newsroom.

But at first, they still rehearsed together and did gigs whenever they could, which wasn't often. When she wasn't in class or in the library, Susan practiced for hours a day, in the good weather, sitting out on the front porch of the old house where she was renting a room in Cabbagetown, and sitting cross-legged with her guitar on her bed, in the bad. One day, Corey showed up, knocking on her door and explaining that he'd heard the music and had to follow it to the source. He worked as a bellhop at the Royal York Hotel and played a little piano himself. He was looking for a band to join, and somehow, he shoehorned himself into theirs.

At first, he'd treated Susan well, and it hadn't taken long for her to develop a crush on him. But as soon as she showed her interest, he changed. He began to talk to Susan as if she were some sort of pest, hanging around. He tolerated her and let everybody know that's all it was. Eventually, Susan got it, too, and broke it off.

That's when he decided he did want her, after all. He didn't know he'd miss her till she went, he said. He chased her for a few weeks, but once Susan made up her mind, it was made up. She told him, again and again, that she didn't want him around anymore.

Lillian hoped he'd got the message.

After the first few jazz sets that evening, a tall, thin folk singer took over the stage just before ten. By the third verse of the first song, Lillian knew she was going to enjoy the show, despite feeling annoyed about the news that Corey might show up. Phil was a talented singer, his guitar playing was top-notch and his material was relevant. Not moon/June/spoon love-song stuff. Protest songs, songs about racism, war, changing the world.

She'd just settled in for a great show when the mellow vibe was ruined by Corey's arrival. He made a lot of noise coming in, although it wasn't hard to drown out an acoustic guitar and a folk singer. He bumped into a couple of people in chairs on the way in, muttered a "Sorry, sorry man" to a few people, and cursed once or twice before he finally arrived at the chair beside Susan.

He looked a mess. His hair was getting shaggy, his striped shirt had stains down the front and he was wearing some kind of weird, crocheted thing as a belt. He didn't listen to the music for long before he started whispering in Susan's ear, putting an arm around the back of her chair and a hand on her knee. She smiled politely for a while, then exploded.

"Corey! Stop it! Listen to the music!"

Corey glanced at the stage, then pulled his chair around so that he faced Susan and had his back to the singer. "I don't want to, he's crap. Come on, baby, let's get out of here."

Susan folded her arms and shook her head.

Des decided to step in. "Come on, man, give it a rest. She'll talk to you after the show."

Corey wasn't having it. "She'll talk to me when I say, man, not when you say. Come on, Susan, don't be such a little bitch."

The word was gunpowder. "Corey!" Susan snapped. "Shut up or get out of here."

Corey swayed in his chair. Lillian was sure that if there were any light in this room, they'd be able to see that his pupils were dilated to about the size of dinner plates.

"Come on, baby, let's go."

Susan stood up. "No! If you won't leave, then I'm going. I'm sorry," she said to the singer on stage who had stopped mid-song when the confrontation grew impossible to ignore. "I'm sorry I interrupted your set."

Corey gripped the arms of his chair and tried, unsuccessfully, to rise. Wow, he was really wasted.

"No, don't get up!" Susan hissed at him. "If you follow me, I'll make you regret it."

She wove her way between the tables, every eye in the place on her. When Lillian described the scene later to their friend, Penny, they both agreed that it was the sort of thing that would make most people shrivel up with embarrassment.

But Susan wasn't like everybody else.

Lillian knew that even if Susan didn't want Corey to follow her, she wouldn't want to be alone. After the singer got back on track, Des busied himself with finishing the beer and Corey put his head down on his folded arms on the table. Lillian slipped out of her seat.

She found Susan in the ladies' room, smoking a cigarette by the open window. Her mascara was smudged and her face looked like she'd had the flu for two weeks.

"You have to cut him loose." Lillian leaned up against the sink.

"I thought I had. I wrote him a letter."

"Don't cry, Sue, he's not worth it," Lillian said. "You just have to be firm with him."

"You're right. I just hate confrontation."

"But you've told him. The hard part's over," Lillian said.

"I've been worried about how he'd react. He's been quite volatile over this past month," Susan said, her hand shaking as she lit her next cigarette.

"Is he on drugs, do you think?"

"Might be."

"Do you think you could get him to stop?"

"I've talked to him. It's no use. He won't listen."

That night was the last time Lillian saw Corey with Susan. And now she was gone.

Lillian hadn't thought she'd ever want to speak to Corey again, but here she was, walking up the broken pieces of sidewalk that led to his front door. She had to take two streetcar rides to get to his place on Bathurst Street. It was a glorious September morning, and the blue skies and sunshine combined to make her forget Susan's death—for a moment or two, not much more.

She wasn't really sure what to say to Susan's ex-boyfriend, but she knew she had to see him, to find out whether he was as shaken by the news of Susan's death as she was. If she got the chance, she was going to confront him about the drug use, too.

The old house he shared with three other guys was sagging in the middle. A few tarpaper shingles had come loose and a drainpipe at the corner had come apart. The green paint job on the siding was about forty years old and the sidewalk to the front porch was cracked and broken.

Lillian wasn't inclined to hold the decrepit state of the house against Corey; he and his friends were just renters, after all. But the state of the inside? That was completely up to him. As he led her into the living room, she caught sight of a kitchen with a sink piled high with dirty dishes. The couch and chairs had clothes thrown all over them, the coffee table was covered with pizza boxes and every other flat surface was covered with empty beer cans and bottles.

Corey left her to figure out her own seating, watching silently until she finally pulled a jacket from a chair and sat down. Neither one spoke for a few minutes, then Corey asked, "Why are you here?"

"There's been some bad news about Susan."

"I know," he said. "The cops came over to tell me. Wanted details about when we met, how long we'd been dating, stuff like that." He took a long swallow of his beer.

Really? At 8 o'clock in the morning?

Lillian felt anger rising in her like crashing chords at the end of a Russian concerto. "Aren't you shocked?"

"Not really," Corey said, in a slow drawl that made her just want to bash his face in. "This is the big city, right? I mean, I know it's not New York, but bad stuff happens here, too. Why would you think nothing bad would ever happen to your friend? Or to you?"

"You think something bad happened to her?"

"What else?"

"Maybe she just died," Lillian said. "I haven't heard anything about what caused it, have you?"

Corey shrugged, then finished the beer. "Nothing official. But it's the first thing you think of, isn't it? Although . . . how do we know she didn't do it to herself?"

Lillian's eyes widened, and she felt her stomach turn. Was it possible that Susan, somebody she thought she knew as well as anybody knew anybody, carried around some thoughts and secrets that would make her want to end her life?

No way.

"Anyway, maybe you're right," he said. "Maybe she had a heart attack or a brain tumor or something. It means nothing to me. Susan and I were done, you know that. I moved on, she moved on. I told the detective he'll have to look somewhere else for his answers and I'm telling you, too." Corey walked to the front door and opened it. "So long, Lill."

***

Lillian had a million questions and even though she was burning to get home and stay there for a while, when the phone rang with the request that she come down to the police station for a meeting with Detective Sinclair, she didn't hesitate to say yes. It only took a few minutes for her to get through the formalities at the reception desk. Sinclair ushered her into a small room and closed the door.

"Miss Clarkson, once again, let me say how sorry I am about your friend's death."

Lillian shook her head. "I still can't quite believe it. I go to call her and then I remember that she's gone. What have you been able to find out? Was it some condition that she had? Her heart or brain or something? Something that no one had known about? Or maybe something that she kept a secret from all of us?"

Sinclair made direct eye contact, his gaze kindly and sympathetic. "I'm sorry to have to tell you about this. We've talked to Mr. and Mrs. Taylor and we'll be issuing a press release later today. Your friend's death is now being classified as 'suspicious.'"

Lillian stood up. "What do you mean, 'suspicious'? Do you know the cause of death now?"

Sinclair nodded. "We found needle marks on her arm and drugs in her system. We assumed that meant an accidental overdose. But the coroner's report is in now, and there's something else."

Lillian was aware that he was watching her eyes. She wanted to cry, but she forced herself to stay cold. "What is it?"

Sinclair shook his head. "I have a few questions first. Tell me about Corey Lang and his relationship with Susan Taylor."

"He was her boyfriend."

"For how long?"

"About a year."

"What does he do?"

"He used to work at the Royal York, handling luggage. He hasn't had a job lately, but I heard somebody saw him working in a kitchen at a restaurant."

Sinclair had his pen out and was making notes. "Which restaurant?"

"The High Park Diner on Bloor Street."

"You said 'was' her boyfriend. Was, because she's gone now, or—"

"Was, because they broke up. A few months ago. He became very weird, hung out with some strange people. And she didn't like how possessive he was."

"Possessive? In what way?"

"He was jealous of the time she spent in the library and of the time she spent on her music. He was jealous of Mountain Sky, too."

"Mountain Sky?"

"That was our band. He was in it for a while, too. We officially closed it down about six months ago, but a few of us still get together once in a while to jam. Corey didn't like that, and he didn't like that Susan still spent time practicing her guitar. So, they had a big fight and then they broke up."

This was strange. Hadn't Sinclair already been over to talk with Corey? Hadn't he been told that they'd broken up—in Corey's words, they'd "moved on?" Why was Sinclair asking her these questions?

The detective stood up and walked around the desk to face her. "Miss Clarkson, Mr. Lang would not answer our questions at this point, and I appreciate your responding so easily. I know this will be hard for you to hear, but . . . Susan didn't die of natural causes. It was a lethal dose of street heroin."

He crossed his arms and waited. Waited for what? It was as if he thought Lillian would have something to say.

She was reeling. Heroin was something she'd heard about; the news magazines were beginning to discover it and she'd seen a few articles about it in the newspaper, too. But it wasn't part of her life or anybody's she knew. Crazy, wild people smoked marijuana and one or two very strange people dropped acid. Heroin was for the lost, unfathomable creatures at the very edges of the world. What on earth would it have to do with Susan Taylor?

Ever since the meeting with Detective Sinclair ended, Lillian had had a shrill, ringing sound in her ears. She didn't remember getting home, or curling up in her favorite angora blanket. She'd been in some kind of weird state ever since the cop told her about Susan and the drugs.

Through her window to the willow tree outside, Lillian could see that the end of summer was coming soon, even though it was only the eighth of September. No one waited until the twenty-third to say "Summer's over" up here; there was often snow on the ground by then. The tree branches had already lost most of their leaves and the entire street had a dead, shriveled look.

Just like her heart, whenever she thought of Susan.

The rest of the day passed like the last seconds of the minutes before dismissal time on the last day of school before vacation. Lillian felt as if she were under water. Heavy, thick water. Quicksand. Trying to move a foot forward and mired in mud.

Somehow, though, Lillian knew that the worst thing she could do was curl up in the fetal position, alone in her apartment, as appealing as the thought of that kind of with-drawal might be. She had to distract herself with work.

Chapter 4

September 9
1964

Fortunately, the morning news run on Dawn Patrol the next day was at the busy end of the scale. She arrived at work to find Chuck already there, with a stack of wire copy at his elbow and muttering about the ridiculous time limit on his newscast. It would be a big news week: it was back-to-school time, and in the U.S., students were returning for the first time since the Civil Rights Act had passed in early July.

"It's the biggest piece of legislation in decades. Maybe ever!" Chuck paced around the newsroom. "Desegregation. President Kennedy's legacy. It's the lead again today. And I need three more minutes on the 7:30 cast."

"What about the flag debate, though?" Josh loved the chance to debate the lineup with Chuck. Lillian was never sure whether he disagreed as often as he let on, or just liked to ruffle Chuck's feathers.

"Second item!" Chuck pounced on Lillian. "Lill! I've got two clips from CBS ready to go and Josh has an interview with a school principal from Virginia at 7:15, but we could use some Toronto actuality. Can you find me a prof who studies race relations? Or maybe somebody here who is a product of the American school system?"

"I'm on it," Lillian said, grabbing two phone books and heading into the recording booth.

She put the headphones over her ears and started calling around.

The newscast always had to find the Toronto, or at least the Canadian angle, on these American stories, and some days, that could be hard to do. For a talk show like Maggie MacRae's, it was easier to fill the air time: regular feature guests could be focused on any number of subjects.

The Legal Beagle, Glenn Lewis, was coming in today and he was ready to talk about the U.S. Civil Rights Act. They also had "Book Time", with an excerpt from *To Kill a Mockingbird*. But it wasn't all politics: Gilbert the Gardener would be coming in Thursday to talk about planting bulbs, the "Weekend Guide" was on Friday, and Dr. Arnold was a regular on Mondays with medical advice. Each item was a five or ten-minute change-of-pace from the pop songs and the chat from Maggie.

Each of these people was what was known as a "good guest"— able to translate complicated stuff into plain English, always on time, even early for their spots. Each of them except Dr. Arnold— he was a bit of a handful. He was a lot of a handful, actually, always tense and anxious about going on air, always demanding feedback on how his interview had gone and then pouting (or worse) when the comments weren't a rave review. When he came in to the station, he somehow managed to upset just about every person whose path he crossed.

Lillian vaguely recalled Dr. Arnold passing in the hallway Monday morning. She wondered if he knew about Susan. But how could he have missed seeing all the police cars and the ambulance? She was pretty sure that everyone in the station knew that a young woman had died.

Smoking was Dr. Arnold's topic that day, she recalled. It was a two-parter, with the first segment, last week, exploring the report of the Surgeon General of the United States, declaring that smoking causes cancer, and the second part, looking at the reception since its release last January.

It had been a few years since Lillian quit, but she'd had moments since Monday when she could have used a butt or two.

She worked her way through three professors' names from the U of T political science department, called their numbers, and got no answer. It wasn't often easy to get people on the line at 5:45 in the morning. She was about to give up and tell Chuck no dice on the local angle for the school desegregation story when she decided to try a fourth number. She heard someone pick up and a man's voice say, "Hello?"

"Thank you for taking my call! This is Lillian Clarkson from CUBR news and we're wondering if we could ask you a few questions about the U.S. Civil Rights Act."

He agreed, and she raced through an interview, getting the twenty seconds of tape they needed to put in the middle of the clip-and-script. She wrote the copy for Chuck, printed it out, wrapped the page around a tape cart, and brought it over to his desk.

"Good work, Lill!" He barely looked up from the stack of papers and tapes surrounding him. His hubcap-sized glass ashtray was almost heaping with cigarette butts and he had one going, holding it between two stained yellow fingers while he used his thumb to sweep through a newspaper. She'd been told that Chuck read eight newspapers a day, and she could believe it.

"Take a break, kid," he said. "I'm good for the 7:30 and the 8:00, but I'll need you to chase something for 8:30."

Lillian went off to the farthest desk in the farthest corner of the newsroom and sat down with the muffin and soda she'd brought in a bag from home. She didn't actually have a desk of her own in this newsroom yet, but since most of the reporters or producers would arrive for work for another hour or so, she had her choice of where she wanted to sit.

She popped open the can for her drink, then picked up the phone and dialed Penny's number.

"Hey, wake up, Penn," she said.

"I'm awake," she said. "Just watching the news on TV."

"Traitor. We have better stuff."

"I know you do, and I have the radio on, too. I heard the overnight guy, and Josh and Eddie sign on, and I know all about the hockey game, back-to-school, and the flag debate," Penny said.

"You had trouble sleeping?"

"Yeah. You?"

"Oh, yeah." Lillian munched on her snack. "I've been thinking about Susan non-stop."

"And about what happened to her," Penny said. "Tell me something, Lill. Does it make you scared?"

"Not particularly."

"I've been afraid of my shadow ever since you told me what the cop told you." Lillian could hear the strain in Penny's voice. "That somebody could have deliberately injected her with something. In the radio studio!"

"Well, they haven't said that for sure yet, Penny. All Detective Sinclair told me was that she died of a heroin overdose."

"I don't believe for a minute that she did that to herself! I'm not sure how, exactly, but isn't it possible someone did it to her?"

"I don't know, Penn. I really wasn't in much of a state to ask the detective any follow-up questions. Maybe I'll get a chance some other time."

"So, somebody might have killed her. It just blows my mind."

"Yeah."

"Do you think it happened at the radio station?"

"I don't know, Penny. Could somebody have injected her somewhere else and then she came over to the station for her interview taping? Maybe she felt relatively normal and then the stuff overwhelmed her? Or. ... maybe she shot herself up in the women's bathroom at CUBR!"

"I don't believe that for a minute! And I know you don't either."

"I don't know what to believe."

"Believe in our friend, that's what."

"I don't know anything about heroin, do you?"

"Nothing. P.J. did a mini-doc here about six months ago, about the increase in soft drug use. I could ask him."

"I don't think we call heroin a soft drug!" Lillian said.

"No, I know, but it's the closest we've come over here to any coverage about heroin use."

"I'm surprised by that, actually, Penn. I would have thought CBC Radio, with all the time you guys have for long-form interviews and documentaries, would have done some coverage on drug use."

"We have done some, as I said, but . . . yeah. It's not a subject that's come up much."

"Maybe that will change."

"You think I should suggest a story?"

Lillian considered this. "I think I'd probably wait until we know more about Susan's death. If it's going to have any impact."

"What are the police going to say about it, I wonder."

"Detective Sinclair said there would be a press release."

"I'll watch for that when I get in to the station. I have to go in early today."

"Why?"

"They called me in to do the morning chase, in addition to my regular stuff on the afternoon show."

"Wow, that'll be a long day."

"Yeah, well, we all have them from time to time, don't we? Last night, I stayed around a bit late, too, because they were having trouble filling the story spots for 6:45 and 8:15, and nobody could leave until that was done and they did the split."

"Did the split? What's that?"

"We type up each story on green paper that comes with five pages separated by carbon paper. Each story usually has two or three newspaper clippings with it, too. When everything is ready for the show, we split the pages into five piles—for the host, the producer, the technician, the researchers—usually, it's around 6, but sometimes it's as late as 10 o'clock. I feel sorry for a lot of those people, the ones with lives, you know, wives and husbands, children. So, I pitch in whenever I can. I felt like I should be the one to stay and help because I took off early on Monday to go over to your place."

"How many stories are in each show?"

"Well, the morning show is three hours long. We have the cutaways for the national news on the hour at 6, 7, and 8, and we have our local news at 5:30, 6:30, 7:30, and 8:30. Everything in between is talk, so that's usually about eleven or twelve stories."

"And no commercials."

"And no commercials."

"When do your hosts ever go to the bathroom?"

"During the newscast. Only option. I heard they had a guy a few years back who insisted on deking out for a break whenever there was a prerecorded taped interview in the lineup. The producers hated it because they thought it was too risky. Sure enough, one day, the tape broke while they were on air and there was no host in the chair to pick up the baton. There would have been about four minutes of dead air."

"Would have been?"

"Technician saved the day. He had a backup tape of the Prime Minister making some speech about something or other and he slapped that on the playback machine."

"What did you end up booking for the 7:15 slot today?" Lillian asked.

"Another Beatles panel. We did one Monday but there's so much interest, we figured we could get away with another one. And it was easy to do. Not hard to find four Beatles fans in Toronto this week who want to come on the radio and talk about those boys."

"How about tomorrow?"

"We've got a bagger with a Soviet specialist on east-west relations."

"Wow, that's a bit out there."

"Yeah, it is. This new exec producer we've got seems to really want to stir things up. I watched them have a hell of a fight at the story meeting last week about booking this guy versus the Beatles panel. Pavel Andreyevitch is his name. In the end, it was the fact that he was actually from the Soviet Union and not just some professor of Russian Studies from U of T that made the difference. We couldn't get the actual Beatles, of course, just some fans. So, it's Pavel Andreyevitch on tape for replay September 10th at 7:15, and Wendy, Helen, Vicki, and Sharon, the Beatlemaniacs, are on standby."

"What was the Soviet guy like?"

"You would have been impressed. What you'd call good-looking. Dark hair and skin, eyes the color of a midday sky in May, great cheekbones and jawline, with a neck and shoulders designed to hold up an expensive suit just like the one he was wearing."

"Sounds like you're the one impressed," Lillian said.

Penny laughed. "Yeah, I guess I was."

"And what about the girls on your Beatles panel? Were they excited?"

"That's putting it mildly. Huge fans with very cooperative parents, who took them out to the airport Monday to see the group arrive. Ten thousand fans at the airport, behind a chain-link fence at 12:15 a.m. Monday. Thirty-six fainters. Our Wendy and Helen got to shake hands with them. Apparently, the Beatles are famous for coming over to talk to fans, sign autographs, shake hands, and give hugs. Sharon said she'd read that they've said in interviews that they thought that was one thing that made them different from the other groups. She *also* said she heard John wandered off and met a group of fans at the hotel before the show and went out to see some of Toronto with them."

"Ha! I'll bet that set off a frenzy."

"None of our four did any tour-guiding for the Beatles. But a handshake for our Helen and Wendy was pretty exciting, anyway."

Lillian and Penny giggled together on the phone for a few more minutes, and then the memory of Susan pierced the moment.

"I miss her, don't you?" Penny said.

"Absolutely. It's only been two-and-a-half days, and it feels like a year," Lillian said.

"And it makes me feel antsy about everything. Jumpy."

"We should take up martial arts or a self-defense course or something. Listen, I'd better go. I'll call you later."

Lillian hung up the phone and stowed her brown paper bag in the garbage bin. She would take a break in the ladies' room, redo her lipstick, then help Chuck get on with the rest of the morning's newscasts.

Detective Sinclair was waiting for Lillian when she came out of the bathroom. She had no idea how he'd gotten past the front desk receptionist, but she supposed that's what cops were trained to do.

"Miss Clarkson? I have a few questions. Could we go somewhere to talk?"

"Let's go into the staff meeting room." Lillian led the way down the north hallway.

"We've been piecing together Susan's last day," the detective said after they sat down across a table from each other. "I have a couple of gaps and I'm hoping you'll be able to fill them in."

"Of course," Lillian said.

"Susan's death *was* an overdose. Heroin, and a really bad batch. New stuff on the street and we want to track it down before too many other kids OD," Sinclair said. "Do you have any idea where she might have obtained it?"

The room was suddenly very stuffy and warm. Lillian shrugged off her jacket. "I don't," she said. "I had no idea she was using anything."

This was all overwhelming. How could she not have noticed that Susan was into drugs? She'd always known that Susan could be quite a private person. It was the way Lillian had been brought up, too; her parents were just as uncommunicative about personal things. Her mother said that she had been urged by *her* parents "don't tell anybody our business" and that was why she was as secretive as she was. Lillian wondered whether *they* had something to hide.

Since they'd come to Toronto, Susan had become even more reserved, but Lillian had just assumed that had to do with the fact that she knew Lillian didn't like her boyfriend. Once they broke up, things started to open up quite a bit, but Lillian's and Susan's paths had diverged since their Mountain Sky folk group days. It was no surprise that there were major areas that they no longer had in common and that Susan had secrets. Actually, Lillian had a few of her own.

But nothing like drugs! That hadn't even occurred to Lillian, and she was still having trouble focusing on this new information.

Sinclair was staring at her. "I can see it was news to you. It was news to her advisor at the university, too."

Lillian managed to choke out a question. "What did you find out about her last day?"

"The day before her last day, really," Sinclair said. "In the morning, coffee, classes, lunch with another computer engineering student. All afternoon in the library. Her evening hours, nobody seems to know."

"I can help you with that. She was with me, with us."

"Us?"

"The five of us had a Labor Day weekend get-together. Sunday night, because I had to work Monday morning, Glenda was on standby to go in to her office, and Susan had a media interview to do. Joyce came down on the train from Ottawa. We got together for a potluck dinner and a few glasses of wine."

"I'll want to speak to them all," Sinclair said. "I assume you can give me phone numbers and addresses?"

Lillian nodded, but the request left her with an unsettled feeling. Losing Susan was bad enough; now, with the police involved, she also felt like her own life barely belonged to her anymore.

"I still can't get over it," she said. "Susan was a clean-living person. She hated drugs. It's one of the main reasons she dumped Corey."

"People change," Sinclair said. "Especially young people."

That much?

***

When she finished work around noon, Lillian found herself on the way to Corey's house for the second time this week. He opened the door and she brushed past him on her way to the living room.

"Sit down," she said, and if he was surprised by her taking over, he seemed willing to go along with it. "The doctors found heroin in Susan's system. What was going on?"

Corey leaned against the couch, spreading his arms over the back. "We didn't really intend to use, but nobody who hasn't tried it can really understand," Corey said. "Drugs expand your mind. And it was something Susan was interested in. Thousands of people have done it . . . . millions. Susan was a seeker. I am a seeker. We were experimenting with a few different things. All kinds of serious people, beautiful people, people like Susan are interested in trying new things."

"I call bullshit," Lillian snapped.

Corey made eye contact with her for the first time since she'd arrived. "It was Susan's business, Lill. Look, I gotta go meet a guy."

As he walked to the front door and held it open for her to leave, Lillian still wasn't buying it. As far as she was concerned, Corey was a pompous jerk who had Susan under his thumb for a little while, for God knows what reason. It just didn't ring true. She also didn't think much of Corey's suggestion that she not poke her nose into Susan's life and that Susan had a right to privacy. As she found out more about Susan's secrets and started to suspect that she'd lost her life because of one of them, she was becoming convinced that a friend has a duty to snoop around.

Chapter 5

September 10
1964

It was another busy morning in the newsroom, with phones ringing and the rattle of typewriters going nonstop. While she worked, Lillian watched the sun rise, then bathe the city in a beautiful, end-of-summer-in-Toronto golden haze.

During her break, she called Susan's parents. They'd taken on the sad and necessary job of packing up their daughter's apartment. A lot of her things had been turned over to the police, Mrs. Taylor said. Lillian had no idea whether this was normal procedure in a case of a heroin overdose.

When Eugene Lamont, the news director, got into the station, he called Lillian into his office. It was a tiny space right beside the bull-pen of six desks that the reporters, researchers, and technicians used interchangeably. It looked like Lillian's teenaged brother's room back home in Albany—a pile of books serving as a place to hang a jacket, shelves full of papers and folders, posters on the wall of sports cars and busty, half-naked girls.

"Lill, I've got an assignment for you," Eugene said. "I know you have a lot going on right now, and it's tough, with what happened to Susan, but—"

Shoot. She certainly hoped it had nothing to do with his latest side project, to create and produce a mystery book show. She'd heard he'd been cornering people in various departments to ask them to suggest possible titles for it.

"I know it must have been horrible for you, to be the one to find her," he said.

He looked so uncomfortable that Lillian had to cut him off. "It's okay. I'm okay. More work to do would be good. What is it?"

"The Royal Tour."

Well. This *would* be good. The Queen and Prince Philip were to visit Ottawa, Charlottetown, and Quebec in mid-October, and like any Royal Tour, this one was bringing lots of buzz. People just loved to see royalty. Lillian remembered her mother in New York, talking about a Royal visit with President Eisenhower in the late 50s, and the way people lined the streets to see the Queen and Prince Philip. Her grandmother loved to discuss any bits of Royals news in the papers. Not the Americans' Queen, but they did love the pomp, circumstance, and glamor. And here in Toronto, well … it was a Royal Tour. Big news.

"Your job will be research," Eugene was saying. "Putting together background notes for Dominic. He'll be reporting the Tour. He's been prepping for months but there's a lot of last-minute stuff to do, it turns out, and he's screaming for more help."

"Thanks, Eugene. This is far out."

"You're sure? That was quite an experience you had on Monday. Maybe you need a little time to get over it…"

"No, I don't. I'll be fine."

"The … uh … timing's okay? It's October 10th to 12th, about a month away."

"The timing is fine," Lillian said. "Is there going to be an interview?"

"No, never. But he'll be talking to many people on the fringes and there are rumors of a protest in Quebec City, where the Queen is scheduled to be October 10th, after she's in Charlottetown. Then, on October 12th, they'll be in Ottawa for a Thanksgiving Day luncheon and there will be a reception for reporters." He consulted a clipboard on his desk. "We want you to go to Ottawa to do some advance work."

"Will I be there in October when the Royals are there, too?"

"We'll see." Eugene picked up one of the newspapers from his desk. The meeting was over.

If Lillian said she was anything less than thrilled, she'd be lying. It was the glamor of a Royal Tour, yes. This was one of the plum assignments in any newsroom, seen that way by anybody but the most jaded, and past-his-stale-date, reporter, and here she was, being given a chance to be part of it. On the edges, yes, but still a part of it.

But that wasn't the only thing. It was also the vote of confidence in her skills as a researcher and as a valuable member of the news department.

She couldn't wait to get on the phone to Penny.

"The Royal Tour! Holy moly! That's fantastic, Lill!" Penny said. "And you get to travel?"

"To Ottawa, anyway, as part of the prep," Lillian said. "A chance to meet up with Joyce for a drink or dinner, too."

"This is just so great. You know, whether it was a Royal Tour or a tornado or an election . . . just 'a big story', right? You'll be out in the field and in on the action. I'm so excited for you!"

"I think it's great they picked me, too, you know?" Lillian said. "Not that they had a lot of other choices, for a researcher. The news department isn't all that big. But there are the two junior reporters, Leo and Christie. They might have liked to go, but Eugene asked me instead!"

"Yeah, that kind of surprised me."

"You mean, because they're guys? Yeah, me too. I would have expected your people at the CBC to be faster to give that kind of break to a girl than a private station like this."

"I don't get the impression that CUBR is a hotbed of male chauvinists, though, from the things you've told me."

"No, it's not," Lillian said. "That's all Eugene. He just treats me like anybody else. I don't think he's ever even noticed that I'm female."

"You are lucky. We have a couple of jerks here who seem to think they have to point it out to you at least three or four times a week."

"Yuck. I've run across a few of those, too. Out on stories, not in the newsroom. In the bar. The worst was a six-foot, five-inch guy who insisted on telling me that he was 'built to scale.'"

"My worst was a guy who put his arm around me when we were being introduced to one of the mucky-mucks from head office and said 'isn't she cute? She really improves the visuals around here.' Pigs."

Lillian sighed. "Well, what are you going to do? They run the world."

"Just be grateful for the good ones like that Eugene guy running your shop. We've got more women, over here at the CBC than you do, and that keeps it under control." Penny covered the mouthpiece with her hand, but Lillian heard her muffled voice, "I'm almost done. I'll be there in a minute. Hey, how are you doing today, Lill? About Susan, I mean."

Lillian sighed. "I've had better days."

"Yeah, me too."

"I just keep thinking that there should have been something else I could have done to prevent it, you know? If we were close, and I thought we were, she would have talked to me, would have told me what she was doing."

"Maybe she was really embarrassed. Or afraid you'd get her in real trouble."

"What do you mean, turn her in, in some way? Never! And why would she ever feel embarrassed with me? Or with any of us? I don't think I ever showed her I disapproved of her or was judging

her, and that she had to walk on eggshells with me. But maybe I did."
And there, it was out. The guilt had been eating at Lillian for days
now, and finally, it was out there.

"Lillian, listen to me. Susan probably had her own reasons for
not telling you she was experimenting with drugs. Or she was just
about to tell you, in a day or two, and she just ran out of time.
Or that she wasn't doing that at all! There was nothing you could
have done to prevent what happened. Susan was living her life
and you're living yours. You can control yours, but you can't control what others do, or what happens to them." Penny waited for
a while for Lillian's agreement with her words, but it just wasn't
coming. "Hey, I've got to go. Are you home tonight?"

"Yeah, call me later."

When Lillian got back to her desk, she found a stack of pink
message slips and a note from Chuck, saying that Raymond, their
regular radio technician, had been in, looking for her. She glanced
through the messages, feeling reluctant to phone anybody back,
and decided to find out what Raymond wanted first.

Lillian checked the cafeteria, Master Control, the technicians' lounge, and several of the studios before she located him in
the Music Library.

Valessa Gulliver, the music and reference librarian, sat on a
high stool in front of a counter where she presided over the station's assets and history.

Not many radio stations had a room like this, or a caretaker
like Valessa—the quirkiness of CUBR was one of the things about
it that appealed to Lillian. She knew that if she wanted to find almost any piece of music, even recorded on a 45 or a 78, she could
find it here.

The station owner, Atwood Brooks, had begun collecting
in the 1930s and the legend was that he refused to let anyone
ever throw anything away. The entire room had floor-to-ceiling

shelves, some crammed with albums, some with books and magazines, and some with tapes. The music collection covered every style, even though most of the station's programming these days was Top 40.

The research collection covered every decade, with particular emphasis on the events of the 30s and 40s. Lillian had been told that every item in the whole place was meticulously catalogued, and the one person who could put her hands on anything, within minutes, was Valessa.

Her long, silver hair was tied back, kept out of her way with a plain elastic band at her neck. Black turtleneck, black pants, and black ballet slippers—that was Valessa. You could count on her to dress the same, every day, and you could count on her to care about research and history.

A row of soundproofed listening rooms ran the length of one wall and that was where Valessa directed Lillian. "Raymond Chernowski? He went into room D with an armful of albums. Country, I think, maybe bluegrass," she said. "I tried to push a couple of classical disks into his hands, but he wouldn't take them."

She probably wasn't kidding.

Lillian tapped at the door of Room D and Raymond pushed it open to let her in. He had an LP spinning. "Hi, Lillian. Candace has me in here, timing some intros for Maggie's show," he said, waving toward the turntable with the stopwatch in his right hand.

"Chuck said you were looking for me."

Raymond stopped the music and motioned for her to sit down in the room's only chair. "I want to tell you something about myself before the gossip finds its way to you. There's already a few people who've heard and are passing it along, and I don't want it to get out of hand or exaggerated. I'm speaking with everybody I know here, one at a time. Privately, you dig?"

Lillian nodded. What on earth could this be?

"It's not the sort of information I would feel obliged to mention, normally. It's my business, and nobody else's. Well, I guess it's Oscar's, I told him when he hired me. But nobody else in the tech department knows and certainly nobody else in the newsroom or the office."

He took a step backward and leaned against the wall. Lillian was suddenly acutely aware of how small the listening room was. They were definitely inside each other's personal space.

"Ever since it happened, I've been thinking about you and wondering how you were taking it. I mean, it would be disturbing to find anybody's body on the floor of your radio studio but to have it be one of your best friends . . . When I saw you, looking at her and then on the phone, calling for the ambulance, I just had this realization of how *young* you are, and how you probably never had anything traumatic happen to you."

"I'm twenty-two," Lillian said. Was he insulting her? "I'm about the same age as you."

"I'm forty," Raymond said.

Well, shoot. But guessing people's ages had never been one of her skills.

"All right, then. What is it, Raymond?"

"I got this job, thanks to Oscar and Eugene being very open-minded." He shifted from foot to foot and she could see a sheen of perspiration on his upper lip.

"Just *tell* me, Raymond. I have to get back to my desk and my phone."

"Yeah. Okay. I was in prison for six months a while back. I have a criminal record."

"For doing what?" Lillian wasn't sure what her reaction was to this news, but her curiosity never rested.

"Drugs. It was supposed to be just some weed, for my own use, but the guy who sold it to me asked me to hold some extra, plus a few pills, and they got me for trafficking," he said. "So, the lesson is, never do some guy a favor when he asks you to hold something for him."

"No kidding." Lillian couldn't believe anybody would be this thick. Was he making a joke? "No, Raymond, the lesson is don't buy drugs, any quantity, from anybody. You ended up in jail, for heaven's sakes!"

"Yeah, yeah, I know," he said. "I learned my lesson. I was just kidding. But look, I wanted you to know, and a few others to know, direct from me. So that you know exactly what it was about. So that if you hear anybody trying to tell you I was in prison for ten years for robbing a bank or that I hurt somebody or something, you'd know it was just gossip. And maybe you could correct anything like that if you hear it, okay? It was six months, just marijuana. That's all."

"When was this?"

"Seventeen years ago."

"A long time."

"Yeah, yeah, it was. Something like that shouldn't follow you around for years after but you'd be amazed, some people's attitudes. I've lost a couple girlfriends after telling them. One of them was cool with it, but her mother freaked out."

"Why are you telling me about this now?"

"I overheard Maggie chatting with one of the news guys. She doesn't know it's me, I don't think, but she was saying something about someone with a criminal past working here. So, I just thought, if there is talk, I want the truth out there. I wanted to get things straight with a few people who seem trustworthy. Like you."

Lillian stood up and reached for the doorknob. "Thank you, Raymond. I appreciate the vote of confidence. Is there anybody else you've talked to, anybody else who knows, and that you don't mind if I talk to?"

"Oscar. Eugene. Mr. Brooks."

"Mr. Brooks, the owner?"

"Yeah."

"Chuck?"

"No, not Chuck. Not yet. I might speak to him, too. Yeah."

"Alright. I have to go. But yes, you can count on me not to listen to any ridiculous rumors about you."

When Lillian got back to her desk, she had a message to call Detective Sinclair. Darn. She hadn't thought to ask Raymond whether she was compelled to keep his secret from this police officer. In fact, she'd been so startled, she hadn't really asked if it was a secret she was supposed to keep. She understood Raymond wanted her to challenge anybody who was passing along outrageous, untrue gossip about him, but did that mean she was free to bring it up and state the facts? She'd have to get back to Raymond and ask him about that.

In the meantime, she'd decided she wouldn't discuss it with Detective Sinclair. She needed some time to figure out just what she did think about Raymond's revelation. Mostly, she wasn't impressed with people who'd been to jail, but she hadn't really thought about it much. She didn't think she'd ever met anybody with that experience. She didn't feel judgmental about it; probably, every case was different and who was she to say what she might do herself, in certain situations?

Sinclair wanted to meet with her to ask a few more questions about Susan. She headed out for the coffee shop just down Yonge Street that she'd suggested. Walking in and doing a quick scan around the room, she saw that there was no sign of him yet. She took a table as far from the door and as far into the back corner as she could get.

He didn't keep her waiting long.

"Lillian, hello. Thanks for taking my call and coming over to meet me. I want to ask you a few more questions about Susan, her friends and associates, her job, her background and so on." He sat down and nodded a yes, as the waitress waved the coffeepot in his direction. He looked warm; it was a warm day outside but he'd probably be a bit more comfortable if he weren't wearing a heavy, dark blue suit with a long-sleeved white shirt buttoned up to a collar that was too tight.

His glasses were sliding down his nose a bit and he took them off, wiping them on one of the table napkins.

"Yes, of course, Detective Sinclair. What do you want to know?"

"We need to know more about her associates outside of the university. Please tell me about the rest of the girls in your group. How many were there, again?"

"Six. Glenda, Penny, Joyce, Rhonda, me . . . and Susan."

"I'll get their surnames from you in a minute." He had his head down over a notepad, scribbling furiously. "They all live here? No, wait, you told me one lives in Ottawa."

"Joyce lives in Ottawa, works for the government. Rhonda is in New York."

"Okay, let's start with Glenda."

"Well, Glenda has been our friend for almost ten years. We were all about twelve years old when we met at a school track and field meet. In high school, Glenda was the wild one, dating boys who'd already graduated and who spent their days in dark garages crammed with machinery, vehicles and grease. Her parents gave her free range as soon as she became a teenager," Lillian said. "My parents were never quite that easy to manage. Glenda grew up to be so beautiful that she had to beat the boys off with a stick, so to speak. But even though she spent her time in circles far more grown-up than the ones that Susan or I could get into, she never dropped us as friends."

Sinclair was making notes. "I take it you approved of Glenda and appreciated her."

"We did. She had a boyfriend in senior year with a very kind heart, too. I remember one Friday night when the rest of us had no dates and lots of depression coming on over the idea of yet another evening walking from the bowling alley to the diner and back, Spike invited us to come along with him and Glenda, to hang out with his boys at the baseball diamond."

"Gave you a little prestige, did he?"

"Exactly! We thought Glenda should hang on to that one, but she moved on to somebody else before the year was over."

"How is Glenda feeling about Susan's death?"

"She's devastated, just like the rest of us."

"When did she move to Toronto?"

"Not long after Susan and I left Albany, with Des. She got a job, answering the phone and filing in a doctor's office and she seems to like that pretty much. She goes to church quite a bit and she has a lot of friends I haven't met, but we try to get together every few weeks."

"What about Penny? Is she from Albany, too?"

"No, she's a Toronto girl. I met her when one of the producers at my station took me to a bar one night. A "Media Ladies of Toronto" night. She works at CBC Radio."

"And you? How did you get your job?"

"I think I told you that Susan and I were in a folk group, with a friend named Des. His older brother, Josh, Josh Marshall, is the Josh in Josh and Eddie on *The Dawn Patrol.* He got the job for me."

"And Rhonda? Where does she work?"

"An advertising agency in New York. She's a friend from university."

"And Joyce works for the federal government."

"Yeah, I'm not sure what she does. Something with files and stats." Lillian fixed him with a serious look and tried to be as authoritative as she could. "Now, I think it's time you answered a question for me. Why such interest in Susan's friends? Is this what's done whenever somebody overdoses on heroin?"

Sinclair closed his notebook. "We have more information, Lillian, and I'm going to share it with you. It won't be easy to hear. Susan's death has now been classified as a homicide."

"What does that mean?"

"In this case, murder."

Chapter 6

The sound of a car horn honking startled Lillian just as she was about to step off the curb on her way back to the station. She had been in a daze ever since her meeting with Detective Sinclair. It was bad enough, when she thought Susan had overdosed on heroin, but that she might be a murder victim? This was worse.

Now that she knew that the police thought Susan wasn't responsible for the drugs found in her system, she could give in to her anger and turn the blame for Susan's death on some unknown 'other'. Someone had stolen her friend away from her, away from her family, away from *herself,* her future, her career dreams, her own desire to be a mother and a grandmother. Someone had injected her with a lethal drug and left her to die. Alone. On a floor. Was she in pain? Lillian had no idea and didn't want to know. It didn't really matter—no additional detail could make her any more furious than she already was about this.

Someone had killed her friend, and that person would be exposed and punished.

Then, maybe she could get over this feeling that it was her fault because she hadn't saved her.

***

Lillian could barely keep her mind on her work and as soon as she could acceptably punch out for the day, she was out the station's front door and on her way to Corey's place.

It always looked bleak, but today it looked particularly rundown and dreary. Deserted. Lillian rang the doorbell, then pounded on the front door. When no one answered, she walked around to the backyard and hammered on the back door. Still, no reply.

She tried peering in through the kitchen and then the living room windows, but they were so grimy she really couldn't see anything inside. She even lay down on her stomach and tried to see in through the ground-floor windows, but they were even worse.

After half an hour, she gave up. No one was home. Or willing to answer.

***

Her phone was ringing when she walked into her apartment. Mrs. Taylor was on the line.

"Lillian, dear, I just wanted to let you know we're having a small service for Susan tomorrow. At 2 o'clock. At the Anglican church on King Street. It will be very small, and we might have something more later, in Albany. Where she grew up." Mrs. Taylor had held it together pretty well until that last sentence, but she lost it then, and the sobs came on, with no possibility of stopping them. Lillian understood, and she just waited while Mrs. Taylor got herself back under control.

"The police aren't releasing her body yet. Apparently, there's suspicion of ... of ..."

"Yes, I've heard, Mrs. Taylor," Lillian said, rescuing her. "Yes, of course, I'll be there for the service. I'll let her other friends know, too."

"Thank you, dear. I've already heard from Glenda. She called yesterday. I remember her so well from the neighborhood. She's connected with some church community in Toronto, apparently, and she was offering her pastor to conduct a service. Do you know anything about this?"

Lillian didn't know about this specific offer, but she knew about Glenda and her pastor. It was the wrong word for him, really. Lillian thought of him more as a guru and Penny thought he was an out-and-out cult leader.

Howard Ronson was his name, and Glenda had met him shortly after arriving in Toronto. After attending his 'church' for a few months, she asked Susan and Lillian to come along to a meeting with her. Afterward, Susan was very vocal about not liking the way he encouraged people to fawn over him. She also thought he made it too easy for them all to make financial donations. Lillian didn't like the way he looked at Glenda and the other young women in the crowd.

She and Susan had politely declined any more invitations to attend evening prayer meetings or Sunday afternoon gatherings with The Called, as Howard referred to his followers.

Lillian just couldn't get over it. Growing up in Albany, Glenda had never been a religious person. But, after eight years of calling her own shots and getting zero supervision, guidance or expectations from her parents, maybe Glenda was enjoying the rules and the demands of Mr. Ronson and his crowd.

And now, Glenda was calling bereaved parents on Howard's behalf to try to get another stage for him to spout on. At least, that was the way Lillian saw it.

She didn't share her opinions with Mrs. Taylor though, and when she arrived at the memorial, she saw Howard Ronson standing beside Glenda, in the congregation. The service was conducted by one of the Anglican priests connected to the church, but Pastor Howard was invited to the pulpit to say a few words about Susan, along with several others: her brother, one of her close friends at the university, and some others that Lillian didn't recognize.

It was a quiet, dignified service. The music was thoughtful and the atmosphere was respectful. Afterward, Mr. and Mrs. Taylor seemed to be grateful to have had Glenda and Pastor Howard, among others, to help in accomplishing one of these sad, last duties for their daughter.

But Lillian resented every moment that the guru took in the middle of the ceremony, to talk about his beliefs and to offer a better life to those who would agree with him.

After the memorial service, she tried to dodge Glenda and her pastor friend, but Glenda intercepted her.

"I have to ask your advice on something," Glenda said. "I'm thinking of giving up my apartment and going to live in the community."

Lillian was shocked. "What does that mean, 'in the community'?"

"It's a farm north of the city. I've been to visit a few times. A beautiful landscape, animals, an orchard, vegetable gardens. We grow all our own food. We rely on ourselves for everything."

This all sounded quite strange.

"What about your job in the doctor's office?"

"They've agreed to have me work part time, just filling in. Some weekends, when it's hard to find people to help. Anybody with a family and kids in school doesn't want to work weekends. And they'll call me in to work sometimes when too many people are off sick or on vacation."

"But Glenda, why do you have to make such a big change? If you're interested in his message, just go to the meetings, or the gatherings or whatever you call them. But don't *move* there!"

"You're being very judgmental, Lill. You never used to be this way. Is it because of working at the radio station? Susan knew all about this and she wasn't so critical."

"Susan knew? Since when?"

"She met quite a few of the people through activities at the university. We had dinner once—her, me, Jordan, this guy I've been dating, some student she started dating after Corey was gone, and Howard."

"Howard? Your church group leader?"

"He's a brilliant man. He gave books to all of us and he put Susan and me on a reading program."

Susan hadn't mentioned any of this to Lillian. How did she ever find the time, with her engineering studies at the university?

What other secrets had she had?

When Des called that evening, Lillian felt as though a gentle summer rain had started to fall in the middle of a six-week drought. Their friendship in Albany went back to fourth grade, and their years together in their band, Mountain Sky, were some of the best she'd had so far. She would be forever grateful to him for helping to arrange her job here at the radio station and he was grateful to her for making it so easy for him when he wanted to pull out of the music world and pursue his interests in politics and finance.

"You must be feeling rotten," he said. "Let me take you out. You'll have somebody to talk to."

His choice for the evening was the drive-in theater. Quite a good choice, really; they could talk with no risk of being overheard. The movie was something with a complicated plot about a jeweled dagger being stolen in Greece or Iraq or somewhere. They didn't watch much of it, but got right into a discussion of Susan's death.

It was just so easy being around him, always had been. He was a shoulder to cry on, and she needed to talk about Susan. He'd been her best listener during her adjustment to working at the radio station, and he was particularly interested in what she had to say about his older brother, Josh.

Des was just as shocked as she was, that drugs had been found in Susan's system and that the cops were calling it murder.

"It just makes me so flippin' angry," Lillian said. "I want to find whoever did that and hold him down while he gets a taste of what it was like."

Des tried to defuse the moment. "Whoa! Remind me never to get on your bad side."

He changed his tone when he saw how intense she looked. "Sorry, I didn't mean to joke."

"It's alright, Des. I'm just so . . . I feel so helpless. . . but I feel like I have to *do* something. I mean, I know the police are investigating and they know what they're doing and I don't. But I don't think any of them care about her the way I care. Cared."

Des held out an arm, and she moved in against his shoulder. He hugged her for a moment, and then she pulled away.

"Thank you. I think you understand."

"I do. I cared about her, too. I've known her since elementary school. She was a good person, and whatever the reason, no one had the right to do that to her."

Lillian stared at his face in the semi-darkness. "That's right. No one had the right. So much goes on in this world, where people just do what they want, because they have the power. Nobody thinks about what's right, or who has the right. But nobody had the right to do that to her, and somebody should answer for it."

Des nodded. "And I get the feeling you're going to make that happen?"

"I am," Lillian said. "Just watch me."

Chapter 7

September 14
1964

Lillian listened to Josh drum his fingertips on the table. The story meeting for the *Dawn Patrol* show on Monday dragged on for a full hour. Usually, Chuck attended as the newsroom rep but he was snowed under, getting ready for coverage of the Royal Tour and the flag debate, and so he sent Lillian in his place. She watched the sweep hand on the clock move at a turtle's pace. Whoever had the bright idea of calling it a sweep hand? More like a creep hand.

Even though one part of her mind was calling it excruciating, and reminding her how much she hated meetings, another part was grateful for the distraction. Her weekend had been just hours of eating too much pasta, trying to read some massive novel about Afghanistan, and watching TV until her eyes ached. Monday morning was welcome.

One by one, the hosts, the researchers, and the producer discussed that day's sound and presented their ideas for the next one. Josh was tactful in shooting down some of the comments but he was tough too, and if he didn't think an idea was focused or major enough for the morning show, he said so. No sparing the feelings, playing personal favorites, or promoting his own interests and hobbies. He was all business. Mostly, he wanted light, bright, and trite, with plenty of pop songs in between the chat. Stick to the program profile.

Oscar, the producer, by contrast, liked to follow his nose. Two weeks ago, it was all about sailing stories for him, because he'd had his first cruise on Lake Ontario, thanks to a friend who'd invited him. Last week it was back to the news and the excitement over the Beatles concert on September 7th. If Lillian were making a bet, she would have guessed that this week it would be something about the Tokyo Olympics—when was that, now? She glanced into her daytimer. Opening October 10th.

But this week, Oscar was interested in Russians.

Last month, a world-famous first violinist, Anna Kogonov, had jumped ship in Montreal when the Moscow Philharmonic made a stop en route to a performance at the World's Fair in New York. When the performance began, the conductor raised his baton and looked toward the strings section—and the woman was gone.

After a few moments of confusion, the house lights came up, according to the daily newspaper, and the rest of the musicians were hustled offstage by a dozen burly men in dark suits.

The Soviet government had just issued a formal demand for information from the Canadian and U.S. governments about Anna Kogonov's whereabouts.

"So, it's officially a defection?" Oscar asked. "Like that ballet dancer who bailed on the Soviet Union when he was on tour in Paris?"

"That's what it looks like," Josh said, scanning the headlines.

"And where is she now?"

"Nobody knows," Josh said.

"Okay. Lillian, I'd imagine the news will be all over that one. We'll be doing lots of chat about the details of the Royal Tour and the Olympics Opening. Anything else?"

"You said we needed to pay attention to the last few weeks of the World's Fair, too," Josh said.

"Oh, yeah, we do." Oscar reopened his notebook. "Mr. Brooks is making some sort of speech about trends in broadcasting down there, and we'll need to do something with that. Maybe news would want to get some clips or something."

Lillian jumped out of her thoughts when she realized he was talking to her. "Maybe. I'll mention that it came up. Chuck or Eugene might have an opinion. But . . . "

"But what?"

"But it's not really news, is it? I mean, 'trends' . . . right there, it's not news."

"Well, it's not really chat for the morning show, either," Oscar snapped. "We'll sort it out later."

As the group dispersed, Josh signaled to Lillian that he wanted her to wait for a moment until the room had cleared. "How are you doing, Lill?"

"I'm hanging in there." She spoke cheerfully, but when she met Josh's eyes, she knew that he really was asking, not just going through the motions. Just like his brother, Des, he cared.

"I have a lot of moments when I can't believe it's true, though. It's only been a week and I just miss her so much."

Josh nodded. "Des told me the police think it's foul play."

Neither of them spoke for a few minutes, then Josh said, "If there's anything I can do, you know I will."

***

When Lillian got back to the newsroom, Leo, the junior reporter with the checked sports coat and the brush cut, held out a phone to her.

"Hello?"

"Lillian, it's Corey. Corey Lang."

"Corey. I'm glad you called me. I went by your house the other day. I want to talk to you."

"I want to talk to you, too. That's why I'm calling. Have you talked to the police lately?"

"If you mean about Susan being murdered, yes, I have."

"Good God. Is that the word? Yeah, I guess that's the word." He sounded scattered and almost hysterical. "Look, Lillian, I want to make sure you didn't misunderstand our talk the other day."

"About what?"

"I didn't mean to imply that Susan and I were using drugs all the time. I was just . . . generally, you know . . . I was just being cool, you know? To a lot of people, drugs aren't that big a deal. People are experimenting a little, that's all. People that I know, that is. But you've never seen me under the influence, have you?"

"Is that what you think Detective Sinclair will ask me? Corey, this is your chance to come clean. Be straight with me. Was Susan experimenting with drugs? With hard drugs? With heroin?"

You could have read an eight-hundred-word story out loud in the silence that went by before Corey finally answered.

"As far as I know, Susan never willingly touched drugs."

***

When Lillian hung up the phone, Chuck handed her three pink message slips. Penny, Detective Sinclair, and Raymond Chernowski.

Raymond. Now that was weird. Why was he calling her? She picked up a phone and dialed the extension for the tech department.

"Lillian, could you meet me for a coffee in the cafeteria?" His voice was slow and low.

When they sat down across from each other with two vending-machine coffees well-diluted with powdered milk, Raymond lost no time in getting to the point.

"Detective Sinclair from the cop shop asked me questions."

"What questions?"

Raymond fiddled with the plastic spoon. "Why did I leave the station so fast last Monday morning?"

"It's a good question, Raymond. We'd just found Susan Taylor's body. Then, you just disappeared—before the ambulance even got there! It was like a hit-and-run . . . WAS it a hit-and-run, Raymond?"

Raymond's eyes were haunted. "No! You're off on the wrong track, Lillian. I didn't hurt Susan, I never would. I . . . I cared about her. I saw her all the time, when she'd come in to the station to meet you, and I even ..."

"You even what?"

"I even asked her out one time."

This was news to Lillian. "What did she say?"

"That she appreciated the invitation, but she had a boyfriend and wouldn't go out with anybody else."

"And how did you react to that?"

Raymond looked at her sharply. "You sound like Detective Sinclair. That's what he asked me, too."

"You told him all of this?"

"Yeah. He asked me if I knew Susan, how well, and so on. What I remembered about everything that happened that morning." Raymond gulped his cold coffee. "And why I left in such a hurry."

"Had he looked up your record? Did he bring that up?"

"No, but it's just a matter of time, I think."

Raymond was the picture of 'worried', Lillian thought. Maybe it was grief. He had said he was attracted to Susan; maybe he was as shaken up by her death as Lillian was.

She studied his face and his hands. No, that was worry, not grief.

But why would he be worried if he was innocent?

That afternoon, the final assignments for the Tokyo Olympics came out. Lillian had no illusions that her name might be up on the assignment sheet pinned to the bulletin board. Covering the Olympics was a plum job, handed out to seasoned, deserving reporters, hosts, and technical people. Senior people.

Still, she lined up in front of the board with the others because she was curious to see who would get an all-expenses-paid trip to Japan. The thought was so exotic that it gave her shivers.

Maggie Macrae. No surprise there. *Josh, Eddie, Eugene,* three or four reporters, and a dozen technicians she'd never met.

Lillian glanced at Raymond, who was standing to her right. His face was contorted.

"What is it?" she asked.

"My name's not there."

Lillian wasn't sure what the right response was. "Did you think it would be?"

"Eugene as good as told me I'd be going."

"What does that mean, 'as good as told me'?" Lillian asked.

Raymond took it as a rhetorical question, glared at her, then marched off toward Eugene's office. She heard raised voices for a couple of minutes, then Raymond came rushing out.

That afternoon was filled with Royal Tour prep. Lillian lined up the Tour reporter, Dominic, to do a pre-tape for Maggie MacRae's show. Raymond was the technician assigned to run the board for any interviews today and but he didn't show up in the studio. After they waited for him for ten minutes, Dominic got restless; he was eager to get out of the station to work on a story.

Lillian went looking for the technician, but Raymond couldn't be found in any of the usual places. He had started very early that morning and she only had a window of about fifteen minutes when the availability of the reporter and the end of Raymond's shift overlapped.

She couldn't spot Raymond anywhere. Was he that upset about not getting the Tokyo assignment? Apparently so, according to Chuck. He told Lillian that Raymond had called Eugene and announced that he was quitting. He didn't want to get up at 3 a.m. and come in even one more time, he said. They didn't appreciate him and they didn't respect him, he felt, and he wanted to be done with CUBR.

Lillian was back in the newsroom, explaining to Dominic why he'd been held up for so long, only to find out they wouldn't be doing an interview taping after all, when Chuck called out that he had a phone call to transfer to her.

"Lill! I just have a ten-minute break, but I wanted to remind you that I'm moving next weekend."

"To that commune."

Glenda inhaled deeply. "To The Farm, yes, with Howard."

Lillian looked around the newsroom, then turned her back and spoke quietly. "You know what I think of this plan, Glen. I don't see why you can't continue to belong to the group without actually moving there."

"Howard thinks this is the best thing for my personal development," Glenda said. "Come on, Lill, don't be like that. I'm going to try it, and if I don't like it, I'll be back."

"Are you keeping your apartment?"

"Well, no, I had to give notice. I can't afford to pay in both places, so ..."

"So Howard Ronson *charges* you to do what he tells you?"

"Lill, you're being a witch. Come on."

Lillian could hear that Glenda wasn't standing up well under this pressure, and she decided to back off. "Alright, alright. Do you want any help with moving?"

"Oh, would you? We could use your car."

"Sure thing, Glen. I'll be there Saturday morning."

After Lillian hung up the phone, she wandered into the wire room. Her shift was finished, but she just didn't feel like going home yet. She stood in front of the Associated Press machine and watched the words appearing on the yellow paper.

Hundreds of bishops and archbishops beginning a meeting with the Pope in Rome. Speculation about an election call coming in Britain in the next day or two. Ottawa and Quebec City getting ready for the Royals while politicians worried about the possibility of Quebec nationalists disrupting the visit.

A feature about Dr. Martin Luther King Jr. and the likelihood that he'd be receiving the Nobel Peace Prize this year. Another reaction piece to the news in August that South Africa would be banned from competing in the Olympic Games because of its official policy of apartheid.

Lillian stood and stared down at the machine while the paper continued to spill out, line after line of news and information about people around the world, taking action on their beliefs.

And what was she doing? Her best friend had been killed, in this very building, and what was she doing? She knew she couldn't suddenly get herself onto the homicide squad. But surely, there would be something she could do to get involved in finding out what happened to Susan? In getting justice for her? She had experience as a journalist and she had access to all the perks and privileges the media have. Couldn't she put those to use to try to do something to help find the answers to Susan's death and to get rid of this awful emptiness she felt?

***

That afternoon, Candace Barkley, producer of *The Maggie MacRae Show*, positioned three chairs in the studio for a taping of a conversation that would be replayed during the 9:15 time slot tomorrow. The topic was women's rights, a subject that had circled the runway for about six months before Maggie finally agreed to have it booked. Lillian had been assigned to help out, since she was one of the few women who worked at CUBR: she, Candace, and Maggie were the total female contingent.

There wasn't much interest, and often a lot of sneering at the issue among the men who worked at the station. Lillian actually felt appreciation that the topic was being touched at all.

She and Penny had often discussed the differences in the way CUBR and CBC handled the job of covering the news and current affairs.

At CBC Radio, although they did pre-tapes throughout the day, a taping like this would sometimes take place during the World News report, while the national crew took over the airwaves from a local show like the one Penny worked on.

They had about ten minutes to get the guests in, ask the first question and get a compelling, seemingly live segment recorded and ready to roll. Sometimes it was scheduled to air within the same hour and sometimes, Penny said, when her producer was feeling particularly ambitious, or when the flow of the show called for it, scheduled to air right after the World news. Why not just do it live, then, if there was only a ten or fifteen-minute difference? Sometimes it was a guest's timing and sometimes it was the need to know what they had, on tape, before going to air with it, she said.

Candace Barkley had become one of Lillian's idols the day she heard her mutter "idiot" under her breath, when Eugene turned down another one of Candace's suggestions for coverage of a women's rights protest in Washington D.C.

Candace been working toward getting today's taping set up on the show for months. When Betty Friedan arrived, she and Lillian hovered in the control room, watching as the feminist leader strode into the studio with Maggie and two other women in her wake. Her trademark curly hair was almost vibrating with frizz in Toronto's late summer humidity.

"I can't believe we got her in here, can you?" Candace whispered.

Lillian shook her head.

"Did you read *The Feminine Mystique?*"

"Of course! Blew my mind."

Candace beamed, then rushed out of the control room to meet Betty and show her to her seat. About fifteen minutes into the interview, Lillian appreciated the fact that they didn't have to squeeze it in during a national news taping, the way they did it over at the CBC. Betty had a lot to say, and she said it in long sentences. Paragraphs, even. It would be an interesting challenge to find clips short enough for the newscast.

When they walked Betty and her entourage out through the newsroom and past Eugene's office, Lillian saw the boss sitting behind his desk with his arms crossed and an irritated look on his face. Might be that any clip from Betty Friedan would be too long, as far as he was concerned.

Well, for every barricade that Eugene had up, Candace had three ladders. She was practically dancing because she was so thrilled with the way it had gone. Maggie was satisfied with the result, too.

Was it Lillian's imagination, or had Candace given Eugene a little wave as they passed by?

Chapter 8

September 15
1964

Even though she was only about forty feet down the hall from the newsroom, Lillian could hear the shouting as soon as she opened the bathroom door. Eugene was not thrilled with the clip they had supplied for use on the morning newscasts. Livid would be a better word.

"Drop that item!" he yelled at Chuck over the phone. It was so loud that Lillian could hear him from her seat halfway across the newsroom.

"You got it, boss," Chuck said, raising his eyebrows at Lillian as he hung up the phone. "Told you so."

"I don't see why it's such a big deal," she said.

"We hear the opening shots across the valley," Chuck said. "And the drums. Maybe we're scared."

She thought she knew what he meant, but she wouldn't want to take a test on it.

"What he's saying out loud is that it's just a clip from a soft feature. From the daytime ladies show. It's not news."

"Then what is news?" Lillian asked.

Chuck grinned. "Whatever he says it is. Or any other news director, wherever."

Lillian shook her head. "I'm so confused. But thanks for the weird explanation."

"Isn't it time for you to go get Dr. Arnold from the lobby?"

"Oh, yeah, thanks. I'd completely forgotten we bumped him from his usual spot yesterday." Lillian grabbed for her clipboard and stopwatch, while she checked the time on the one of the enormous clocks that showed the eastern time zone. "I'll put him in Studio 6. Raymond should be there."

"Raymond is not there. It'll be Dennis this morning."

"Raymond didn't change his mind about quitting?"

"Even if he did, I don't think Eugene would let him back in the door," Chuck said. "What's the doc talking about this morning?"

"Smoking and Lung Cancer, Part 2. After he's done the live interview for Josh and Eddie, we'll clip it for the news kicker at 8:30."

Before Lillian got across the lobby from the elevator, Dr. Kevin Arnold rose from his chair. He carried a black medical bag with him, a move that Lillian had seen as an affectation until one morning last winter, when he was called on to revive a fellow guest. She'd never forget how they'd all watched as a woman gasped for breath and then passed out; Dr. Arnold had brought her around in minutes.

His brief items on medical topics were popular with the listeners and he was one of the most reliable sources they'd had—both in the quality of his information and the consistency of his appearances every Monday. He was sometimes rude and grumpy, but overall, the good outweighed the bad.

"Hi, Dr. Arnold. Thanks for coming in."

"That's okay, Lillian," he said. "How are you? Glenda's told me you've all been having a rough time after losing Susan last week. I was so sorry to hear about it."

"Thank you," she said. "Let's go down to the green room. We have about half an hour before your item and Oscar asked me to get a list of the topics you're going to do for the next month or two."

Once they were settled in the waiting room outside the studio and Lillian had supplied Dr. Arnold with his black coffee and an ashtray, she took out a notepad. "Now, what will the topics be?"

"Symptoms of appendicitis. How to prepare for an operation. Fathers in the delivery room, yes or no? And why you should watch your blood pressure."

Lillian finished making her notes just as the door opened and Oscar appeared. "We're ready for you now, Kevin," he said.

"Okay," the doctor said, butting out his cigarette. "Oh, and please add the Surgeon General's report, Part 2 to that list, Lillian. Today I'm going to talk about ending pregnancies."

"But I thought you were doing the Surgeon General's report today!"

She was speaking to a closed door.

Lillian hadn't seen Dr. Arnold since last week, when Susan died. She'd called him to confirm this week's topic, and he'd called back to confirm that it would be about smoking.

So why was he talking about abortion?

Josh looked as shocked as everyone in the control room felt. Eddie threw his piece of copy across the room, as a signal about the way he felt about the item. When *Dawn Patrol* was over, and *The Maggie MacRae Show* started, from Studio 1 with a taped debate about merits of The Animals versus The Dave Clark Five, the two morning men stomped out of the room. Dr. Arnold followed, saying something about a medical emergency he had to get to. Lillian was too stunned to say anything to him as he left.

Chuck appeared in the control room doorway.

"What the hell? Lillian, did you prep this topic with him?"

"No! He's supposed to be talking about cigarettes!"

"Well, he didn't! Damn! Somebody's calling." Chuck picked up the phone and from his comments, Lillian could tell that it was

Mr. Brooks. She had never heard the station owner call in during a show before this.

But Dr. Arnold's comments had been quite inflammatory. The choice of topic was bad enough—abortion was a subject that wasn't discussed as everyday conversation, particularly between men and women. It was even worse because of the harshness of Dr. Arnold's statements.

She knew she was paraphrasing, but Lillian was sure her recollection was accurate.

"There is no way abortion should be legal. It is damaging to the physical and mental health of the mother, and it is damaging to society. Not to mention the religious implications! The rights of an individual can't be allowed to trample on the greater good of the whole. Rights? What am I saying, rights? Nobody, no woman has the right to end a life, no matter how convenient it might be, for her. I'm sure murder often uncomplicates the killer's life, but that doesn't mean we allow it!"

Eugene was so furious he called a special programming department meeting. He'd calmed down a little by then . . . but not much.

"I know some of you have been wondering why I'm going ballistic on this. Yes, of course, we cover controversy from time to time. And we have opinions expressed on the air. But that's in the designated spot for it! In the editorials, on the panels when we explain that we have both points of view represented in the weekly round-up that I do! Nobody can just go on the air and give his opinion like that. Okay, maybe sometimes, we did hear the Legal Eagle say last month that he believes the War Measures Act should be repealed. But he showed us the script for that ahead of time! It was vetted by me, and by Mr. Brooks. Dr. Kevin Arnold didn't let anybody know what he was going to say!"

"Do you disagree with him?" Candace asked.

"That's beside the point!"

"What about freedom of speech?" Dominic asked.

Eugene glared at him. "What would you have? Airwaves that are wide open, just anybody can flip a switch and start talking about anything they want, with any opinion they want? It would be chaos!"

"The end of the world as we know it," Candace said. Eugene's head whipped around so that he could look directly at her, then back at the crowd. He wasn't sure he'd heard sarcasm there, and he'd decided to give her the benefit of the doubt.

Lillian was very sure that was what it was.

"The point of this meeting is to remind you all to keep close tabs on your shows and your newscasts," Eugene was wrapping up. "And to let you know, in case you are wondering, that the doctor has been warned. If it happens again, Dr. Arnold won't be allowed on air again." He stood up and stormed toward his office.

"No time for questions, I take it," Candace muttered.

Lillian grinned. She didn't feel the blame was being directed her way, and she wasn't sorry to see Dr. Arnold go. Even if it was just for the lack of pre-approval of his remarks, she wasn't sorry to know that his opinion wouldn't get any more air time at CUBR.

But it would get lots, in Parliament, while some of the MPs lobbied for changes to the abortion law.

***

From home an hour later, Lillian called Detective Sinclair. He'd invited her to call him any time and, for some reason, she felt she wanted to talk to him.

"Miss Clarkson," he said. "What can I do for you? Anything new?"

"Nothing to tell you." Lillian said. "But if I do come across something, or hear something, I'll call you."

"Glad to hear that," he said. "Never too many ears and eyes open."

"I wanted to ask you," Lillian groped for the words she wanted to say. She had nothing to say or ask, really, but somehow, she wanted to stay connected. "The person who did this . . . will you be able to find him? Or her?"

Sinclair seemed to chuckle. Or maybe it was a snort. "The official answer would be 'yes'. The more accurate answer would be 'it depends'. But we've gathered a lot of solid information at the scene and we'll be talking to hundreds of people. I'm very confident."

"What would you want me to be looking for, or listening for, if I could be helpful?"

There was a short pause, as if Sinclair were considering. "I'm sure you know most of the people at the station. Just keep your eyes open for conversations I might never hear about. Anyone who might have been at the station that morning, for example. Someone we don't already know about, someone we haven't interviewed yet."

"I'll do that," Lillian said. "I want to help in any way I can. The person who . . .why do you think they did that?"

"No idea at this point," the detective said. "That's another thing we'll look for. Motive. Who might have wanted Susan Taylor dead? Who stood to gain from her death? Did she have any enemies that you know of?"

"None that I know of," Lillian said.

"This . . . whoever it was, probably has gone to some effort to cover his tracks. Might even be setting us up to follow a false trail. You might be able to keep us away from any blind alleys."

"I'll do my best," Lillian said.

***

After the call, Lillian curled up on her couch for a nap. After only fifteen minutes, she woke up in a fog. She headed out, but nothing pierced it—not the late afternoon sun, not the fantastic aroma of the coffee she stopped to drink at a diner on Queen Street, and not the two-hour walk on the lakeshore.

She was lethargic and yet she felt restless. Somehow, she felt herself compelled to talk to Corey again. But not on the phone.

The streetcar clattered and clanked like it was about to fall apart. Would they ever replace them? The back of her cotton blouse was beyond damp; she was sticking to the old leather seat.

Two men with crewcuts stared at her, and then one tried a wink. Men! Did they think women were on earth just for their personal entertainment? Not all, of course, but some.

She remembered how one night she, Penny, Joyce and Susan had shared stories, over long-necked bottles of wine, of men accosting them. Lillian had had her share of wolf whistles and crude remarks shouted as she'd walked past construction sites. Penny told a story of a man sitting across from her on the subway, exposing and fondling himself while he watched her reaction. She was frozen, she said, and she was more upset by that, by her own reaction, than by her first view of a penis.

Joyce had had a man try to kiss her when he drove her home after babysitting for his kids, and she said she'd heard similar conversations with other women. Every time, every single person had a story.

Susan's was the worst. She hadn't been willing to go into details, but if it wasn't rape, it was pretty darn close. Done by a university date, someone she knew, not a stranger in a back alley when she'd made a bad decision and taken a shortcut in the dark. (This was Lillian's biggest fear.) Forced by a boy she'd daydreamed about, Susan was left with no bruises, no marks on her body, and no obvious wounds. Hurt without violence, if that was possible. The wounds were the kind that don't show, but go much deeper, inside.

On the latest phone call, Detective Sinclair told her his next steps would be to retrace all of Susan's activities over the past month and to interview all of her friends and contacts. He brought Raymond's name up again. Everybody thought he'd quit because of losing out on the Tokyo assignment, but maybe the timing of that news had been a lucky coincidence for him. Did he have another reason for wanting to get out of radio, a reason that had to do with Susan's death?

Detective Sinclair asked Lillian if she knew of anyone who might be considered an enemy of Susan's, and she had no answer. Susan was the sweetheart of the town, the queen of the prom. People admired her and sought her company. They loved to hear her talk about how much good she planned to bring in to the world, with her inventions and discoveries.

Mail was piling up outside Corey's front door. Lillian picked the envelopes up, then knocked. When he opened the door, she handed them to him, then pushed past him to go inside.

"Corey, I want to know what happened with you and Susan."

Corey had on only an old pair of jeans. He looked like he hadn't slept in days. Avoiding her eyes, he turned and walked into the kitchen, opened the fridge, and pulled out a can of beer. He held it out toward Lillian.

"You drink too much, " she said. "No."

Corey shrugged and snapped off the top, then took a long gulp.

"What can I say? She dumped me."

"Why?"

"Long story."

Lillian stared at him. "And how did you react? Did you hate her? Enough to want her dead?"

As soon as she said it, she saw his eyes go narrow and felt his heart harden. Wrong question, wrong approach.

Corey drank for a few more minutes and Lillian had the sense to stay silent. Finally, he said, "I didn't hate her at all. She was my girlfriend."

"But she dumped you."

"Months ago. Wouldn't you think that if I was that kind of guy, if it was a crime of passion, it would have happened sooner than this?"

"Maybe it took you a while to get up the nerve. Or to realize she wasn't going to change her mind. Did you try to get her to change her mind?"

A fly buzzed in through the open kitchen window and settled on an open-faced bologna sandwich on the table.

"I went to talk to her a few times, yeah," he said.

For a few minutes, the sound of the fly buzzing was the only sound in the room.

Then Corey cracked open. "I love her, Lill. I told her that, she told me that back. We were good together for quite a while, even though I didn't live in science world and she didn't care enough about music."

"Why did you break up?"

"Just started fighting too much. About how late to stay out at the coffeehouse. We'd be there seeing some fantastic group and Susan would want to leave at 9:30. She didn't want to hang out. I started playing on a softball team. She didn't want to join and play, too, and she didn't want to come watch the games. So, we broke up."

"When, exactly?"

"Last May."

"Last May! But nobody knew you weren't together anymore until a few weeks ago!"

"I asked her not to tell people. I didn't want to have to deal with the questions, and a few of them would be upset as soon as they heard. My mother, for one. Maybe you, her friends?"

Lillian shook her head. "I wouldn't have cared."

Corey drained his second beer. "What did you think of us?"

"Mismatched," Lillian said.

"Maybe I'm a better match for you?" He leered at her.

She knew it was the beer talking and that he would be easy to fend off.

Lillian shook her head. "So, you broke up four, five months ago."

"Yeah, and she got a new boyfriend pretty quickly. A grad student in the physics department, just down the hall from where she is at the university."

"Did that make you mad enough to shoot her up and leave her to die alone?"

"Christ, Lill! I didn't do that!" Corey was pacing the kitchen like a caged tiger. "Is that what you think? Is that what the cops think?"

"I just have one word of advice for you, Corey. Alibi."

***

Penny called just minutes after Lillian arrived home.

"We're just around the corner. Come out for a bite of dinner. We'll have you home before eight."

"Who is 'we'?"

"Des and me."

"I'll be right there. Where, exactly?"

"Duke's for cheeseburgers."

The restaurant had the homey vibe of a 50s diner, black and white checked floor, turquoise fake-leather benches, and tabletop jukeboxes. They did hugs all around and then chatted about music, the latest news, the clothes the British bands were wearing. But they all knew that they'd come around to talking about Susan's murder, eventually.

Des opened the subject. "Have you talked to the cops again, Lill? Do they have any leads?"

"Nothing they've told me about," she said. "Detective Sinclair seemed to be interested in her ex-boyfriend the most."

"Do you really think Corey could have killed her?" Penny asked.

"No, I don't think so. Somehow, I can't imagine him stringing together enough coherent thought. And at the radio station! It doesn't make sense. If he wanted to inject her, and maybe kill her, wouldn't you think he'd get her over to his place and do it privately?"

"Maybe he tried and she wouldn't see him," Des suggested.

Penny shook her head. "I think it's more likely that it was some kind of weird stranger. Or a stalker thing."

"But most violent crimes involve somebody you know, not a stranger, Detective Sinclair told me," Lillian said. "What I want to find out next is who this new boyfriend is." She took a bite of her apple crumble. "Or 'was', I guess I should say."

Chapter 9

September 17
1964

After knocking on the professor's door, Lillian looked up and down the hall of the fourth floor of the Science Building. The University of Toronto was not a place where she'd spent a lot of time since she'd moved to the city. Actually, the only places she'd seen much of were the coffeehouses in Yorkville and the radio station. But after she walked around campus for half an hour, the Science Building wasn't hard to find.

A low voice ordered her to come in. A wave of cigarette smoke curled out through the open door and dispersed into the hallway, looking for other lungs to invade.

A large black ashtray, overflowing with butts, and a package of the same cigarettes that Lillian had seen advertised on a bus on her way over here sat by Dr. Berman's right hand. A book the size of a suitcase was on her left. Lillian had not seen many college or university professors, but she'd seen enough TV and movies to know that this one was probably not typical. Her carrot-red hair sprang from her scalp in waves that looked vaguely electric, as if she'd put her finger in a socket somewhere. She wore a flowing garment made of some sort of silky fabric covered in a batik print. Every one of her fingers carried a ring and the hoops in her ears were about four inches in diameter.

"Can I help you?"

"I'm a friend of Susan Taylor. I was told you were her thesis advisor," Lillian said.

Dr. Berman stubbed out her cigarette and motioned toward the chair facing her desk. Lillian had to move half a dozen journals and file folders from it to the corner of Dr. Berman's desk before she could sit down.

"We are all missing her very much," Dr. Berman said.

Lillian looked around the room at the floor-to-ceiling bookshelves and the tiny window, propped open with a long pencil. "I don't know if you've heard that the police now think that she was . . . that it was a . . . " She couldn't quite get out the words.

"A murder? Yes, I have." The professor's eyes were kindly. "What can I do for you?"

"I've just heard that Susan was dating a grad student, a physics major. I wonder if you know anything about that?"

Dr. Berman stared at her for a few moments. Making up her mind, probably.

"How well did you know Susan?" Apparently, she had a few more questions before she did.

"She was one of my best friends," Lillian said. "We were in school together and we came up to Canada from New York to try to make it with a folk group in Yorkville."

"But Susan decided she'd rather go to university," Dr. Berman said.

"And the rest of us decided we wanted something else. I work in a radio newsroom."

Dr. Berman looked at her sharply. "Are we on the record here?"

"I'm only talking with you out of personal interest, Dr. Berman," Lillian said. "We're not covering Susan's death in my newsroom. Maybe we would, if the police were releasing information about the case, but they're not."

The professor leaned back in her chair. "Aright, then. Yes, I was Susan's thesis advisor, but I was also her friend. She was a remarkable young woman and we had big plans for her, here in the department. The work she was doing was very cutting-edge. She's been assisting with some of my research, but she was also doing original work of her own and I think she would have been publishing by the spring. She was supposed to be doing a presentation on her results at an ACM meeting in New York as part of the World's Fair."

Lillian was fighting with her mixed feelings as she heard all this. Proud, because Susan was doing so well, but sad, so sad. None of this was news, though. It was Susan's social life that was a blur to her.

Dr. Berman noticed her distress and stepped in to rescue her. "Now, you were also asking me about Susan's relationship with Mikhail."

Mikhail?

"Mikhail is one of the brightest lights in the physics department. He's working on a combined master's and PhD, and even though he's only been here a few years, his name is better known than some of the profs over there."

"Where is he from?"

"He did his undergrad at NYU. He and Susan met at a faculty mixer at the end of last year. She told me he hit all the right notes with her from the beginning."

Dr. Berman's phone rang, but she made no move to answer it. She just sat there, very still, and looked into Lillian's eyes. And waited.

"Thank you for telling me about him, Dr. Berman," Lillian eventually said.

"Does this help, Lillian? I hope so. It must have been very hard for you, having your best friend die so unexpectedly."

"I think it would be hard to have a close friend die, whether you expected it or not," Lillian said. "But I get what you mean."

"You're right. And is it ever 'expected'?" Dr. Berman pondered the point. "Even when the person is elderly, or is doing something self-destructive. It's probably almost always a surprise."

She smiled. "I don't mean to cut you off, but I have a class starting in ten minutes and I have to go. But you're welcome to come back any time, to talk about Susan."

Lillian stood up. "Thank you for your time, Dr. Berman. I just have one more question. Could you tell me where I might find Mikhail?"

***

When Lillian walked back into the newsroom, she discovered that her absence had been noted.

"Where have you been?" Chuck asked. "Eugene's roaring around, demanding that I call a meeting of everyone assigned to the Royal Tour coverage and I've been stalling him, waiting for you. Come on, grab your notepad."

It turned out to be one of those meetings that it didn't really matter if Lillian attended. Or anyone else, for that matter. One of those meetings that only the organizer got anything from. She hoped it reassured Eugene that all their plans were on track, because it really didn't seem necessary for Chuck, Leo, herself, or the Maggie MacRae crew.

Man, she was hungry. After the meeting ended, she was on her way down the hall toward the vending machines when the main newsroom line rang. Leo picked up. He waved the receiver toward Lillian.

"It's that detective," he hissed.

Lillian headed for an editing room, a tiny space with a reel-to-reel tape recorder, a supply of razor blades and splicing tape, and a phone extension.

"I'll take it in here," she called over her shoulder.

"Lillian, we found something in Susan's apartment, and I want to ask you about it. It's her daytimer."

"Yes, I suppose that would be helpful," Lillian said. "I'm surprised no one found it before now."

"Kincaid turned it up. It's a black, book-type calendar, with a spiral binding. Your friend was keeping it in the milk bottle return spot outside the old house where she was renting. It was our third time going through the place before someone thought of looking there," he said. "We're using it to trace her movements on her last day, her last week, her last month. What we're finding so far is mostly the university, a couple of doctor's offices for appointments, your place, the train station. To New York. Why would she be going to New York? Did you know about that?"

Lillian shrugged, even though Sinclair couldn't see her. "Yeah, I knew she made a trip. She had some research to do for her thesis advisor. And we have a friend living there, Rhonda Sheridan."

She could hear Sinclair making his notes. "I'd like any information you have about this Rhonda. Address, phone number, and so on."

"Sure."

"And what were the doctor's appointments about, do you think? Did she have any sort of condition that you knew of? Something that required multiple visits?"

"Susan was completely healthy," Lillian said.

"Maybe she was going to someone else's appointments? Going along with a friend?"

"Could be. That would be like Susan to do that," Lillian said.

"There wasn't much noted about things coming up for late September or into October, but we did see a note about a train departure on September 28th. Going to New York. Any ideas about that trip?"

"For the World's Fair. We were all going to go, to see it all, and to be in her corner cheering for her while she did part of a presentation at the Canada Pavilion. Her advisor, Dr. Berman, actually, is the one whose discovery it is, but Susan is . . . was . . . part of the team and Dr. Berman was sharing the stage."

"Just a personal trip for you?"

"I think I'll be getting an assignment to gather tape for my radio station, too. Man-in-the-street stuff."

"You're still going?"

"Oh yeah. Who passes up an opportunity to go to the States, ever?"

"There's also a frequent reference, throughout Susan's planner, to the initials MK. Do you have any idea what that's about?"

Something made Lillian feel she wanted to keep this news about Susan's boyfriend to herself for now. She wanted a chance to meet him herself, before the police appeared on his scene. Who knows, it might spook him so much that he'd never agree to meet Lillian.

"No idea," she said.

***

Lillian found Mikhail Kogonov in a small office on the top floor of the science auxiliary building, a beige box that also housed the machines where students could book a time to keypunch the cards they'd use to run the numbers for their research projects. Susan had told Lillian that the facility was in such demand it ran twenty-four hours around the clock and she was often there in the middle of the night to get her raw data processed.

Mikhail was a tall, thin man with the long, slender fingers of a pianist and the build of a competitive swimmer. Just Susan's type.

His face was not friendly. "My office hours are Tuesdays and Thursdays, two to four."

"I'm not a student," Lillian said. "I'm a friend of Susan's." She blurted it out quickly and loudly, so that he would stop pushing the door closed.

And he did. He took a deep breath, and she thought she saw a flash of pain in his eyes. Stepping back into the tiny office, he waved her toward a chair.

"Are you the friend who works in news at the Top 40 station or the one who is at the CBC?"

"The private radio station," Lillian said. "Susan told you about us?"

"All of you. The one at the government, the one working for the doctor's office, the boy who was in the folk singing group with you, his brother who is on the radio."

"She didn't tell us anything about you."

He smiled, and she had a glimpse of what might have been the attraction for Susan. "I asked her to keep our relationship a secret. I didn't want others in the faculty thinking that she was gaining any advantage because of dating me. She was brilliant, all on her own, and I didn't want that undervalued, or her reputation affected in any way."

His English was very good but Lillian could detect just a trace of the eastern European accent.

"But Dr. Berman knows," Lillian said. "She's the one who pointed you out to me."

"Now that Susan is gone, those other things don't matter. I think I can speak about her now. She was so good to me, and to my sister."

"Your sister?"

Mikhail suddenly looked stricken. His gaze went to the window, then back to the phone on his desk. "They never met. They exchanged letters from time to time. They liked each other, I think."

"What does your sister say about Susan's death?"

"Anna is very upset. As am I."

Lillian nodded, then handed him a card. "Here's my number at the radio station. You can reach me there any time. Maybe you'd like to meet a few of Susan's other friends?"

"I'd like that," Mikhail said.

***

Back at the station, Lillian lost no time in getting to the library and asking for Valessa's help. On her way in, she passed Josh, who was carrying a big sandwich and an armful of LPs.

"Hi, Lill," he said. "If you run into Chuck or Eugene, please don't tell them you saw me down here. They think I'm gone for the day."

"Sure thing," she said.

"It's a great place to come for a little downtime," he said. "They've got some fans they want me to meet and some commercials they want me to do, and I'm trying to duck them."

"It must be a drag, sometimes, to be so public."

"No kidding. It's not much fun to be recognized in public when you're just running out to the grocery store and you look like hell. Or to have your voice recognized on the phone."

"Some people would love that. They get into your line of work exactly because they want that attention."

"That ain't me," Josh said.

"I'll keep your location a secret," Lillian said.

Valessa had a stack of newspapers in front of her, but she readily put them aside to listen to Lillian's request.

"Okey-dokey. Anything I have on a physics student named Mikhail Kogonov," Valessa said.

"Or a violinist named Anna Kogonov."

Valessa cocked her head to one side. "Don't you read the papers?"

"Ha, very funny. Come on, Valessa, what do you know?."

"Anna Kogonov is . . . was . . . first violinist for the Moscow Symphony. Defected last month in Montreal."

"Where is she now?"

"Don't know. I think the Canadian government stepped in and maybe she's in Ottawa. But if you're interested, I can hunt through the back issues of the Globe and the Telegram and the Star."

"I'm interested! Thank you so much."

Valessa slid her reading glasses down on her nose. "Is this something the news department is researching? Plans for a series, maybe?"

"It's early days," Lillian said. "Just a fishing expedition."

As she walked down the hall back to the newsroom, Lillian tried to figure out why she couldn't get her mind off the information about Mikhail Kogonov and his sister. If Susan was in the early stages of a new relationship and was happy with it, why hadn't she told Lillian about him? If he was in love with her, why hadn't he seemed more upset about her death?

Lillian instinctively felt that perhaps she was judging too much. She'd only just met the man—how could she evaluate whether or not he was upset? Maybe if she'd talked to him ten days ago, right after it happened, his reactions to her questions would have been different. Maybe he was just the type who didn't show emotion easily.

And what about this sister? Why had she decided to leave her home country? Over here, we vault to the conclusion that anybody who gets a chance to leave the Soviet Union and live in a free country would do that, but presumably there must be many people there who are content to remain there. Wouldn't the star violinist of a symphony orchestra live a comfortable, even luxurious life?

Obviously, she had her reasons, because she'd done it. *How* had she done it? Was it like something from a James Bond movie, where she ran through the dark of night, down a lonely alley, climbed a wall, ducked a bullet, then burst into a brightly lit hotel lobby, shouting for directions to the Canadian embassy?

Lillian shook her head. She was getting silly. Who did she know that she could ask about this?

Maybe Joyce. Her work for the government in Ottawa might give her some knowledge of this.

The desk in the farthest corner of the newsroom was Dominic's. He was out, covering a political press conference, and wouldn't be back for a few hours. She could use his phone.

"Are we off the record?" Joyce's first question caught Lillian off guard.

"Yeah, I guess so," Lillian said. "Yes, yes, we are. I'm just asking for background."

She could picture Joyce pulling her long hair back against her neck, the way she did when she was on a serious topic. "Yes, I can confirm that Anna Kogonov is still here in Canada and that her brother is a PhD student at U of T."

"Loosen up, Joyce, this isn't official. This is friends," Lillian said. "I talked with Mikhail Kogonov at his office at the university this morning. He says he was Susan's boyfriend."

"Yes," Joyce said.

"Come on, Joyce! Did you know about this? Did you know about this Mikhail?"

"Susan told me, yes."

"Why would she tell you and not tell me?" Lillian heard how she sounded, her voice pitched high and her words angry. "I'm sorry. I just mean . . . I thought we were close. I was one of her best friends. Why would she tell you about something as important as a new boyfriend and not tell me?"

"It was about something much more than a new boyfriend," Joyce said. "Think about it, Lillian. You're in the media. Susan had something that needed to be kept quiet. A secret that wasn't really hers. It belonged to Mikhail. To Mikhail and to Anna."

"Anna, the sister."

"Yes. She defected a month or so ago, in Montreal, then ran to Toronto to get to her brother. From what I heard, that was not easy. Then, once she got there, Mikhail told Susan about it and asked for her advice."

"Did he know you work for the government?"

Susan paused. "You know, I don't know if he knew beforehand. But obviously Susan told him about me, eventually, because they called me to ask how to get help."

"Why didn't she just go to the police or the embassy when she first got away?"

"I guess she's had some experiences with police and government in the USSR and her trust level wasn't high, as they say around here."

"Wouldn't the authorities or the media look for her at her brother's place?"

"That's why she stayed at Susan's apartment. They called me from there. I spoke with my boss, and he brought in the right people."

Lillian put her head down on Dominic's desk, exhausted. These were her friends and yet they kept such huge secrets from her? She understood that, because of her job, people might think they had to hold back from her, but didn't they know that she wouldn't reveal a confidence if they asked her to keep it? She could compartmentalize, keep the walls up between her work life and her private life, and they should know that.

What other secrets were there?

"Where is Anna now?" she asked.

"In Toronto," Joyce said.

"Who else in your department knows about all this?" Lillian asked.

"My supervisor, of course. And one other person that I had to bring into the situation because I had to miss a few days because of going to the doctor."

"You've been sick?"

"Yeah, I was away a bit. But Mikhail and Susan were okay with me asking this other person to help and, in the end, everything was handled."

"Who was it?"

"I can't say any more."

"Do you think Susan was in danger because of helping them?"

"She might have been. The Soviet Union is a culture that's very different from ours. People play for keeps. They don't want you to leave, and mostly, you can't."

"It's hard to imagine," Lillian said.

"It is," Joyce agreed. "I've gone to all the briefings here and I've read a lot of books and I still don't think I really get it. They map out your whole life for you from a very young age, if you're behind the Iron Curtain. Many people hate it and they're desperate to escape. Look at the Berlin Wall, my God. People are shot just for trying to cross what was once an ordinary city street."

Lillian felt slightly sick to her stomach. "I can see why Susan felt so compelled to help. Did Susan stay in touch with Anna?"

"I can't answer any more questions, Lill. I probably said too much already. We're off the record, right? From the beginning of this phone call? I need to hear you say it out loud."

"We are off the record," Lillian said. "I'm not sure I'm any closer to understanding why or how Susan died, anyway. Even if someone did kill her—"

"You have to accept that someone did," Joyce cut in. "The police say so, and they have a homicide investigation underway. They'll get to Mikhail and Anna eventually, and we'll have more answers."

"Do you think Mikhail or the Soviets had something to do with it?"

"No idea." Joyce went silent, and Lillian waited her out. "But what I really don't get is how they could have had anybody go into your radio station who could have injected her. Don't you have security? It had to have been somebody inside the station."

Chapter 10

September 18
1964

The door from the parking lot creaked as Lillian pulled it open at a quarter to four. The truth was that the security at the radio station was as relaxed as a suburban house party.

During the day, there was a receptionist at the front desk, a sheet of paper for signing in and out, and a middle-aged security guard who sat in an armchair by the door, ready to answer questions from any visitors. Through the night and into the morning hours, the night-shift guard was supposed to walk around the premises, checking door locks and dark hallways. Even in the aftermath of a murder, CUBR had not seen fit to add more security or tighten up the rules.

Lillian took the stairs up to the office and dropped into her chair. The line-up for this morning's news run was thin, and she knew Chuck would be looking for at least two fresh items from her. The nighttime news guy had left an apologetic note: *Hey, Chuck and Lillian, sorry I couldn't leave you more tape. There was no actuality from the political meeting in Scarborough. I had an interview with another flag debate protester lined up, but he canceled on me at 11 o'clock. I just couldn't stay any later. But I left you some ideas with names and phone numbers. Most of them are pretty soft, though, so do better if you can.*

Lillian settled down with the newspaper and the summaries from the wire machine. She listened to the CFRB newscast at 4:30 and reread the previous afternoon and evening casts, looking for follow ideas.

Then something caught her eye. *Cult leader accosted by parents trying to rescue their daughter.* The dateline was New York.

Apparently, a young woman had joined a religious group and cut off her ties to her family. Her parents blamed the minister for her decision not to see them anymore and had driven over to his home, taking a reporter and photographer with them. The reporter had witnessed a shouting match on the front doorstep and a desperate father trying to gain entry to find his daughter.

The phone rang and Lillian picked up.

"Lillian, hey."

"Glenda! What are you doing awake at 5 in the morning?"

"I could give you some b.s. about not being able to sleep, Lill, but actually, I got a phone call from Howard, asking me to call you."

"Howard? Howard Ronson, your . . . your . . . "

"My spiritual leader, yeah. He wants to know whether you'd like him to comment on the story out of New York today about the girl whose parents are trying to kidnap her."

"I just saw that story," Lillian said. "I think it's a bit more complex than that."

"That's what Howard said!"

"Look, Glenda, I don't think we need a clip on the news with a local angle on this New York story. Thanks, anyway."

"There's a lot Howard could add to your coverage of the faith-based and spiritual community," Glenda said.

"We don't really do coverage of the faith-based and spiritual communities."

"Exactly! And there's a lot to say."

"Glenda, I can't really talk about this now. I have a lot of things to do in the next half hour."

"Right, of course, you're right. We can discuss it when you come over to help me move tomorrow," Glenda said. "About 10?"

Lillian agreed, just to get her off the phone, then sat back and stared through the newsroom windows at the streetlights throwing pools of yellow onto the city sidewalks below.

Who was this Howard Ronson? What were his credentials? What did he have going on that her friend Glenda would pack up and want to move?

Lillian shook her head. She didn't need this distraction. She was already stressed over this morning's news run. Usually, she only had one hole to plug. She didn't much like phoning people at 6 or 6:30 in the morning, and Chuck was unpredictable about how willing he was to do the calling.

To be fair, it also had to do with how busy a day it was in international and national news, and how much rewriting he had to do on the wire copy before it was ready to be read on the CUBR airwaves. He'd been hunched over his typewriter, headphones on, for over an hour. Lining up two or three more items would be up to her alone.

She chased a local reaction to the King of Greece getting married and then tried to track down a home number for one of the members of the new political all-party committee given the job of sorting out the flag issue. She came up dry.

At 7:30, she still had nothing. Nobody in Toronto (no one in the Greek-Canadian community answering their phone at 7:15 in the morning, anyway) cared to comment about the King's marriage. None of the politicians' names were in the Rolodex.

She called the number Glenda had given her.

"Howard Ronson?"

"Yes, that's me. Who is this?"

"Lillian Clarkson, CUBR News. Could I speak to you for a few minutes?"

"Absolutely!"

It was only a ten-minute conversation, but by the end, Lillian could see the attraction for Glenda. He was charming and charismatic—at least, Lillian thought so. And she'd been inclined to dislike him. She could only imagine how quickly he made a conquest when there was no previous opinion.

"Of course, no bona fide spiritual leader makes any effort to separate a child from her parents," he was saying. "I think we might find, as more details about this case come out, that there's been a lot of misunderstanding. On all sides."

Lillian made her decision. "Are you available for an interview on air later this morning, Mr. Ronson?"

"Please. Call me Howard. Yes. How about if I come over to the studio? What time do you want me there?"

"Oh, that's okay, we can do it over the phone," Lillian said.

"I'd really prefer to come in person." Howard had a voice that was simultaneously authoritative and gentle, almost hypnotic.

"Whatever you wish," Lillian said. "I'll meet you at the front door in half an hour."

When she went down to meet Howard, she found him chatting with Marcus, the security guard. It was the first time that Lillian had seen Howard up close. It was difficult to see much detail of his features, because he had a full beard and moustache, the color quite a few shades darker than the salt-and-pepper color of his hair. He was very tall, and Lillian had to tip her head back to talk to him as they walked toward the elevator to the studio.

She planned to put him into Studio 22, do a brief interview on tape, then cut it and turn it around in time for the last local newscast on the Dawn Patrol show. If it was good enough, maybe they'd use it throughout the morning.

"I was so sorry to hear about your friend, Susan," Howard said. "She came along with Glenda to a meeting one evening, the same as you did. It wasn't for her, but she was friendly."

"She was friendly to everyone." Lillian, unexpectedly, became choked up in the moment. Howard stopped walking and looked at her with eyes that seemed to pierce right through to the back of her head.

"She was lucky to have such good friends," he said. "Although I guess, in the end, that didn't change the outcome of her life."

What the hell did that mean? Was he implying that she, or Glenda, or any of Susan's other friends were somehow responsible for preventing what had happened, and hadn't been able to?

"How are Joyce and Rhonda taking it?" he was asking. Did he know everybody's names? How did he know so much about Susan's friends?

Through Glenda, of course.

Later that morning, Lillian called Glenda, to let her know that she'd invited Howard on the air to talk about religions and cults, after all. Glenda was pleased, to put it mildly.

"Oh, Lill, I'm so glad you did that! He knows so much and he has so much to say!"

"He certainly was confident," Lillian said. "Have you told him a lot about me, and Joyce, and Susan?"

"And Penny," Glenda said. "He is very interested in all his disciples' families and friends."

"Disciples? Is that what you call yourselves?"

"Oh, that's just me, exaggerating." Glenda's laugh seemed a little embarrassed. "Are you still available to help me move tomorrow, by the way? I've found a friend with a truck who will help, but that's still only two of us."

Lillian sighed. "Yeah, I'll be there at ten."

Later that morning, when she was circling through the lobby on her way to the library, Lillian saw Marcus, the security guard.

"Marcus! Lillian from the newsroom," she said.

The elderly man had a big grin for her. "I remember. How's your day going?"

"Just fine. But I wanted to ask you about the guest we had come in this morning. Howard Ronson is his name. Do you remember him? Fiftyish. Tall guy, beard and moustache."

"Yeah, sure. I know him."

"You know him? Have you seen him before today?"

"See him all the time. At the Y. He drops in for a workout at the same time as me, a lot of days. Nice guy."

Through the rest of the day, Lillian chewed this over. If Marcus knew Howard, was it possible he had let him into the station on other occasions?

Chapter 11

September 19
1964

The alarm was ringing. The clock on Lillian's night table showed the time as 9:00. Was that possible? She was supposed to pick up Glenda at ten—she'd never make it in time.

Maybe the clock was wrong. She was still getting the hang of reading the numbers on this new digital clock Des had given her for Christmas. Maybe that nine was really a seven? She grabbed her watch to check. Nope, there were the two hands, clearly pointing at a nine and a twelve. She must have set the alarm time wrong last night.

As she groped her way toward consciousness, the phone started ringing, too. Lillian reached for the receiver.

"Hello?"

"Lillian, this is Mrs. Taylor. Susan's mom."

"Hello, Mrs. Taylor." Lillian sat up in bed.

"I'm calling because we had something happen last night. Did you, by any chance, stop by Susan's apartment to pick up a few things?"

This was weird. "No, no, I didn't. What do you mean?"

"Well, someone went into Susan's apartment last night and took some things. We've checked with the landlord and he hasn't given a key to anyone else. Then, we thought maybe she'd given you a key some time. Maybe when she was away and wanted you to check her place?"

"No, never," Lillian said. "Did someone break in?"

"There's no sign of any break in. But things are missing. Her winter coat, her new boots, a few of her books and some other things from her desk." Mrs. Taylor's voice caught, and she had trouble getting the next words out. "And the pearl earrings we gave her for her twenty-first birthday last year."

"I'm sorry, Mrs. Taylor, but I don't know anything about this. How horrible. You should let the police know."

"Yes, of course we will. How are you doing, Lillian?"

"I'm getting by, Mrs. Taylor. Day to day."

"I understand, sweetie." They sat in silence for a moment. "We were thinking of heading home to Albany, but apparently, there's going to be a get-together in her honor at the university later this week, so we'll stay on for that. Did you hear about that?"

"No, I didn't," Susan said.

"Well, I'm sure you and any of Susan's other friends would be welcome. A Dr. Berman is organizing it."

As soon as she hung up, Lillian pulled on a pair of jeans and a T-shirt. Furniture moving clothes. When she got to Glenda's apartment building, she was happy to see three large young men loading clothes, books, and tables into a truck. Glenda was right behind them, carrying her spider plant and a macramé mandala.

"I see you're taking your weird eastern fabric craftey things with you," Lillian said with a grin, as she gave Glenda a hug.

"You laugh, but you wait. One day, everybody will be doing it." Glenda lifted the plant and the wall hanging up to one of the men inside loading the truck. "Thanks for coming to help."

"What do you want me to do?"

"I've got more books upstairs that need to come along. Could you bring some of those?"

"Sure thing," Lillian said, as they walked into the building together. "So, you're really doing this."

"I am," Glenda said. "By the way, I wanted to tell you. I ran into Corey Lang yesterday."

Lillian had a sudden queasy feeling. "Lucky you. Did he stop to talk to you?"

"Oh, yeah. I was coming out of the doctor's office, on my way over to the lab to deliver some samples, for him and for Dr. Arnold. You know, the one you have as your regular medical news guy at CUBR? He's on our floor, in our building, and we do favors for him sometimes. Anyway, there was Corey Lang, walking along the sidewalk. Weaving, I should say. Looked like he was on something. Came up to me and said hello. Called me 'Susan's friend'. 'Yo, Susan's friend', that's what he said."

"Did he talk about her?"

"A little bit. Said he'd been having nightmares about her."

Lillian shook her head. "He is such a weirdo. Anything else?"

"Wanted to know if I'd seen her parents lately. And whether the police had been calling me. 'No, have they been calling you?' I asked him, but he didn't answer. Have they been calling you?"

"Detective Sinclair called to tell me they've found Susan's daytimer. Wanted to know if I knew anything about people she mentioned and appointments she'd had."

"And did you?"

"Not much. A bunch of them were doctor's appointments. Do you know anything about that?"

Glenda reached for an armload of coats on hangers in the closet. "No, not doctor's appointments. Here, can you carry some of these?"

Lillian held out her arms for Glenda to pile on the clothes. "Are you letting your apartment go entirely?"

"I sublet it to a couple of nursing students at Toronto Wellesley," Glenda said. "There was just too much stuff to take out to the farm."

"Where is this farm, exactly?"

"Muskoka," Glenda said.

That covered a lot of territory, if you thought about geography, and none at all, if you thought about communication.

"You might even have to quit your part-time job then," Lillian said. "That's about a hundred miles from here."

She stopped and put down the armload of books she was holding. "Glen, I have to talk to you about this. I just feel as though you're diving into something and you don't know how deep the water is. What do you really know about this man? Or the rest of the people? What are you going to get from living there that you couldn't get from being here in Toronto, with your friends and your job? You could still go to Howard Ronson's meetings, still belong to his church—without giving up everything."

Glenda sighed. "Lillian, I know it's hard for you to understand. But . . . I've been so stuck lately. Stuck and yet changing so much. Toronto didn't work out for me the way it did for you. Or Susan, Des, Joyce. Rhonda went all the way to New York, for heaven's sake. And there I was, working in a doctor's office, doing work I didn't like, no foreseeable future. None. At Howard's farm, I have a place. I belong."

"What about Jordan?"

"I broke it off. He didn't mind. I was just one more, in a long line, to him. It's strange, I know, but at The Farm, I'm not just one more. Howard sees me as unique, and as a precious soul. Nobody's ever done that, not even my mother."

"Will you come back to town if it doesn't work out?"

"Of course she will!" Lillian jumped almost out of her skin when she heard Howard Ronson's voice behind her.

Glenda's face broke into a beautiful smile. "Howard! Thank you for coming!"

"You're very welcome, my dear. I see the boys got here ahead of me. I hope they're doing everything you need to have done to get this move happening."

Lillian looked at him. This was her chance to find out a little more about this man who had drawn her girlfriend so far into his circle.

"Howard, it's nice to see you again," she said.

"Lillian. I hope everybody at the station was happy with the context I provided for your newscast."

"It's always good to get a local angle on an international story," she said.

"I'd be pleased to be your local expert on spiritual issues any time."

"I have to say, though, that I was surprised to hear from Glenda that she's moving to your farm."

Howard beamed at Glenda. "She is one of The Called, yes, she is. We're very much looking forward to having her join us up north."

"How much time do you spend up there, Howard?" Lillian asked. "You seem to be here in Toronto a lot."

"Oh, I travel back and forth frequently. I've been here longer than I expected this time, because Glenda needed my support after Susan was killed . . . to go to her memorial service and so forth. And then, I was doing some media interviews, as you know."

"What will Glenda be doing up there? And what are the accommodations like?" Lillian directed her second question to Glenda.

"Her secretarial skills will be very welcome, Lillian. We need some help—you wouldn't believe what a mess our filing cabinets are! And she'll have five new roommates who are just dying to meet her."

"Five roommates?" This seemed to have caught Glenda's attention. "In what, like a large apartment? Or one of the houses on the property?"

"More like a student dorm," Howard said.

"You haven't seen the place where you'll be living?" Lillian made no attempt to hide her disapproval from Glenda.

"I've seen pictures," Glenda said. "But I didn't see anything about a dorm."

"You'll love it." Howard's confidence was compelling. "But I think we'd better get a move on. We want to get on the road. Long drive ahead of us."

"Could I see some of these pictures?" Lillian asked Glenda.

"No time, no time." Howard's smile was completely gone. He picked up one of Glenda's suitcases and took her arm. "Come along, my dear."

"One more thing, Howard," Lillian said. "I'm sure you can imagine, but I've been preoccupied with what happened to Susan. I think a lot of us have. The police have interviewed me quite a few times and people at the station are all asking questions." She crossed her arms across her chest. "Where were you on Sunday night and Monday morning of the Labor Day weekend?"

Lillian watched his eyes as closely as she could. The right one seemed to flicker a little, but she couldn't be sure.

"Why, Lillian, you sound like Joe Friday from *Dragnet*. Let's leave that to the cops, shall we? I was here, with my angels. Anyone can tell you that. I know your job makes you feel like you're some kind of investigator, but you're not." He held her gaze, even smiled a little. "Try to keep your nose out of my business, will you?"

He said it jokingly, but the "or else" was clear.

Chapter 12

September 21
1964

The mood in the meeting was gloomy and even the sound of the radio playing a Beach Boys tune quietly in the background didn't help. It was definitely shaping up to be what was called a 'slow news week', even with all of the events on the national and international stages. Thanks to a recent order from what Chuck called "on high", to chase local stories and not pay so much attention to the rest of the world, the whole team was digging around in any nearby corner they could think of.

"The biggest local story I've got is a car accident in Streetsville," Leo complained.

"There's a parade down at the Beaches in favor of the Maple Leaf design for the new flag," Lillian suggested.

Dominic threw a crumpled-up piece of paper at her. "We're sick of talking about the flag," he said. "How about a local crime story? Susan Taylor's murder."

Eugene sighed. "Bloody touchy, covering a death that happened in your own studio," he said. "Mr. Brooks is not happy about that. Even though it is our own media mystery, right here in our own backyard, he's not happy."

And of course, we have to keep the station owner happy, at all costs, Lillian thought.

"I think we'll wait for the police on that one," Eugene said. "Cover it, of course, if they put out a release or call a presser. Otherwise, we'll leave it alone."

"How about something about the Royal Tour?" Lillian said.

Chuck pulled out a cigarette, his fourth of the meeting. The butts in his ashtray threatened to spill over onto his desk. *Did he ever empty it?*

She glanced at the line of windows. None of them opened, and they had to rely on the ventilation system to clean out the smoke. It wasn't as bad as being in a bar, but at least in a bar, you had live music and maybe some dancing to make up for the haze in the air.

"Have you got anything new?" Chuck asked.

"Well, it's not exactly local, but my friend Joyce in Ottawa said the security arrangements that are being made are like nothing we've ever seen in Canada before. The talk is that specialists are being brought in from other countries—"

"You'd expect that the Brits would have their own security teams traveling for the Queen," Ron cut in.

"Yeah, but the host country contributes, too. They're putting together a really huge briefing book in Joyce's department. Nobody will talk about it, but maybe . . . "

"Maybe if you went there, someone would let you have a look at it. And maybe if you're right there, someone would talk to you about it." Chuck caught her drift.

"Someone who wouldn't take a phone call about it but might speak to someone right there," Eugene was buying in.

"Might speak to someone who had been vouched for by someone working in their own department," Lillian said.

Silence held sway for a few minutes while Eugene decided. "Alright, let's send Lillian. Take the train, be back tomorrow."

Chuck was not impressed. He dragged his focus back from the window where he'd been watching raindrops carve downward patterns through the grime, sighing and then dropping his head to bang it three times on the desk.

"What is it?" Eugene demanded.

"We've done the Royal visit prep story six times this month already," Chuck said.

"Do you have a better idea?" Eugene challenged in a tone of voice that made it clear that it was a rhetorical question. "Let's get the features machine in gear. Find as many locals as you can who love the Commonwealth and the Queen. Places—maybe a tea shop? Collectors of Royal stuff. Maybe someone who was in London for the Coronation in '53."

"More than ten years ago." Chuck seemed to mutter and yell at the same time.

Eugene snapped. "Alright! I hear you. It's your newscast, you figure it out. Come up with something better."

If he expected Chuck to feel squelched, he had to be disappointed. Lillian (and everyone else) saw the tiny smile on Chuck's face before its mask went back on.

Lillian tried to step in to be the peacemaker. "I think I can get a couple of clips from a couple who are planning to camp out along the Royal routes in both Ottawa and Montreal."

"Camping out—big deal." Chuck lit his fifth cigarette.

"We need enough Royal Tour feature material to fill the next four weeks," Eugene said. "I don't hear a lot of help from you."

"It's actually two weeks, six days," Lillian said.

Eugene glared at her. "Details. Make it work." He gathered up his clippings, his file folders, and the vile pipe that he used to spew a sickly sweet swell that he said was called Joe's Chocolate Flake. Didn't smell like any chocolate she'd ever known.

Just before he disappeared through the door, he tossed over his shoulder, "Thanks again for your help, Lillian. Speak to Lois in the front office about your Ottawa train ticket. And by the way, next week I'm sending you to New York to do some advance work for our World's Fair opening coverage in October."

Well, yeah. Now, she had to take back every cranky thought she'd ever had about the news director. New York!

Lillian was thrilled and sad at the same time. New York! She and the girls had talked about exploring the Big Apple together and now there was no chance of that ever happening with Susan.

That evening, over a bottle of wine at Penny's apartment, she and Lillian toasted Susan once again. "I still pick up the phone to call her," Lillian said. "And then I remember."

"I do the same," Penny said. "I like to take little moments to acknowledge her throughout the day. Otherwise, it feels so final, like there's just this big void."

"Like what?"

"When it's my turn to program music for the show, I choose songs she liked. Yesterday, I played three Lesley Gore songs throughout the show. She was Susan's favorite, you remember?"

Lillian nodded. "The host was a bit ticked off, but he backed off after I agreed to have a drink with him Friday afternoon."

"Are you going to show up?"

Penny shook her head. "Of course not. But by then he'll have bigger problems than Lesley Gore and he'll forget all about it."

Lillian poured them both another glass of wine. "Why does it have to be so difficult?"

"Things are changing for women. They are! Look at us, Lill. You're working at a major station in the newsroom. I'm working at the CBC, doing current affairs, and drama, and music."

They clinked glasses and enjoyed the moment. Yes, Lillian thought, it is getting better for us. Except for Susan. She wouldn't be around to see or hear any of it.

"Your New York trip is mid-week, isn't it?" Penny asked.

"Yeah, Tuesday to Thursday. I'm going by train."

"Maybe I should go, too," Penny said. "I could pitch my producer on having me collect some tape for the show, maybe get an early tour of the Canada pavilion . . ."

"That would be great!" For the first time in two weeks, Lillian felt her heart lighten a little. "Will we need a passport to cross the border? Or to get back?"

"I think a driver's license is enough," Penny said, then went to her purse to find her wallet and pull it out. "I haven't been to New York in ages."

They looked at it together. "Your photo's not bad," Lillian said. "Margaret."

"There were six Margarets in my class when I started school. So, five of us got nicknames and we could pick whatever we wanted."

"I've always liked Penny," Lillian said.

They gazed at the driver's license for a few more seconds, then Lillian raised her glass. "We'll dedicate this trip to Susan."

"It will be lovely to have something to look forward to after her memorial service at the university next week."

"Oh, are you going to that too?" Lillian asked. "I heard about it from Susan's mother."

"Yes, I'll be there. I think Glenda's coming down."

"I'll tell Joyce about it this week."

"I think there will be a public notice somewhere. In the Telegram, or maybe the Varsity, anyway."

"Then the police will probably know about it," Lillian said. "I wonder if we'll see Detective Sinclair there?"

Penny refilled her glass. "Don't think about it. Here's a toast to New York!"

"And once more, to Susan."

***

But before she got to the Big Apple, she had work to do in Canada's capital. Bytown, as they called it in the newsroom. An early morning train set her down in Ottawa three hours later. Joyce had offered to put her up for the night, after she went to the press conference at five o'clock, but this was official CUBR business and Lillian decided to take the opportunity to stay in a hotel. They agreed to meet for lunch at the Chateau Laurier.

Joyce's hair had changed since she'd seen her two weeks earlier. Hugging her friend, Lillian said, "I like your hair."

"Thanks, Lill," Joyce said. "I like to change it a lot. As you know." She opened a menu the size of a large bed pillow and looked over the choices. "Let me get breakfast."

"No, let me," Lillian said. "I'm on an expense account."

"So am I!" Joyce laughed. "I'll get breakfast, you get dinner. Give the Canadian taxpayer a break. Did they give you a credit card?"

"No, I still can't qualify," Lillian said. "So infuriating. Leo, Dominic, Ron, Chuck . . . they're all walking around with credit cards. Meanwhile, I have to carry all this cash."

"The times they are a-changin' ," Joyce said.

"Well, I hope they change enough that I'll be able to get a credit card. Or not face mandatory retirement at age thirty-two if I wanted to be a stewardess. Or firing from my job if I get pregnant."

Joyce's face darkened and she put her lips down to the coffee cup she'd lifted.

"But I guess that's changing, too," Lillian went on. "In the States, anyway. The Civil Rights Act makes pregnancy discrimination illegal. But let's get on to talking about the Royal Tour first," Lillian said. "I have to get my work done, even if I am enjoying myself with one of my oldest friends."

"There's a protocol briefing for the journalists who will be covering the visit," Joyce said.

"Yes, I know. They have them regularly, with updates, don't they? Ron's been up here to a couple of them. He's the reporter who'll be actually covering the story."

"And your job is . . . ?"

"Research." Lillian held her gaze as Joyce stared at her for a long minute. "But they are talking about putting a female voice on the morning news one day soon."

"And what can I help you with?"

"This security briefing book you told me about. Can I see it?"

"No."

Lillian went back to reading the massive menu. Much to talk about.

***

When Lillian walked through the foyer of the government building , she was very aware of the echo her heels made on the marble floor. She had to wrestle with the heavy doors at the back of the East Block theatre where they were holding the press conference. Dozens of backs in brown jackets and navy blazers blocked her view of the stage and podium area at the front. The room was too small for the number of news reporters they'd invited—or perhaps a lot of unexpected people had decided to attend at the last minute.

Lillian was conscious of all the eyes on her as she picked her way through the room to the one empty chair she could see. It was probably due to the fact that she was only three minutes away from being late, but she knew that the other major reason was that she was female. She was the only one in a room filled with about sixty men.

Four speakers sat in a row at a long desk at the front of the room, facing dozens of microphones that had been taped to a long-necked stand. Most were connected to reel-to-reel tape machines, but some were part of the new gear: the portable cassette tape recorder. Lillian hadn't brought a tape machine, planning instead to rely on her note-taking, since she would not be filing anything for newscasts out of this press conference. Eugene wasn't interested in putting tape of any bureaucrats on the air, and this meeting was unlikely to draw the attendance of any cabinet ministers.

The day's announcement was made quickly and within minutes of Lillian's getting settled, the gathering was breaking up. A couple of minor changes to the Royal itinerary, half a dozen new names of dignitaries added to the guest lists at various parties, and details of a reception for reporters, to happen in Ottawa just before the Queen and Prince Philip departed for Quebec City.

When Joyce and Lillian got together for dinner that evening, Lillian had to find out more about this reporters' reception. Did the Queen really drop by to have a drink with reporters?

"Yeah, apparently they do," Joyce said. "Every tour, as a sort of thank you to the journalists. I heard from a friend who went that you don't actually get presented to her. You go, you stand in one place while she circulates through the room. You only speak to her if she speaks to you first. You don't reach out to shake hands unless she does."

"Far out," Lillian said. "I would imagine if anybody goes from CUBR, it will be Ron. Or maybe Eugene."

"Nobody at my level in my department will get an invitation to any of the Tour events," Joyce said. "But that's alright. It's an experience to work on the advance prep, anyway. How's everything else going at the station?"

"I don't know. I'm having a hard time keeping my mind on things, you know?"

Joyce nodded. "Susan."

"Yeah, Susan. I still . . . just feel so bad."

"And shocked."

"And shocked," Lillian agreed. "One day she's there, the next she's gone. Forever. It's just surreal. I feel empty. Lost, somehow."

"Are you going to the memorial service at the U of T?"

Lillian nodded. "I wonder if the new boyfriend will be there, too. I'd like to get to know him a bit."

"He's nice, you'll like him."

At this moment, the waiter arrived with their drinks and Lillian had a few minutes to collect her thoughts. How did Joyce know whether he was nice?

"You've met him?" she asked as soon as the waiter left.

"Yes." Joyce seemed a bit flustered and wasn't making eye contact. She wasn't serving up the details, either.

"When?"

"Susan and Mikhail made a trip up to Ottawa mid-summer. I had a quick lunch with them."

Lillian stared at the menu while she thought about this. She was sure Susan had never mentioned it, and that seemed weird. They all chatted all the time about what they were doing and where they were going.

"Joyce?"

The young woman who stood at the side of their table clutched a brown woolen scarf around her throat with one hand and a black gaucho handbag with the other, its outsize front buckle tarnished and the leather ripped at one corner. Her hair looked as if it hadn't been washed in a month.

"Joyce Lansing?"

Joyce frowned. "Do I know you?"

"Maybe . . . maybe you don't remember me," the girl faltered. "We met at the . . . the meeting at . . . the meeting last Thursday night."

Joyce stared at her, hard. Then, as Lillian watched, she decided. You could see it on her face, as clear as an August day. She stood up. "Come with me, dear. We'll take care of you. Lill, I'm sorry but I have to go. You can stay, they haven't brought dessert yet. You have mine too. Here, here's some cash for my share of dinner."

Lillian got up and reached for her shoulder bag on the back of her chair. "I'll come with you. I don't need dessert."

It seemed that Joyce barely noticed Lillian over the next half hour. She was completely absorbed by the young woman who had joined them. Once they got the bill and settled up, Joyce put an arm around the girl's shoulders and the three of them walked out to the street in front of the restaurant. It was a short cab ride to Joyce's walkup apartment. Lillian watched while Joyce made the girl a cup of tea and then tucked her into bed. She carefully closed the door and sat down on the couch across from Lillian.

"Aright," she said. "I'm ready to answer your questions. I'm assuming you have some?"

Lillian smiled. "Is my curiosity that obvious? Yes, I'd like to know what's going on. But first, can I get some of that tea, too?"

Joyce brought them both cups. "This is a young woman I met at a meeting of a group I belong to. It doesn't have a name. All you need to know is that I help girls who are in trouble."

Lillian sat in silence for a few minutes, considering how much she wanted to know about this and what questions she wanted to ask.

"We have to help them, Lillian. It started for me with a friend who was raped. By a married man with a family. She didn't think she'd be believed . . . not by the police and not by her family. Then, she found out she was pregnant. I went to visit her, and she was practically suicidal! Nobody should be thinking of killing themselves just because they're expecting a baby. Nobody should have to choose between becoming a mother or being dead."

"Nobody should be faced with a choice like that," Lillian jumped up and began pacing the apartment. The subject was so upsetting. She just had to move. "The third choice should be a legal abortion."

"Well, and we all know how hard that is to get," Joyce said. "It's been banned here in Canada almost a hundred years. Doctors won't even say the word."

"I thought there was talk in Ottawa about bringing in a new law."

"There is, but the woman will still need a committee of doctors to swear that her health is in real danger because of the pregnancy. And there's no option to just go across the border to get a pregnancy terminated safely," she said. "The U.S. doesn't allow it either.

So, we have the back-alley abortionists. I've heard stories about women going to a street corner, meeting a stranger who puts a blindfold on them, puts them in a car and drives them to a hidden location. After collecting hundreds of dollars from them. They know they'll be treated like criminals if they get caught. And a lot of them get horrendously sick afterward and don't get the proper medical care."

Joyce was becoming upset. She stopped for a moment to get herself under control. "It doesn't always happen like that, and we do have some physicians who handle it safely and humanely, though."

"And you've been helping women to get these abortions," Lillian said.

"I probably never would have discussed it with you if Pearl hadn't come up to me in the restaurant," Joyce said. "It's my thing. There's no reason for you to approve or disapprove."

"I am shocked."

Joyce paused while she sipped her tea. She seemed to be considering her next words—censoring herself, and then deciding to go for it. "I think you're naïve and overly judgmental. These young women could die if they don't get help. Tens of thousands of women are dying every year. Because of unsafe abortions. Because they're so desperate they try to do it themselves, with a wire coat hanger. Or they go to somebody completely unqualified, pay them a pile of money, and then get butchered on a table in a room that isn't sterile."

"But what if you get caught?"

"There's a sisterhood here in Ottawa. There are dozens of us helping, and nobody is going to rat on anybody else. I won't get caught."

Lillian watched Joyce for a few minutes. "I feel like I don't know you," she finally said. "I don't think any of us really know you."

"Any of us?" Joyce repeated. "Lillian, you don't know. We've all been helping girls in trouble. We have . . . one of us . . ."

"What are you saying?"

Joyce took a deep breath. "You have to promise this is all just a conversation between you and me."

"I promise. What else?"

"A friend of mine got in trouble last spring. We helped her. She took a few weeks off from her job and she came here. I made the contact in Toronto but Susan was the one who went with her to the appointments. Penny went home with her on the train. We all helped. Susan, me, Penny, Glenda. The doctor she works for put us in touch with a doctor on her floor who does them."

Lillian had a thought that came to her out of nowhere. "Was it Dr. Arnold? Dr. Arnold performs abortions?"

"I've said enough. You have to promise to keep all of this to yourself now."

"Yes, I promise."

"Why don't I believe you?" Joyce took a deep breath.

Lillian glared at her. "I don't know. Why don't you?"

"Oh, Lillian, don't be mad. We kept it just among us because you're in the media."

"Penny works for a radio station, too."

"It's different. Penny's show is different from the newscasts you work for."

Lillian didn't see it. All she saw was that all of her friends were closer to one another than to her. "I don't understand why you didn't tell me about it before this. You've all known me a lot longer than you've known Penny. You trust her, but you don't trust me."

"It's not a matter of trust," Joyce said. "It's just . . . different kinds of friendships, different people, that's all. We didn't know what you'd say. If you want to help, and you can keep it confidential, we'd like to have your help. Lill . . ."

By this time, Lillian had her jacket on and her purse over her shoulder. She grabbed her overnight bag from the place where she'd dropped it by Joyce's door. "I have to get back to T.O."

***

Lillian's first call, the minute she got back home to her apartment, was to Penny.

"I just don't understand why you knew about it and I didn't!"

"Why does it matter?"

"And not just you, but all of you!" Lillian shrugged off her jacket and let it fall on the floor.

"I think it was one of those things where the fewer people know, the better," Penny said. "We each had a job to do, but why tell anybody else and risk having it blow up? And it all happened really fast, Lill. Rhonda called Joyce, looking for an answer to her friend's problem, Joyce and Glenda found the doctor, Susan went with her to the appointments and I took her home afterward. There was no reason for anybody else to know."

No reason except friendship, Lillian thought. No reason except history.

"Look, I don't know what else to say. I did what I was being asked to do. It wasn't my secret to tell, it was Rhonda's friend's. Maybe you should talk to her." Penny waited a minute, probably trying to assess whether the timing was okay for changing the subject. "How was Ottawa, anyway? How is Joyce?"

"Why do you ask? Is there something going on with her that I should know about?"

"Aw, come on, Lill. This is getting silly."

"I have to go."

She hung up and went foraging in the refrigerator. She was absolutely starving, even though she had had a very satisfying dinner with Joyce in Ottawa before the whole day went south. On board the train, the only things available came in plastic bags and aluminum cans, but despite the lack of appeal, she'd loaded up on a few salty and sweet distractions.

Now she was home and still feeling hungry. There wasn't much in this kitchen, though; a few crackers and slices of cheese would have to do. And there was always the peanut butter jar.

Her phone rang. She wished there was a way to tell who was calling, so that she could decide whether or not she wanted to take the call. If it was Penny—or Joyce—it would be a very brief call.

"Miss Clarkson? Detective Sinclair here."

Lillian put down her plate and sat down on the couch. "Yes, Detective. I'm here."

"I have a favor to ask."

"Yes, of course."

"Are you going to the memorial get-together they're having for Susan Taylor at the university the day after tomorrow?"

"I am. I didn't know they were calling it a 'memorial get-together' but yes, I'm planning to go."

"That's more my term, I think. I mean, we wouldn't really call it a 'wake', like one of the Irish classic ones. And from what I've heard, it won't be a service. No hymns or Bible readings, no sermon. But I won't really know, since they haven't sent any invitations to the police. Did you get an invitation?"

"Yes, I'm invited."

"So, the favor is that you'd be my eyes and ears at this thing. I'd like to be there myself, of course, and I supposed we could insist. Make it clear that as private as they might want it to be, the police have an interest in being present, and need to be present. Or we could work with the family to find ways we could be there, secretly."

"Both ideas seem kind of awkward."

"Exactly. So, I thought I might be able to accomplish my purpose just by giving you a heads-up on what I'd like you to watch for and by talking to you after it's over."

Lillian chewed this over for a few minutes. It didn't seem that it would be that hard to do, and if it helped them get any closer to solving the crime and finding Susan's killer, she was all for it.

But it occurred to her that there was an opportunity in the situation for her, too. "I'd like to help, Detective Sinclair, I really would. But I wonder if we could talk about one other aspect of the case."

"Which is?"

"I'd like to hear more about Susan's daytimer."

The silence after this statement left her feeling that she'd over-stepped some boundary of some sort.

Then he surprised her. "Alright. What do you want to know?"

"What does the book have for April and May? And the summer."

"That covers a lot of territory," Sinclair said. She heard him thumbing pages. "Alright, we've got some pages that say 'doc' and a time on them. We've got the second weekend of April with a 'R' at the top of Saturday. The doc times are the week after that. We've got a few evenings in May with 'M'. Oh, and here's one in June with 'P', 'G', and 'J 'on a Friday night, circled."

"Those are all her friends," Lillian said. "Penny, Glenda, Joyce. R is our friend, Rhonda, from New York. And I'd guess that 'M' is Mikhail, her new boyfriend."

Lillian felt slightly sick to her stomach. She hadn't seen Susan at all in June, and there wasn't a Friday night when all of them were together. Was she wrong to feel so left out? Was she wrong to feel that she must have done something really horrible, must be a very undesirable, unlovable friend, to be so clearly deserted? She felt betrayed, and yet the logical part of her brain was asking 'By whom?' and 'How so?' She didn't expect that she had to be included in every single gathering or conversation that her friends had—or did she?

"Thank you, Detective," she said.

"You know, I'm thinking it might be useful to have you go over Susan's daytimer page by page with me. Do you think you could free up some time tomorrow?"

"I'd be very interested to see it, Detective, and if I can help in any way, I want to. Where are you at with the investigation, anyway? The last I heard was that it was . . . murder. Who do you think might have done it?"

"Well, usually in these cases, we look at the husbands or boy-friends, first," Sinclair said. "I can't tell you much, but I do appreciate your helping me with her daytimer. And maybe there are some thoughts you might have, things you might have witnessed with one or more of these people, that could help.

Corey Lang, the ex-boyfriend. We've been talking to him. Most of the people who were in the station that morning have been interviewed and cleared. There weren't a lot of you, it was so early. I won't upset you with the details, but we know from the examination of her body that she was killed there. She wasn't killed elsewhere and then moved there. The one person I'm watching carefully out of that morning is your technician."

"Raymond?"

"Yes, Raymond Chernowski. He left the station shortly after she was discovered. Then a few days later, he quits his job. Have you seen him since?"

"No, I haven't. But why don't you just find him at his home?"

"He hasn't been there either. Don't worry, we'll find him. But I'm nowhere near arresting anybody. I'm just telling you about the people we're looking at."

"Anybody else?"

"You mentioned she has a new boyfriend."

"What would be the motives of these people?" Lillian asked.

"Old boyfriend, could be jealousy. The radio technician, maybe he had a crush on her and she wasn't interested? New one, who knows? You'll probably see him at the memorial. Maybe we could talk afterward and you could let me know what you thought of him?"

Lillian didn't answer.

"One more question," Sinclair said. "Is there anyone else, anything else Susan might have been mixed up in?"

Twenty-four-hours ago, Lillian would have said 'no' to that question, and been sure of her ground. But now? She just didn't know.

Chapter 13

September 23
1964

Rain hammered against the window, and in the corners of the old building, the wind bayed like some far-off wolf talking to the moon.

Lillian's mood that morning was bleak. The primary reason was the weather. A rainstorm had rolled in off the lake and it was coming down like a cresting wave when Lillian ran from the parking lot to the back door at four a.m. The rain itself wasn't so bad, but it was cold. Just a few months from now (perhaps even weeks), the Arctic air would arrive, the temperature would fall below freezing, and the snow and ice would take over.

Another reason was that yesterday was Ratings Day. Eugene had called a special meeting to discuss the BBMs and had photocopied the pages where CUBR's numbers showed up, distributing a copy to every single person working on the newscasts or the shows. News had the biggest numbers, so maybe that explained why he was making such a big deal about the quarterly report on audience size. *Dawn Patrol* did fairly well, too, with about ten percent of the market, but everybody else was looking at single digits. The exception was the middle-of-the-night show, which had so few listeners they couldn't be counted and whose slice of the audience was reported as zero.

"Do we really care that much about all this?" Lillian whispered to Chuck while Eugene continued his pep talk.

"It's the bread and butter," Chuck said. "The advertising fees they can charge depend on the audience numbers. Unfortunately, big numbers for the newscast won't get them to the 'most listened to' status. They need the rest of the programming to hold up."

"And I heard the next book will be done using computers," Leo whispered. "It'll be a total drag, watching how important those numbers are going to be after that."

"Our jobs will depend on those computer numbers," Dominic hissed.

"Your jobs depend on these numbers!" Eugene boomed, well into full speech-making flight. "These numbers aren't good enough. We have to do better."

Lillian could see it, but she was finding it hard to care in the midst of everything that was going on. She listened politely to Eugene, but was relieved when the meeting was finally over and she could go home.

The third reason for her gloom this morning was that Susan's memorial gathering at the university was scheduled to start at two p.m. She had promised to pass along her observations to Detective Sinclair and she felt uneasy about that. Even though it was a personal, not a professional event, it felt weird to be on the lookout for information for the police, rather than for the newsroom.

Aside from that, it was just going to be a rotten afternoon, no matter what. She wouldn't bail out on it; that would be disrespectful to Susan's memory. But she was depressed, thinking about it, and she knew she'd feel miserable afterward.

The phone call came through shortly before noon.

"Lill! Line three!" Chuck shouted in her direction.

"Lillian? Lillian Clarkson?" The man's voice was deep and commanding, somehow. Like an army sergeant.

"Yes, this is she."

"Lillian, this is Kevin Arnold."

Lillian was at a loss for a minute. Why would he be calling her? It was Wednesday, and he'd already recorded his item for next

Monday's show. Maybe he wanted to change the topic, like he had last week? Well, better to do it in advance than to surprise them all, the way he did.

"Yes, Dr. Arnold, what is it?"

"I want to talk to you about Glenda."

"Glenda? My friend, Glenda Levy?"

"Yes, the one who works for Dr. Rand, in my building," Dr. Arnold said. "And about your friend, Joyce."

Wait, how did he even know Joyce? Or that she was a friend of Lillian's?

"I've got about ten minutes until I have to leave for an appointment, Dr. Arnold," she said.

"I'm here at the station," he said. "I'll meet you in the lobby."

As she watched him walk toward her when she got off the elevator, Lillian was impressed, once again, with what a snazzy dresser he was, for someone over thirty. His suit fit just so and his topcoat was black and rich-looking, not a beige trench coat with epaulettes like so many of the reporters in this building liked to wear. His hair was neatly cut but longer, the way the stylish men were wearing it.

She stopped about three feet away from him. "What's up, Dr. Arnold?"

"Dr. Rand tells me that Glenda has given her notice," he said. "No notice, actually. Today is her last day and she's moving up north."

"Yes, she is," Lillian said. Why did he think this had anything to do with her? Or with him?

"Meanwhile, Joyce Lansing isn't returning my calls. And now Rhonda Sheridan is MIA."

Rhonda? He knew Rhonda, too?

"Dr. Arnold, why do you want to reach them?"

He looked into her eyes and she saw a shade drawn down over them. "It doesn't matter. I just thought you might know. Maybe they'd all gone off on some trip together or something. I know they are your friends. Glenda talks about you all the time."

He said nothing for a few minutes and seemed to wait for her to get uncomfortable with the silence and rush in to say something. She had no intention of doing that.

"Well, thank you for coming down to meet me," he said. "I was concerned, that's all. I have to get going now. Nice to see you, Lillian."

Now that was all very weird, she thought as she watched his back disappear out the station front door.

The scene at the U of T campus was even stranger. But that was probably because her heart had snapped back into aching mode and she knew that everything she saw, smelled, and touched during the memorial service would remind her of Susan and how much she was missing her. The Science Department professors had booked the Faculty Club on Willcocks Street and when Lillian arrived, the ballroom was already three-quarters full. A podium had been set up at one end and she saw Dr. Berman there, chatting with a club employee about the microphone.

"Hi, Lill." Lillian turned to see Glenda. With Howard Ronson.

All she could manage was a brief nod.

"Thank you again for helping me move my things on the weekend. I came back and finished out a few more days at the office. I wanted to be here for this—" she waved an arm toward the crowd in the room—"but then I'm going back up to The Farm."

"And you asked Howard to come along with you?" Lillian scanned the room for someone else she knew who could be her escape.

"No, no, I invited myself," Howard said in his smooth way. "It seemed like an interesting event and I thought Glenda might need some support, since her boyfriend couldn't be here."

"Jordan's not here?" Lillian asked.

Glenda frowned. "No, we decided it was better if he didn't come with me to this. We've had some disagreements lately . . . mostly about my decision to quit my job and move up north for a while."

"Is it just for a while, Glenda? Is it?" Suddenly, this felt like an urgent question to Lillian.

"Yes, a while. I'm not sure I'd say it's 'temporary' but I wouldn't say it's a permanent move, either. I'm going there to learn. For a while."

"Yes, of course," Howard said. "The choice is entirely Glenda's."

Lillian looked at him. "You know, her friends will all be here. Hers and Susan's. I don't think she really needed your 'support.'"

Howard smiled. "Probably not, Lillian. But I have another reason of my own for wanting to be here. Two reasons, I should say. Just look around—there are a lot of interesting people to meet here. And I thought I might run into you, as well. I've been wanting to talk with you about the media here . . . how it works, who the people are, the best way to get a press release out. Maybe we could chat for a few minutes before they start the ceremony?"

Lillian felt as if she needed a shower. "I actually promised to speak with Dr. Berman before it begins, so I'm going to have to say 'no', Howard. Maybe some other time."

She still had words she wanted to say to Glenda about her evening with Joyce in Ottawa, but clearly, that was going to have to wait, if Howard Ronson was going to be at her side during this event.

Dr. Berman looked pleased to see Lillian when she approached her at the front of the room.

"I'm glad you could make it here," the professor said. "I think it's going to be quite a turnout."

"Susan had a lot of friends wherever she went," Lillian said. She was making conversation and doing all the normal things, but the last thing she felt was normal. There, on the table, was an LP-sized photograph of Susan, her dark hair down to her waist, her summer tan, and her bright smile. She was wearing a blue gingham kerchief bandana on her head and a rope of beads around her neck. One look at the photograph and Lillian almost melted into tears.

"Oh, excuse me, I see the dean coming in," Dr. Berman said. "I'll be back in a minute."

Lillian clutched the edge of the table, then swayed backwards. This was ridiculous—why would her knees feel weak? Sure, she was sad about Susan and she had been for more than two weeks now: sad, and horrified, and angry about what had happened. But that wasn't reason enough to be passing out in public.

"Breathe deep through your nose." She felt a hand at her back at the moment when she heard the voice. Eugene's voice. Of all people. "You'll be alright. You just have to get through the next few minutes. Then each of the next minutes, one at a time."

She concentrated on breathing in and breathing out. Gradually, Susan's picture came into focus and the temperature in the room went down. "Thanks, Eugene. I'm sorry. I don't know what happened."

His eyes were kind. "A memorial service is usually hard to take. Especially in a situation like this, a really close friend."

Was it only in the newsroom that he was a jerk?

"She *was* a really dear friend," Lillian said. "But I was at the small service her parents held last week and I didn't react this way."

"It had just happened. You were probably still numb, or in shock."

Lillian nodded. "Probably."

She couldn't think of anything else to say to him and he seemed to pick up on it. "Well, listen, I'm going to find some of the others from the station and get a place to sit."

"A lot of people came from the station?"

"Oh yeah. Partly to support you and partly because Susan Taylor is a story right now."

Lillian looked around at the crowd. Up to about two hundred now, she estimated. Counting numbers of people at an event was one of the first reporting tricks she'd been taught. As she looked at the faces, she remembered that she'd agreed to bring Detective Sinclair some sort of report. Who was here? Scanning the people in the seats and the people still milling around near the doors, she spotted Joyce, Penny, and Des. Josh and Eddie, Maggie, Chuck, and Leo from the station. Glenda and that guru. And was that Dr. Arnold with them, the three of them looking over some of the Group of Seven paintings on the walls?

"Hey."

She turned to find Corey Lang standing there, swaying slightly. He'd cleaned up, in a rather pathetic way: dress slacks that were a couple of sizes too big, a grubby white shirt, a crocheted blue tie, and a sport coat.

"Hello, Corey. I'm surprised to see you here."

"I wanted to show up at something that was for her. Her parents didn't invite me to the service last week."

"Maybe they didn't even know you exist."

"I called them and introduced myself," Corey said.

"You didn't."

"Why not? Even if she didn't think I was important enough to mention to her parents—"

Lillian didn't let Corey finish the sentence. "They're in mourning, Corey, for heaven's sake!"

"Yeah, well, so am I. What?! So am I," Corey insisted, in response to Lillian's raised eyebrows. "She was my girlfriend for . . . for . . . well, for quite a while. I wanted to meet her parents." He looked around the room. "Are they here?"

Joyce, wearing black, joined them. "They changed their minds about staying for this and they left earlier this week. Wanted to get home to Albany, for a service there. Hello, Corey."

Corey looked her up and down. "Hello, bureaucrat," he said. It was a nickname, but it didn't sound friendly.

Joyce ignored him. "Lillian, will you come and sit with us? Penny and Glenda are holding seats together."

Lillian's first reaction was to refuse. She was still working through her feelings about her discoveries in Ottawa. But Joyce's face was so hopeful, and she was getting a sense of comfort from just the familiarity of being three feet away from her. They'd known each other a long time. Lillian was so aware that just two weeks ago she'd lost someone who'd known her since grade school. In a way, a whole chunk of her past was now missing. Angry and hurt as she was, she didn't want to lose another chunk.

"Alright. Corey, take it easy. See you around."

Penny had chosen seats in the second row, right behind Dr. Berman. Glenda and Howard Ronson sat to her right. As Lillian and Joyce approached them, Penny jumped to her feet. "Here's a seat for you, Lill." Clearly, she was as anxious as Joyce to put this confrontation behind them.

"Thanks."

Howard reached forward to grasp her hand in both of his. "Once again, I'm so sorry for your loss, Lillian. Susan was a lovely young woman."

"Thank you, Howard." He was so weird. She just couldn't see why Glenda was having anything to do with him and his "disciples." Ridiculous. Jesus had disciples, the Buddha had disciples. Mohammed had disciples. This guy didn't. Shouldn't.

"Thank you again, Lillian, for your assistance on the radio news report." Howard leaned across Glenda's lap and ignored Lillian's efforts to show him she wanted to face the front of the room and sit in silence.

"You're welcome."

"And for your cooperation in having me be a part of Susan's private service last week." *Why would he think she had any say or anything to do with that?* "You know, I'd be happy to be called any time for comment on any items you're doing on religion or spirituality."

"Glenda mentioned."

"Or to do some sort of regular item on one of the shows," he said. "I know *Dawn Patrol* has regular legal and medical speakers. Maybe Maggie MacRae would want to talk about spirituality?"

"I doubt it," Penny put in. Lillian suppressed a grin.

Howard frowned. "Really, Lillian, I think I could bring something of great value to your listeners." He glanced at Susan's photograph at the front of the room. "And there are some things about Susan that I could tell you, things that might help with your adjustment to your loss."

What did that mean? Was there something specific or was he just looking for levers to use to persuade her?

Their murmured conversation had drawn attention. Dr. Berman turned around. "Lillian, I want to introduce you to a few people here. I think you've met Mikhail Kogonov. And this is his friend, Pavel Andreyevitch."

The two men sitting beside her stood up and extended hands to Lillian to shake. Howard reached out as well, but the older man with Mikhail seemed not to notice. Pavel Andreyevitch had high cheekbones, deep-set brown eyes, and a moustache. Somehow, Lillian was reminded of the Hollywood star who'd made his fortune playing Western heroes. Why did so many of the new people she met remind her of old movies or TV shows?

Howard held his hand out just a few moments longer than was comfortable, then dropped it. Neither of the two Russian men seemed to notice.

Pavel Andreyevitch. The name was reminding her of something. A Russian classic novel, maybe?

"Mikhail, how are you doing?" Lillian asked. "This must be a very difficult time for you as well."

Mikhail looked as though he had had little sleep lately. "It is, thank you, Lillian. She was a remarkable person, just remarkable. As you know. I still don't feel it's quite real. Your life can just change in a day. Or a minute."

"I feel the same way," Joyce said.

"Please excuse me," Pavel said, and moved off through the crowd.

"I have a few other people I have to see, too," Lillian said. "Mikhail, this is Joyce. Penny. Glenda. All friends of Susan's."

They all stood and looked at each other, somewhat awkwardly, then Dr. Berman took control of the situation. "It's so good that we are all able to come together like this. To remember her and honor her." She looked over her shoulder at the man in a dark suit taking a place behind the podium. "I think they're about to get started."

Penny shot Lillian a look that meant something; she wasn't sure what.

A pianist claimed the piano bench and began a medley of classical pieces and preludes, as Lillian moved toward the back of the room. She found a place to stand, then focused on Susan's picture. Lillian gave her full attention to her memories as she listened to the speeches people made about her friend.

Dr. Berman spoke of her academic achievements; another professor who had guided her through the three years of her undergraduate studies spoke about her popularity in the department. The dean spoke about her death as a loss to the educational and the scientific communities, then the university chaplain said some devout and comforting things. Almost before Lillian knew it, the pianist was playing a version of "You'll Never Walk Alone" and people were rising and making their way out of the room.

Someone had placed a gigantic bouquet of yellow roses on the front table beside Susan's picture. Dr. Berman went to it and removed four of the long stems and brought them over to Susan's three friends, handing one to each.

"Thank you so much," Glenda said, speaking for all of them, as they nodded and smiled at Susan's mentor.

While she watched the people greeting each other after the service, something made Lillian raise her head and scan the room. Hundreds of people were now funneling through the doors. Was that Raymond Chernowski? She hadn't seen him since the day he learned he wouldn't be sent as part of the coverage team to the Tokyo Olympics.

Lillian crossed the room as quickly as she could, but by the time she got to the door, Raymond was nowhere to be seen. Outside the faculty club, people swarmed around on the sidewalk and although she saw several men in striped shirts like the one she thought she'd seen on Raymond, she didn't spot him.

Lillian stopped to study one of the men. That looked like Susan's brother, Norman. She knew from days gone by, when they were all kids in Albany. He was two years younger than his sister and her friends, and had always been wanting to tag along on their adventures. Many times, Susan's mother insisted they include him.

Now, they were all in their twenties, long past parental babysitting requirements, and Lillian hadn't seen much of him at all over the years. Last week, she'd reconnected with him at Susan's family memorial service, and she'd realized that if she'd seen him on the street, she never would have recognized him. The little boy from the 50s was long gone, replaced by a tall, well-built, tough-guy type.

Two taxis had pulled up to the door of the building on Willcocks Street and she watched to see whether Raymond got into either of them, but the passengers were older couples, the men in tweed jackets and the woman in black suits. Not likely Raymond would have taken a taxi anyway, now that she gave it a little more thought.

She stared down the street, trying to catch a glimpse of him, but saw nothing.

"Lillian? Are you looking for someone?"

Susan's boyfriend and his friend were beside her.

"Yes, I thought I saw one of the technicians from the radio station," she answered Mikhail. "A former technician. He seems to have quit recently. I've been trying to get in touch with him, but I thought he'd left town." Lillian shook it off and turned to face Mikhail and Pavel Andreyevitch. "It was a nice service, wasn't it?"

"Very nice," Pavel said. "Many people liked your friend."

"Yes, they did," Lillian said.

Mikhail looked up and down the street. "We have a car coming. Could we give you a lift somewhere?"

"Thank you, no. I feel like walking and my apartment isn't far from the university."

They said their goodbyes, and she turned back to the faculty club building. *Pavel Andreyevitch.* Then she had it. Penny had mentioned that name as the expert on Soviet life they planned to interview for her show.

Should she go back inside and see what Joyce, Penny, and Glenda were doing next? Just a couple of days ago, that would have been exactly what she'd do, but today she just didn't feel like being in their company.

A man in a striped shirt, halfway down the block, caught her attention. There was Raymond!

Lillian set off at a run. She wasn't sure what it was she wanted to say to him, if she caught up with him, but her curiosity was at a full bark, and she knew that she'd figure out what her questions were as soon as she got him.

Chapter 14

Raymond was about a block ahead now, obviously able to run faster than she did. She shouted his name, but she doubted he'd be able to hear her over the traffic noise. He turned on to Spadina, heading toward Queen's Park. She stopped shouting. Somehow, she had the feeling that he knew perfectly well that she was chasing him.

Lillian's race along the sidewalk led to nothing. By the time she reached Bloor Street, heaving and panting, she knew she'd lost him. Actually, she wasn't even sure she'd had him! She was sweaty, winded, and hurting, and scolding herself for overreacting.

When she talked with Detective Sinclair from home later that evening, he didn't think it was overreacting.

"That's spot-on, Lillian, well done," he said. "I'd been wondering if Raymond Chernowski would show up at the funeral. That's one thing we watch for."

"For what? For terrified co-workers who show up to say good-bye to someone?"

"Well, he wasn't Susan's co-worker, now was he," Sinclair said. "He was somebody questioned by the police in an irregular death."

"Is he a suspect?"

Sinclair paused. "I wouldn't go so far as to say that. We don't have any formal suspects yet. Just 'persons of interest'. "

"If he's one of them, who are the others?" Ordinarily, Lillian wouldn't be quite so direct, but the water was boiling for her tea and the kettle was screaming in a way that implied that any minute the neighbors would be banging on the door, demanding an end to the noise.

"Corey Lang, the ex-boyfriend. He was at the university funeral service. Why? He wasn't a student, was he?"

Lillian snorted. "He wasn't interested in learning anything. I don't think he would have had the stamina or the brains."

"So, he was there."

"Maybe because Mr. and Mrs. Taylor hadn't let him in to the private service last week. Maybe he wanted to pay his respects somewhere?" Lillian said.

"Maybe." Sinclair paused, as if looking through notes. "I also find it interesting, the way Glenda Levy brought along her spiritual guy. What did you think of that?"

Lillian had many things she could say about Howard Ronson, but they were all a matter of opinion. Much as she might dislike his manner or his efforts to use her media job as a stepping stone toward his own fame, she didn't see that as reason enough to link him to a murder, for heaven's sake.

She felt a little mixed up about how much she wanted to tell Sinclair about what was happening with her relationships with her girlfriends. Yes, in one way, she could see that any conversation or development might have relevance for his investigation of her friend's death, but in another way, she could imagine that he might find it all not at all related. She decided to just let his questions guide the way.

"I think Glenda has found something in this group, Howard's 'community', that gives her something she's been needing," Lillian said. "So, she cuts him a lot of slack. And she's so impressed with him, and he's so eager to meet people and make use of them through her . . . through *everybody* in his group, probably . . . that he's inviting himself along to any and every place he can."

"Okay, that makes sense. What about the new boyfriend, the guy from Russia?"

Lillian shrugged. "He seemed pretty normal to me. Nice guy. Very smart, obviously, very well-regarded in the physics department."

"Is it odd to you, at all, that she didn't mention him to you or introduce you?"

Lillian winced, but she didn't want to discuss all of that with Sinclair. "Yeah, I guess, but she's been busy with her studies and getting started in grad school, and I've been busy with things in the newsroom. We probably would have had a chance to catch our breaths and catch up at Thanksgiving."

"Anything else you noticed?"

"Not really. It was a perfect service, just the right tone. I was a bit worried that I'd be in meltdown, blubbering all over the place, but I didn't. It was nice to see how many friends she had and how respected she was in the Science faculty and the computer department. It's funny, you know. You think you know someone well and then something like this happens and you find out they have a whole other group of people, a whole other life, that you know nothing about."

"And what do you think of that?" Sinclair asked.

"I'm happy for her," Lillian said. "I do feel like I have some catching up to do, though, on Susan Taylor 101. And if I can help you catch her killer, I want to do that."

Chapter 15

New York City
September 28
1964

People at the World's Fair were packed in, shoulder to shoulder, and the buzz from their excited voices was louder than Lillian had heard even from people having a blast on the midway at the annual Exhibition.

The top attraction was the Unisphere, and to get a look at it, she had to stretch her neck back a long way. She held her Polaroid camera as steady as she could and tried to fit the image of the giant stainless-steel structure into the frame. It was an artistic, massive representation of the globe, and the message in the name and the sculpture itself set the theme for the 1964 World's Fair: *We Are All One.*

Lillian waved the print through the air, waiting for it to dry before she peeled back a layer to reveal the image of the Unisphere silhouetted against a vivid September blue sky. Eugene had asked her to bring back lots of pictures of the exhibits, in addition to gathering research and finding people to send over to the radio studio for interviews with Fred, the afternoon newscaster.

When Eugene had called her into his office the morning after Susan's service at the university, he'd been very compassionate and careful with her. She sat on the edge of her seat, waiting for one of his characteristic sexist remarks, but none came. *What had happened? Had he had his consciousness raised by one of his daughters? What was it he wanted to talk to her about?*

The trip to New York was the last topic she'd expected. The Royal Tour was just two weeks away, and she was working hard on that, plus there was plenty to do to get ready for the material that the reporters on the ground in Tokyo for the Olympics would be sending. She had needed the time to work on those things so that she could get away for this New York assignment.

"Lillian, sit down," he'd said. "Since I saw you at Susan Taylor's service yesterday, I've been thinking that this might be just one job too many for you."

Lillian stared into his eyes. "Eugene, I want to go."

"You're just back from Ottawa, now you'll have to go again... so soon."

"It's what I want to do."

"You want to go to New York."

"I do."

She had never been to New York, even though she'd grown up in Albany. It was Emerald City, filled with hundreds of wizards, not just one, and she'd never been able to find, or afford, the Yellow Brick Road. But now, she was working in a place where they needed to send people to places like New York and Ottawa and Tokyo!

"I just think you've had quite a shock, and quite a lot of work in the past few weeks, and it might be better if you stay home," Eugene said.

Lillian weighed her next words. Eugene was a good guy, and he meant well, but she didn't need him to be the one to make decisions about her well-being. That should be up to her.

"Eugene, thank you for your concern. But I think work . . . a lot of work . . . is the best thing for me."

He looked at her for a few moments, then nodded. "Alright. Call Fred after you get there and find out what he wants you to do for the afternoon newscasts he's doing from there."

Lillian managed to state her agreement to the plan and in the next few days, she'd packed a bag, picked up her ticket, and made her way to a small hotel room several train and subway connections away from the fairgrounds.

Although she planned to find a lot of stories while she was there, Lillian had also lined up interviews from Toronto before traveling to New York: the head of the Canada Pavilion; Juliette, Canada's songbird; the poet Leonard Cohen; and the actor Paul Soles.

She didn't kid herself that any of these interview guests had any respect for or interest in her; it was CUBR Radio they had agreed to talk to. Whatever the reason, she was looking forward to meeting all of them.

She also had an old friend to catch up with. A call to Rhonda was one of the first things she'd done once she got settled at her hotel. She'd arranged to meet her this morning at the Unisphere, before the workday was to be underway. When she saw Rhonda walking toward her, looking like a fashion model on a catwalk, Lillian felt her heart lift. She'd been hurting so much since she'd lost Susan three weeks ago, but somehow the sight of Rhonda lifted the pain. Even with her uncertainty about her relationship with her girlfriends and her questions about Susan, she was happy to see her friend.

"Rhonda! It's so great to see you! I missed you." It felt as though Rhonda's return hug was just as enthusiastic as hers.

"Same here," Rhonda said.

"Where should we eat?"

"Let's go to the Belgian Pavilion. The girls at work told me the restaurant there has something new called Belgian waffles that is just divine!"

As Lillian followed her friend across the tarmac toward the Belgian Pavilion, she recalled how Rhonda almost always spoke with dozens of exclamation points. In high school, she'd been the one urging them all on to try new things, to meet new people, and to rebel whenever they could. Right after graduation, she'd headed for New York City and found herself a secretarial job in a talent agency. She kept in touch with all the old friends, but she had definitely moved into a new phase.

As they settled into their seats, then watched the waitress deliver massive plates covered in waffles, strawberries, and whipped cream, Lillian felt better than she had since Joyce admitted that there was a secret that she, Penny, and Glenda had been concealing. Rhonda, at least, would be one friend who still wanted to be close.

"This is so groovy," Lillian said. "It's going to be such a blast, visiting all these pavilions."

"I've been here twelve times since it opened," Rhonda said. "It's giving me loads of ideas of places I want to visit one day."

"They're doing a world's fair in Montreal in a couple of years, did you know that? They're calling it Expo 67 and it will be the same sort of thing. Everybody is very excited about it, although there's lots of controversy."

"I *did* hear about that," Rhonda said. "Joyce told me, I think, or maybe it was Penny. Yes, it was Penny. She said the Canadians are really thrilled to have a chance to show off to the world . . . or at least, some people feel that way. She said a lot of people there feel competitive with the United States."

Lillian nodded. "It seems to some of them that the Americans do everything so much better. They copy Americans or buy their stuff in almost every category you can think of. Clothes, music, cars, art, business, sports. They try not to face it, but they think Americans are cool and they're not."

Lillian stepped aside to get out of the way of a passing troop of Boy Scouts, heading for the Malaysia Pavilion. "Yeah, somebody said it's like there's a glass wall at the border and Canadians spend their lives with their noses pressed against it."

"You've been in Canada a few years now, Lill. Do you think Americans are cooler?"

Lillian shook her head. "It's not so much that Americans are cooler. It's that we have *confidence*."

"We have that!" Rhonda laughed. "How are things at the radio station, Lill? Any good new assignments?"

"Well, this is pretty cool."

"Yeah, no kidding. Why did they send you, do you think?"

"I'm really not sure. Maybe because all the senior reporters and the newscasters—even most of the DJs have been here, since the Fair opened last April. They wanted some more coverage and research done. I was the last one left who hadn't been here and who wasn't lukewarm about the idea of going."

"Maybe," Rhonda said. "Or maybe because you're so comfortable about asking complete strangers questions."

"I'm not that comfortable. It depends on the situation. When I'm on the air or covering a meeting, I'm there as a station representative and I feel like it's CUBR they're really seeing, and talking to. But off the air, when people hear what I do, they immediately want to tell me a story I should cover or they want me to tell them entertaining stories about the media. And I'm just not wired that way. They have no idea that most of the time I'm scared to death of saying the wrong thing."

"Anything else going on for you?"

"I'm doing advance work for the Royal Tour. Oh . . . and we had Betty Friedan in for an interview a couple of weeks ago."

Rhonda was impressed. "Cool! What did you think of her?"

"So smart," Lillian said. "But a little scary."

"She scares the old men, too," Rhonda said. "And that's good. Things are changing around here, Lill. You can feel it."

"Probably about five years before we'll feel it in Canada."

"Maybe, maybe not. Canada is keeping up with the States in a lot of categories." Rhonda mopped up the last of her whipped cream and waffles. "And it's just as backward as the U.S. in a lot of others. Abortion, divorce, civil rights. We all still have a long way to go."

"How's it going at your job, Rhonda? Are you enjoying it?"

Rhonda shrugged. "It pays for my apartment and my records. I'm saving up for one of those new Mustangs. It's all okay." She pushed her plate aside and pulled the ashtray toward her. The cigarettes she pulled from her hobo bag were filtered and menthol. She waved the package toward Lillian, who shook her head 'no'.

"How are you feeling now that it's been three weeks since Susan?" Rhonda asked.

"I'm alright," Lillian said. "I think we're all feeling kind of bruised."

"Yeah. We should get together tonight, you and me, and raise a toast or two to her."

"I'd like that. I'll call you after work and we'll meet up."

They sat in old-friend silence for a few minutes while Rhonda smoked.

"Penny told me she's doing a few things to get ready for this Royal Tour, too," Rhonda said.

"I'll bet they're giving lots of attention to it at the CBC."

"A thousand reporters and crew, Penny told me."

"Wow. The Royals are supposed to be at the Fair later on and so, part of what I'm doing is looking for items CUBR could do about that."

"Maybe you could go around with a tape deck and a microphone, asking random strangers if they think the Queen of England should still be the Queen of Canada?" Rhonda said.

"Oh yeah, that would be totally comfortable for me," Lillian laughed. "Are you trying to get me in trouble? Do you have any better ideas for man-in-the-street questions?"

"Dozens! Let's see. How about 'do you think it's right that women get paid less than men for doing the same job?' or 'do you think it's right that a couple wanting a divorce have to run to a place like Reno and pretend to live there?' Or 'who is better, Paul or John?' Rhonda could see that she'd lost Lillian's attention. "What is it?"

"Look over there, in that lineup to the Hall of Science Building. I think that's Susan's boyfriend, Mikhail."

"Where?"

"Behind the man with the really wide red tie. There's another man in front of him, with a white shirt and horn-rim glasses. Then there's an older woman beside him."

Rhonda stared, while Lillian lifted her camera to try to get a closer look through the lens. "That's Dr. Berman!"

"Who is Dr. Berman?" Rhonda asked.

"She was Susan's thesis advisor. They were working together on an experiment, too. Something to do with computer programming, or communications or something. Susan was supposed to travel with her to the World's Fair at some point to present their findings to some kind of international audience."

"That probably explains why Berman's here now then. Maybe Mikhail is here in Susan's place?"

"Let's follow them."

Lillian didn't know why she'd said that or what was drawing her toward Dr. Berman and Mikhail. But ever since she'd decided to try to help find out the truth about what had happened to Susan, she'd felt she was in the wrong place whenever she was doing anything not connected to her friend's death.

Researching Royal likes and dislikes, chasing stories about weird religions, looking for good guests to discuss women's rights or reproductive issues—whatever it was, it felt irrelevant. A beautiful girl, one of her best friends, had died when poisonous crap flooded her veins and it was not an accident. How was she supposed to think of anything else?

Lillian took a look at the lineup. It would take an hour or more to get in. She thought of looking for information on Dr. Berman's talk and going to that instead. But what if it had already happened? What if this lineup and this pavilion were the scientist's last activity before going back to Toronto? Lillian didn't want to take that chance.

She spotted an open loading bay door, far to the right of the lineup at the entrance. "Come on, Rhonda, we're going in the back way."

She remembered a trick that one of the old-timers from the City Hall Press Gallery had explained to her: grab a clipboard and a pen, a white coat if you can get one, put on a look that says 'I work here' and ease your way in, backwards. No one will ever question you, he said.

She led Rhonda around to the back door. No one was around and they strolled in with all the confidence in the world. This was exactly Rhonda's cup of tea—'stick it to the man'.

The interior of the building was a glorious display of futuristic dreaming. Lillian and Rhonda stationed themselves beside the front entrance, behind a pillar so that they'd be out of the eyeline of the ushers, the guides, and the ticket-takers. Dozens of people crisscrossed the lobby from one exhibit to another.

Around them, half a dozen staffers and visitors were taking a smoke break. Lillian watched carefully, and after about ten minutes, she saw Mikhail and Dr. Berman walk in. Lillian decided to take a chance and strode off toward them, leaving Rhonda to follow her.

"Dr. Berman! How nice to bump into you!"

Dr. Berman took a step back. "Yes? Are you one of my students, Miss. . .?"

"Lillian Clarkson. I am from Toronto, but no, Dr. Berman, we first met a couple of weeks ago when I came to talk to you about my friend, Susan Taylor. Then again, at her memorial service. Hello, Mikhail."

"Yes, yes, of course. Lillian."

The two men with them stopped their scanning of the pavilion and its visitors. They looked at Lillian closely and she returned the stare. One was tall and well-built, with perfectly groomed dark hair and moustache. The second was shaped like a bowling pin. Both wore brown, badly cut suits. Lillian thought that one of might be the man who'd been with at Susan's memorial service. What was his name? Peter? Pavel? Mikhail looked ten years younger than they did, with his white jeans, striped shirt and surfer-style haircut.

"Hello, Lillian."

They all stood in silence for an awkward few minutes. Lillian knew she had to get control of her shyness if she were going to hang on in this conversation. *I work here, I work here,* Lillian thought. Then, *No. This is my place, it's a party and I'm the host. I'm in charge.*

"It's an amazing place, isn't it? I just got here, but already I'm dazzled," Lillian said. "I'm here for the radio station, looking for interviews with Canadians and other people who are visiting the Fair. Maybe you've got some observations, Mikhail, about some of the scientific innovations they're presenting."

"Thanks, Lillian, but I'm not giving interviews," Mikhail said. "Dr. Berman would be a much better choice, anyway."

"Would you speak with me?" Lillian asked the scientist.

"I'll get back to you on that. Right now, we have to get to an engineering association meeting. Nice to see you again," Dr. Berman said vaguely.

And they were gone.

"Well, that was weird," Rhonda said.

Lillian was deep in thought. "Let's take a quick walk around. Then I have to get back to the hotel to see if there are any messages."

Rhonda wasn't ready to let it go. She seemed rattled. "Was it just me or were those guys kinda scary?"

"Well, we're all scared of anybody from the Soviet Union, aren't we? We've been trained to fear communism for decades now. Kids in schools these days have to practice 'duck and cover' under their desks for air raid drills, in case the Soviets suddenly decide one day to bomb us. Who wouldn't be jumpy about meeting four of them, just out in broad daylight like this? I don't care about that, though. I don't care who they are, unless they have something to do with Susan."

Lillian grabbed a handful of brochures from a long table up against the wall. "Let's skip the tour. We can find out enough from these brochures.

***

The skies were filling in with ominous, dark clouds, skidding in from the east. The Canada Pavilion executive hadn't shown up for his interview. When Lillian got back to the hotel, she found a message that he'd canceled. Damn. It was too bad that there wasn't a way to get that message faster. She'd worked on a story earlier in the year about an invention called a pager that doctors could carry that would receive a beep tone to tell them they should call the hospital switchboard for a message. Reporters could use something like that.

Lillian had always wanted to see Central Park, and she decided to trek over to Manhattan to fit in a walk before going to meet Rhonda for drinks. They watched as their cocktails were delivered to their table.

"Cheers," Lillian said, lifting her glass. "And a toast to Susan, one of the best friends ever."

"To Susan," Rhonda joined in.

The lobby bar in the hotel had that chill, 'anything could happen here', 'you're in an adventure' vibe.

Maybe Lillian had seen too many movies.

"Do the Toronto police have any leads on finding Susan's killer?"

Lillian shook her head. "No, and the longer the length of time from her death, the less likely it gets."

"What's the speculation?" Rhonda asked.

"The police seem to be most interested in her ex-boyfriend, Corey."

"I remember Corey," Rhonda said. "A kid walking around trying to pretend to be a man."

"Good description. He's into drugs now, and even if you might have thought him completely inept and incapable of killing anybody, drugs can twist things up quite a bit."

"That's true," Rhonda agreed. "What do you think?"

"I just don't know. I wish I did. Might be him, might be one of the radio techs who was in the building the morning she died, might be this creepy religious guy she met through Glenda. He was also hanging around the station. Or we could speculate all over the place, and say, might be her landlord. Might be a club owner where Mountain Sky performed, once upon a time. Or how about somebody at the university? Or somebody from way back when in Albany?" Lillian took a long gulp of her drink. "I just don't know, Rhonda. But I'm trying to find out."

Rhonda looked at her, her eyes brimming with sympathy. "Let me know if there's anything I can do to help."

***

When Penny called her hotel room that night, Lillian had her feet up on the coffee table. They were aching after a full day at the frenzied pace that was New York.

Penny was worried about Glenda. If there was one thing Penny wasn't, with her friends, it was short on things to say. Lillian was still working through her thoughts on their confrontation over Joyce's revelation about helping in someone's abortion, but that wasn't what Penny had on her mind. She was fretting about Glenda's safety. Penny thought Glenda was in danger, associating with Howard Ronson and what he was apparently now calling the Flower Rising World Coalition, and she was concerned that Glenda was going to reverse her decision about getting away from the cult because of Bobby.

"Bobby!" Lillian said. "Who is Bobby?"

"New romance."

"What happened to Jordan?"

"She outgrew him, she said."

"Have you told her what you think?" Lillian asked.

"She shuts me down whenever I bring up the subject," Penny said. "She'll barely speak to me about her opinion on the weather these last couple of days."

"Well, that's nothing new, you have to admit, Penny. Glenda always played her cards pretty close to the vest."

"She did. Do you remember back in high school when she heard that Mr. Dwight got a job as a roadie with The Guess Who for the summer and she didn't tell a soul?"

Lillian frowned. "No, I thought that was Susan."

"Maybe it was both of them. How did you know about it? Did Susan tell you later?"

"No, Mr. Dwight told me. At the time."

Penny laughed. "He told me, too! He probably told a hundred people and swore us all to silence. C'mon, Lillian, we have to figure out what we can do to sort Glenda out. I know you've been ticked at us because we didn't tell you about the abortion thing, but this is more important. And I know you've been busy with work and you've been affected by Susan's death. We all have, but you seem to be almost obsessed."

Lillian could hear Penny take a breath and then decide to go all in. "I think you've decided not to help me help Glenda because you don't like it that Glenda kept a secret from you," Penny said. "But it wasn't Glenda's secret to tell!"

"I'm not obsessed with Susan's death. I just want to find out what happened to her. And I *am* there to help Glenda. I just don't think we should force our opinions on her. She's a grown-up and she can do what she wants."

Chapter 16

Toronto
September 30
1964

Lillian heard the 'bing' noise that signaled Chuck was getting to the end of the line on the piece of paper where he was typing one of his news stories. She watched him as he grabbed the carriage return lever and pushed it back to start the next line. She had no energy this morning to concentrate on anything and all she'd done so far was stare at him, doing his work.

Penny had been calling throughout the morning but Lillian was dodging her calls. She'd had a brutal day already, setting her alarm for 3 a.m. and going in to do the show just four hours after she'd arrived back at Union Station. She just didn't have the energy for another discussion with Penny.

What she really wanted was a break from the station. Lillian swept the pile of pink message slips on her desk to the wastebasket, grabbed her coat, and headed for the door. She was almost through the lobby when she heard her name called.

"Miss Clarkson? I'd like to speak to you for a moment, please."

It was one of the two Soviet men she'd met at the World's Fair and previously, at Susan's memorial service. Dr. Berman's colleagues. The good-looking one.

"Yes?"

"Pavel Andreyevitch is my name."

"I remember."

Pavel looked around the lobby. Marcos was making a point of watching him and it seemed to make him uncomfortable. "Is there somewhere we could go to talk?"

Did he think she'd fallen off the turnip truck yesterday?

"Right here is fine, Mr. Andreyevitch. What is it about?"

"Please. Call me Pavel. I am here to extend an invitation on behalf of Mikhail Kogonov and myself. The Bolshoi Ballet is to be in the city next week and we would like you to see a performance. As our guest."

Lillian had heard about this show from Joyce. The tickets were rumored to cost about half the price of a car.

"That's very kind of you, Pavel. But why are you offering this to me?"

Pavel looked around the station lobby and waved an arm, to take it all in. "I will be straight with you, Miss Clarkson."

"Lillian."

"Lillian. We are doing much work here that we think would benefit from positive coverage in your country's media. We will show our people the reports that are being made here. We would like to offer you this gift, to see the performance, in return for the opportunity to discuss our project with you and perhaps tell your audience about it."

"I think you have a misunderstanding about my job, Pavel," Lillian said. "I don't have any role in choosing the stories that are covered."

Pavel looked at her with a gaze that almost seemed to sift through and memorizing the contents of her brain. "Nonetheless, it would be instructive to hear about what you do and how you do it. We would like the opportunity to tell you about our project, too. It would be just an . . . an exchange, is that what it is called? An information exchange, a cultural exchange."

"What is your project?"

"It is in the new field of computer science. We are building a programming language to build on COBOL and Fortran," Pavel said.

Lillian felt as if she were listening to someone speaking Greek. "I would think that Dr. Berman and Mikhail are in a better position than I, to exchange information," she said.

"Perhaps." Pavel nodded. "But your work in a radio station is also very interesting. How many of you put on each newscast?"

"Two."

"Two! I would have thought you would need many more."

"No, just two. We move pretty fast." She smiled at him.

"I have seen pictures of North American radio studios. Do you also run the technical pieces, play the music and so forth?"

"No, we have specialists for that. Technicians and sound engineers, who handle all of that."

"And you have guests, some days. Experts in some field or other, who come in, to speak on the airwaves."

"Yes, we often have expert guests. Many different kinds of interviews."

He suddenly looked very sad and his piercing blue eyes seemed to Lillian to have changed color. "Your friend Susan, Mikhail's girlfriend, she was to be such an expert guest, I believe. That day that she died."

"Yes, she was," Lillian said.

"That day, still, it was just the two of you, working on the morning newscasts? Were there any other expert guests there that day?"

"There were a few others. I don't really remember."

"And your technician . . . ?"

"Raymond."

"Raymond, he was there, too." Lillian shot him a look. *What the hell was that about?*

"Raymond, I have heard about, from my friend, Mikhail. Raymond, he was attracted to Mikhail's girlfriend, Susan Taylor. Susan thought it was amusing, but Mikhail went out of his way to let Raymond know his attentions were unwelcome."

"What did Raymond say?" In spite of herself, Lillian was interested.

Pavel shrugged. "He said he was going. That there was nothing to be concerned about. That he wouldn't be bothering Susan and that he wished her and Mikhail well."

Lillian felt as if she were frozen for a moment. She took hold of herself. "You must excuse me, Pavel, but I have an appointment I have to get to."

"Yes, of course, my apologies. But truly, we would like you to see the Ballet. Dr. Berman and Mikhail will be attending as well."

Lillian looked at Pavel with a little more curiosity. "Do you work with them at the university, Pavel?"

"Not directly. But I spend a lot of time with Mikhail. Dr. Berman is in a different department, in Computer Science. Mikhail is a physicist. But they are friends because of Susan."

"And you? Are you friends with Mikhail , too?"

"Yes. He's been my friend ever since I promised to help to get them to leave his sister alone."

***

The ducks were screaming at the geese to make room on Grenadier Pond. She sat on a bench, watching their dispute and laying mental bets on which would win. That was the 'appointment' Lillian had used to detach herself from the encounter with Pavel Andreyevitch. The walk in Central Park in New York had been such a thrill and now that she was back in Toronto, she craved a little quiet time in High Park. The leaves on the trees were already changing color and dropping; the summer was over.

She had been still for more than an hour, sitting there hugging herself, and pulling her headband down over her ears. The band was too narrow to help much and had been chosen more for its color coordination with her red skirt than for warmth, but she hadn't stopped to think much about dressing for the temperature. If she had, she'd have remembered that there could be snow in late September.

"Lillian."

She was startled out of her daydream about New York skyscrapers. Just moments earlier, she'd been thinking about Susan and feeling, once again, how incredibly unfair it was that her life should be cut off so soon. Too soon. Before she'd had a chance to find lasting love, have a home and a family, see how far her science career would take her.

Lillian turned sideways on the bench. Raymond Chernowski stood behind her, hands plunged deep into his pockets, denim jacket collar turned up against the wind.

"Can I talk to you for a few minutes?"

"How did you know I would be here?"

"I followed you over. From your place."

"You know where I live?"

He looked out over the pond and after a few minutes, it was clear that he would not answer that.

"Raymond, everybody is very suspicious about you. Do you know that? You quit, out of the blue, no notice—"

"Just a week after a body was found in a radio studio where I was working. Yeah, I get it. It looks bad."

Lillian didn't think he got anything at all. "Why did you quit, Raymond?" She looked around the park as she said it. There was really no one else around and suddenly, she felt exposed and un-safe.

Without being invited, he dropped onto the bench beside her. "I've been in radio since I was eighteen, Lillian. Right out of high school, right out of Radio Club. For me, it was like hitting the jackpot. It was all I ever wanted to do, man the board and play with sound. I've been there twenty years, day and night, working all kinds of strange hours, overtime, double time. Coming in on every holiday. Never a thank you, never any recognition. I got my paychecks, but that's not all a guy needs, right?

"Then, something like the Olympics comes along. I never threw my hat in the ring before because I always thought there were others in line ahead of me. But Bolger retired, McAllister died, and Darren didn't want to travel. I thought it was my turn, finally . . . and then I hear they're sending Nico." Raymond kept his gaze on the far side of the pond. He was intent on pouring out all these words to Lillian without ever looking at her. "I just couldn't believe it, so I took off. But now that detective has been calling me."

"He knows where you are?"

Raymond shook his head. "But he's been pinning notes on my door. Asking me if I remember anything else about that morning. Doesn't he think I'd say so, if I did? Christ, that poor girl."

Lillian stared at him for a few minutes. "Why are you here? Why did you want to talk to me?"

Several more minutes went by. Then, he spoke in a tone that was only inches away from a sob. "Lillian, I didn't have anything to do with her death, I swear it. But I knew they were suspecting me and I needed to get on my way before it got really ugly."

"But you didn't get on your way. You're still here."

"Nobody but you has seen me and nobody's calling me except that cop."

"What are you going to do, Raymond?"

"I'm going traveling. Out west. Leaving today. In fact, I was almost on my way but there is something I have to tell you." A wind had come up and Raymond shivered. His jacket was too light for late September weather. "I changed my mind about six times. Sometimes, it seemed like just too small a thing to mention, but now that I'm going, I just feel like I have to tell somebody."

"Maybe you should tell Detective Sinclair."

Raymond shook his head. "Nope, I'm not talking to that guy anymore."

"What is it?"

"That morning . . . when Susan Taylor died . . . in the studio . . . I saw her old boyfriend near the building."

"Corey?"

"Yeah, that's him. I think I met him in a bar once, when I went out with a gang from the station to see your band play somewhere. Corey." He stared out across the pond. "Susan Taylor's boyfriend."

Lillian could feel about an hour's worth of unspoken pining between the lines. Maybe a lifetime's. "Did you care for her, Raymond?"

He seemed to snap out of something. "Oh, I wouldn't say that. I asked her out once or twice but she told me she had a boyfriend. Of course, I could accept that but you can't fault a guy for trying. But then when I met this guy . . . well, I couldn't believe someone like him was in the picture. I mean, what did they ever have in common?"

"Music."

Raymond nodded. "How do you compete with that, eh? Anyway, I stopped thinking about her after that."

"But you didn't forget about Corey," Lillian prompted.

"That's right. And that morning, about 3:30 when I got to work, he was standing near the front entrance, having a smoke. As soon as he saw me, he ducked around the corner."

"Did he talk to you? Did he say anything?"

"Zilch."

"Did you tell Detective Sinclair about this?"

"I called him, yeah. He said there's really no way to prove Corey was ever there, if he denies it. He was such a pain in the butt that I just stopped talking to him," Raymond said. "But the thing is, there is proof."

"What?"

"I picked this up off the ground." Raymond reached into his pocket and pulled out a book of matches. Printed on it were a logo and the words "The Mynah Bird". Lillian hadn't been near that Yorkville club in quite a few months, but at one time it was almost her second home.

"How do you know this came from Corey's pocket? Can you prove it was on the ground there? That morning?"

"How do you know I'm not just making it up?" Raymond shoved the matches back into his pocket. "Same questions I'd expect Sinclair to ask me." He stood up. "See you around, Lillian."

***

Lillian could hear her phone ringing as she unlocked the door to her apartment.

"Lill, come over to the Purple Onion." Penny sounded more than a little stressed. "Glenda needs to talk to us."

"Oh, Penny, I'm beat. I just want to put on pajamas and crawl under the covers with a book. I picked up a paperback of *Peyton Place.* It's the book of that new TV show, and it's pretty good. I thought I'd see whether I like the book or the TV show better."

"Come on, Lill, she *needs* us, she said."

Lillian sighed. "Alright. Half an hour."

The air in the coffeehouse was blue with smoke but Lillian could see enough to notice that the place was packed. Judy Collins was playing four nights, and it looked as though word of her talent had spread. Lillian saw Penny waving at her from a corner table and went over.

"Where's Glenda?"

"In the ladies room. I think she got kind of choked up and she wanted to be alone for a while."

"Choked up? Why?"

Penny pushed a cup of coffee toward Lillian. "She's really messed up because of Howard. And The Called. That's the other name for this Flower Rising World Coalition."

"A very weird name. They're both weird names."

"Yeah. Well. Anyway, she's fallen for some guy she met there and Howard, the guru, is trying to keep them apart."

"And her guy is agreeing to that? Is that this Bobby you mentioned? Or a different one? Anyway, if he's letting Howard Ronson push him around, it doesn't sound like he'd be too much of a loss."

Penny frowned. "I'm probably not telling it right. Glenda will tell you what's going on when she gets back." She sipped at her coffee. "We have to help her out of this, Lill. I still feel terrible about Susan, you know I do, but there's nothing we can do for her now. We can for Glenda. It's not that we care more for one than the other. It's that we can do something."

"I think you're wrong. We *can* do something for Susan. We can help find out who killed her."

"Isn't that the police's job?"

"I'm not like you, Penny. I don't have the faith in the authorities and the government that you do." Lillian looked around the room, wishing that they had a liquor license here. *Why was it okay to inhale vast quantities of nicotine and swallow a gallon of caffeine but not okay to have a beer? Thanks to some lobby group operating somewhere, or sometime, before she was born.* "But I'm not against doing something to pry Glenda out of this guy's clutches. Is she open to talking about it?"

"She wasn't, before today. You saw that. She seemed to think he walked on water, practically. Moved into his compound, introduced him to all her friends, to Dr. Arnold. Brought him to Susan's memorial."

"Let him badger me about getting him air time."

"Yeah. He's gone around talking about his "profile" the last few times I've seen him."

"So, what's changed?" Lillian asked.

"I think it's mostly because of Howard telling her to drop Bobby, but who knows, it might be something else."

"What are you talking about?"

"I don't think Glenda knew what she was getting into," Penny said. "Howard turned on the charm to both Glenda and Susan at first, but Susan had his number from the beginning and refused to spend any time with him. He called her a bunch of times, and even went around to her office at the university, she told me, trying to get her interested in his group. At one point, she told me, he followed her for five days. Every time she turned around, there he was, smiling and trying to get her into a heavy discussion about metaphysics or philosophy. She just kept on brushing him off but apparently, Glenda was more impressed."

When Glenda got back to the table, it was clear that she had been crying. Her mascara had run, her eyelashes were clumped together, and there were dark smears around her eyes where she hadn't been able to wipe off all the makeup.

"What's wrong, Glen?" Lillian asked.

"Nothing, it's nothing. I'm alright."

"You're not alright. You look like . . . well, you look like you don't care about anything."

Glenda caught a sob and forced it back down her throat.

Lillian reached out for one of her hands and trapped it on top of the table. "What is going on, Glenda Jane Levy?"

Neither Lillian nor Penny said a word during the five minutes it took Glenda to begin speaking. At first, she talked generally about the strange things going on at the community and then she got into the specifics about her own situation.

"Howard insisted I give up all my clothes when I got there. There's a look he wants us all to have, to show we belong, and that we have faith. But he didn't leave me my own clothes, so I could put them on from time to time, if I wanted to. Then, Sister Radha said I should stop looking for them and talking about them. That he'd sold them to a thrift store to get money to buy groceries."

Lillian was so shaken by this she could barely think of what to say. But she felt she had to keep Glenda talking, almost like keeping a stream flowing along a parched creek bed.

"What was the 'look', Glenda? What did he have you wearing?"

"It was a T-shirt with matching pants," she said. "Sort of a beige or light sand color."

"Anything on the front of the T-shirt?" Lillian had a wild, silly moment of imagining a name like The Called or a slogan, perhaps: A Time for Greatness or Things Go Getter With Howard."

Glenda shook her head. "Our appearance was not important. He talked a lot about taking our minds off our clothes and our looks. Putting them on God and getting ready for rebirth. We go on two or three-day retreats, where we fast and pray and cleanse ourselves. Devotion to Howard and the Way, that's what we were working on."

"What's it like, up there in the Muskokas, at the . . . what did you call it?"

"The Farm."

Lillian and Penny exchanged a look. "Did they take good care of you?" Penny asked.

"It was okay," Glenda said. "We all had lots of chores to do, and the angels who had been there the longest had permission to go into town to get supplies."

"And this was all going on over the past few weeks while you were seeing us, too? At Susan's memorial? In between the days you'd be in town?"

Glenda nodded.

"Did you have a job? Did anybody?"

Glenda shook her head. "No, but many people gave to us for collection, when we asked. Most of the angels put Howard on their bank accounts as a joint owner and he goes into town once each week to receive their gifts. And of course, we have the policies."

"The policies?"

"When we join and make a full commitment, we take out a life insurance policy. For Howard."

"What do you think of all this, Glenda?" Lillian asked.

Glenda looked around the room, a little wildly, Lillian thought. "Can I get a coffee? I'd really like to have a cup of coffee."

They signaled the waiter and waited for Glenda to answer the question.

"When he told me it was time to change my name, I felt weird. I didn't even know what he wanted to change it to, but it just felt too weird. I told Bobby I was leaving and asked him to come with me. I thought it was a good idea because he'd been just as upset as I was when Howard told us to stop seeing each other. But he told Howard and suddenly, I was in a room, in front of

Howard, and he said 'Explain yourself, Sister Amor. You can tell us what you were thinking of. We are all one. Even if you stray just a few yards down the road, we will find you. We are your family and we are all one.' " The waiter arrived and Glenda reached for the cup of coffee like a freezing man reaching for a blanket. "That's when I decided to go."

Again, Lillian and Penny looked at each other. This was unbelievable.

Glenda seemed anxious and needing reassurance. "It's okay, Glen," Lillian said. "You're out of there now, and we're so glad you are. You did the right thing."

"What should I do now?" Her hands clutched the coffee cup as if it were a lifeline holding up a drowning woman.

"Change your phone number!" Penny exclaimed. "Don't take any phone calls or have any meetings with that man. Or that other one, Bobby, was that his name? Go completely dark on them. Radio silence. They're dangerous, Glenda. Oh my God. I can't believe we let you get as far into that as we did. I want you to come and stay with me."

"Oh, could I? Thank you, Penn. One of the things that kept me from making a decision there was knowing that I'd given up my apartment. I didn't know where I could go."

"You can always come to any one of us," Lillian said. "Always."

She hugged Glenda and she could feel the intensity of her friend, hugging back. She would be there for her, but deep within, there was still hurt. Glenda and the others had held a secret that excluded her, and at some point, there would have to be a discussion of that.

Chapter 17

October 1
1964

Each time a phone rang next morning in the newsroom, Lillian jumped for it, sure that it would be Detective Sinclair calling her back. When she finally picked one up and heard his voice, she put him on hold for a half-minute and transferred the call to a phone on the most remote desk in the newsroom that she could find.

"Miss Lillian Clarkson! What can I do for you?"

"I've heard a few things in the last couple of days that I think you should know about."

"Excellent. What do you know?"

"Corey Lang was seen near the station in the early morning the day Susan was killed," Lillian said.

"That, I've already heard."

Lillian took a deep breath. "What have you heard?"

There was a long pause as Sinclair lit a cigarette and took a drag. "He came in to see us yesterday. Gave us a detailed statement on his whereabouts that morning . . . and the previous night. He'd been partying around Yorkville and then ended up walking around, walking it off. He passed CUBR and I guess somebody you know saw him then. He got home about five."

"This is all just from what he told you?"

"I know where you're going with that. But the thing is, he was with two other people."

Lillian watched the action in the rest of the newsroom as if it were happening at the end of a long tunnel half a mile away from the spot where she sat. In a strange way, it also seemed as if Chuck, Leo, Dominic, and Josh were all moving in slow-motion. "So, he has an alibi."

"He does. And it's solid. We've checked out the other two people who were with him and there aren't any holes. Also, the three of them were seen together in the club on Cumberland and later walking on Davenport. We have statements from several people who were looking out their apartment windows at several points between three a.m. and five, corroborating their stories."

"You found people who weren't sleeping and just happened to be looking out at the street?" Lillian asked.

"Corey brought his friends into the station to give their information and he had names and addresses of the people who'd seen him go by. We interviewed them and it checked out."

"Corey Lang. Corey Lang did all this." Lillian felt as if she'd suddenly landed on a different planet.

"Yeah. Well. Corey's father might have happened to be with the group that came into the station with him."

"Group?"

"Yeah. Friends, witnesses, father, lawyer."

"I get the picture," Lillian said. "Corey might not be a go-getter, but his father is."

"That's it," Detective Sinclair said. "So, not Corey Lang. You got anything else?"

"Raymond Chernowski has not left town, like I thought."

"Raymond Chernowsi. Okay. What did you think?"

"He was at the station, working, the day Susan was killed. He took off as soon as the police said he could and no one saw him for a few days. Then he was back, got some bad news, bad work news—"

"What was that?"

"He expected to be assigned to the Tokyo Olympics coverage, and he wasn't. He quit his job and sort of disappeared. But then he walked up to me the other day in High Park. He thinks maybe he's under suspicion from you guys . . . and me . . . and he wanted to show me a matchbook he picked up outside the station that he thinks Corey Lang dropped that day."

Sinclair took another drag on his cigarette. "We have Raymond Chernowski in custody right now, but not in connection with Susan Taylor's death."

"In custody!"

He seemed to wait for Lillian to say something else, but she couldn't find any words. "It's drugs."

"It's drugs?!"

"Yes, indeedy. Detective Kincaid has been watching his place because we wanted to ask him a few more questions. When he didn't turn up for quite a few days, she got a search warrant and we went in. Mr. Chernowski came home when we were there, so we took him along, too. Booked him."

"For what?"

"Possession, at this point. The quantity we found wasn't huge. But we're still looking through his things."

"Possession of what?"

"Heroin," Sinclair said.

***

When Lillian got home, she was almost desperate to talk to somebody about this. But who? Penny was obsessed with Glenda's situation. Glenda was *in* a situation. Lillian felt like she and Joyce still had the entire Arctic Circle between them, because of the way Joyce had frozen her out of the group during the abortion episode last spring. Or summer, or whenever it was. Lillian didn't even know.

Rhonda. That was it.

Lillian dialed the New York number, very conscious that it was still early in the day and the charges would be high. The rates hadn't yet gone down to the evening prices. But that couldn't be helped. She needed to talk to Rhonda.

"Hey, kiddo, what's up?"

"Can you talk for a few minutes?"

Well, I'm at work so, no, is the official answer. No personal calls. But my boss is out until three. Phone me back in five minutes and I'll talk to you from his office."

That gave Lillian time to put on the percolator for some coffee and get herself settled on the couch under a blanket. "Hi, Rhonda, is this okay now?" she said, when Rhonda answered.

"Yeah, it's cool. So, what's going on?"

"There are some things happening around Susan's . . ." Lillian got choked up over what to call it, once again.

"The investigation," Rhonda helped her. "What's the latest?"

"The police seem to be convinced it was Raymond Chernowski," she said. "The radio tech who was on duty that morning. They searched his apartment and found heroin."

"Whoa." Rhonda put the phone receiver down, then Lillian heard a door being closed. "What do you mean, heroin?"

"What do I mean? Heroin, the drug, you know, heroin." Lillian could feel herself starting to freak out. She had been counting on Rhonda to be calm and detached, and if she wasn't, Lillian wasn't quite sure what she'd do.

"Alright." She could hear Rhonda swallow. "Alright, they've found heroin in the apartment of a guy who had a crush on Susan. Doesn't that seem to make the conclusion pretty obvious?"

"I know that's what the police think. But I just don't know, Rhon. I've known him almost a year, and he just seems like a nice guy." Lillian couldn't put her finger on what it was; if she could, she'd point it out to Sinclair, right away.

"Well, an intuition about somebody is often worth listening to," Rhonda said. "But if you're right about him . . . that he is not a killer, not Susan's killer . . . what was he doing with heroin in his apartment? Does he seem to you like somebody who would experiment with drugs?"

"No. No, he doesn't."

"Give them to somebody else?"

"No."

"Hold them for somebody else? Maybe he's such a nice guy that he agreed to hold a package for somebody and that's what the police found."

"Maybe," Lillian said slowly. "Doesn't feel right."

"What did he tell the police?"

"Sinclair didn't say, specifically. I think he would have mentioned it, if Raymond had some sort of explanation."

"Does he have roommates? Could it have belonged to somebody else, but he got grabbed because the police already have him on their radar?"

"Maybe." The coffee was ready and Lillian got up to pour herself a cup. "Just a minute, I'll be right back."

When she returned and picked up the phone, Rhonda was ready to give up. "Well, I just don't know, Lill. I mean, it's weird, right? The stuff didn't just fly in through an open window."

"No, it didn't," Lillian said. "But I'm starting to think that maybe somebody carried it in."

"What do you mean, like planted it there, on purpose?"

"Exactly. To make Raymond look guilty."

"Do you have any idea who would do such a thing?"

"None," Lillian said. "But I think the police have to look at that possibility and try to find out."

"They're working hard on it, aren't they?"

"Sinclair says there are two dozen officers and detectives on it, working a lot of overtime."

"So, they're being serious about it."

"They are."

"Is anybody considering the possibility that it was just a random killing? Just some nutcase who happened to be in that building, see Susan, and attack her?

"That almost never happens, according to the stats," Lillian said. "It's almost always somebody the victim knows. But I asked Sinclair about that, way back at the beginning, and he said they were considering that possibility, along with a lot of others.

"Including the possibility that it's not random and that Raymond is being framed."

***

But when Lillian spoke with Detective Sinclair an hour later, it became clear that the police were *not* looking at that possibility.

"I'd say we're ninety-nine percent sure we've got the guy," Sinclair said.

Lillian felt sick. "Have you charged Raymond?"

"Not with the murder. But we're holding him on the drug bust. We just have one more lead to follow but I'm pretty sure it'll end up a dead end."

"You know, Detective, it just doesn't feel right. I know it looks like Raymond was in the wrong place at the wrong time, but that doesn't make him a murderer."

"Of course not. That's why we're gathering evidence. Like a package of the same illegal substance used to kill her, found in his

183

apartment. Maybe it just seems too obvious to you, Lillian, but police work often is . . . just obvious. And mundane."

"Are you sure you aren't just in a hurry to get it wrapped up? Solve the case?"

"I'm going to ignore that, and put it down to you just being very upset about losing your friend," he said.

Lillian hung up the phone.

She paced around her apartment for half an hour and just couldn't get settled. It was dinnertime and she should probably eat but there was absolutely nothing in the refrigerator or the cupboards. Lillian didn't usually like to go out to eat alone but this had been a month of exceptions. She pulled on a jacket and grabbed her purse.

Out on the street, dozens of people were coming and going. It was one of the best things about living in the city. The little Italian place with the red-checkered tablecloths seemed to call her name and almost before she knew it, she was inside and seated at a snug table tucked away in a back corner, a candle burning and an empty wineglass in front of her.

Her mother often said that it was important to be kind to other people and even more important to be kind to yourself, once in a while. Lillian opened the menu and looked over the list of spaghetti dishes.

"Lillian, isn't it?"

She didn't recognize Dr. Arnold at first, because she was seeing him out of his usual environment.

"Yes. Dr. Arnold. hello." She twisted in her chair so that she could make eye contact with him, looming above her. "Lillian Clarkson, from CUBR."

"Of course." He looked around, smiling slightly and seeming very at ease. "Are you waiting for someone? Or are you eating alone?"

"I'm on my own tonight," Lillian said. "Just a quick bite before getting back to work."

"You're going back to work?"

"Oh yes, I often work evenings. I just got back from a research trip and I have a lot to do to pull it all together and type it up for Eugene," Lillian said.

"That's neat," Dr. Arnold said. "Well, I'm just taking a dinner break from work, too, and I couldn't stomach one more brown paper bag sandwich so I decided to treat myself to a nice plate of spaghetti." He looked around the restaurant, then back to Lillian. "I don't suppose it would hurt if we had our breaks together, would it? I have a couple of questions about the items I've been doing for the station that I wouldn't mind asking you."

"Be my guest," Lillian said, motioning toward the chair. Oh no, he wouldn't think she meant 'be my guest' literally, would he?

Dr. Arnold pulled back a chair and sat down. "I guess I created quite a commotion with my item on abortion the other day."

"That's putting it mildly," Lillian said.

"I'm sorry and I learned my lesson. I won't change the topic without getting clearance from the producer ever again." He was looking over the menu. Lillian thought his comments sounded like a throwaway.

"You do get that they'll fire you if you do it again?" Lillian said. "In fact, I'm surprised they didn't drop you after that first time."

Dr. Arnold put down the menu. "Is it that crucial, that I follow orders? Get permission?"

"Well, yeah. They were expecting information about lung cancer and smoking. It had been announced and promoted. But it was also a big deal because of the particular subject you chose for a replacement."

The waitress arrived to take his order. "Spaghetti Bolognese," Dr. Arnold said. "Can I get you something?"

"I'll have the spaghetti marinara," Lillian said. "Separate checks."

"Oh, please, let me—"

"Separate checks, Dr. Arnold."

"Alright, Lillian, but at least you have to let me insist you call me Kevin."

She looked at him. *What was this about?*

"Look, I feel like things have turned sour for me at CUBR and I'd like some help in fixing them. If I'd had any idea that abortion was such a big taboo, I wouldn't have mentioned it."

"Well, it's certainly controversial," Lillian said. "Pretty much everywhere."

"Yeah, I get that now, and I won't make that mistake again," he said.

"You have to come up with a list of safe, popular subjects, then go over them, one by one, with either Eugene or Oscar. Then, you have to stick with them, no changes."

"I just thought it would be a better item, especially since I'd already done something on the Surgeon General's report." He just wasn't ready to let it go. "And not very long ago. It was just that first Monday in September, Labor Day. Chuck told me to repeat the topic, but I just had this feeling that it wouldn't make good radio so I changed it to abortion."

Something clicked with Lillian. "That's right, you were there that morning, weren't you?"

Dr. Arnold looked at her. Did he wince? He certainly had a sympathetic look on his face. "I'm sorry, yes. That's touchy ground for you, isn't it? That's the morning your friend died."

The waitress arrived with two large plates covered in tomato sauce and steaming pasta. Lillian gave her attention to three mouthfuls, then put down her fork. "The morning she was killed."

"Are the police anywhere near making an arrest?"

"They have a prime suspect, yes."

Dr. Arnold ignored his food and gave his attention to Lillian. "That must be a relief to you."

"I don't look at it that way," Lillian said. "The whole thing is just tragic. I don't want revenge and when I think about who the killer might be, I just feel sad for him. But I want him caught, and I'm doing anything I can to help the police with their investigation."

He continued to study her for another moment, then picked up his fork again. "Susan was fortunate to have a friend like you. They all are . . . Glenda, Joyce, Rhonda, Penny. You're quite the group."

Even though Kevin Arnold seemed to know an awful lot about the six of them, it didn't feel comfortable, talking to him about her friends and she didn't feel moved to give him any information. He just gave off a vibe of being too eager for it, somehow. Time to change the subject.

"Even though a lot of the people at the station were in a tizzy about your abortion item, I thought there were quite a few interesting things you said in it. Do you really think countries all over the world are going to be making it legal in the next few years?"

"In certain situations," Dr. Arnold said. "You hear and read politicians talking about it and questioning the status quo already. I mean, how can a civilized society justify forcing a woman who's been raped to go through with a pregnancy and raise a child conceived because of that act of violence?"

He finished his dinner and leaned back in his chair. "I think with all the women's liberation activity we're seeing that contraception will be widely available. 'Every child a wanted child.' Like the slogan. I think when women start pursuing careers the way you are doing, controlling their own bodies and managing unwanted pregnancies will become the norm."

This was not an opinion that Lillian had heard voiced very often. "I guess doctors see abortion differently."

"Not all doctors are the same, just like not all radio reporters. But generally, yes. I think doctors see it . . . at least, I do, as a medical procedure that addresses a medical condition, nothing more. Nothing less, either. . . but just not as a moral or religious issue."

"And a legal issue," Lilian said. "Doctors may think that but they still have to follow the law."

"Yes, they do, and that's why it's so difficult to arrange for a procedure."

"But it does still happen. Women still ask."

"Yes, it does and they do, but most doctors won't go near it. The penalties are severe, if you're caught. It's the sort of thing that's very difficult to keep confidential. I would imagine."

Lillian thought about her own recent brush with this subject and her friends' decision to exclude her. "Not always difficult."

"Although anything can be kept confidential, if an effort is made," Dr. Arnold said.

Neither spoke for a few minutes and Dr. Arnold seemed to go off somewhere in his thoughts. Maybe he was remembering a time when he'd had to turn down a request from a pregnant woman for help? Lillian waited for him to say something more, but when he did speak, it had nothing to do with this delicate subject.

"I have to get going back to the hospital. Please. Let me pick up the check."

Lillian reached into her purse for her wallet and pulled out six dollars. "Absolutely not."

He smiled. "Thanks for the company, Lillian. Good luck with your New York research this evening."

After Lillian had walked about five blocks back toward the station, the question suddenly raced across her brain: How did he know she had been to New York?

***

When Joyce phoned that night, Lillian was *this* close to hanging up on her. The news that her friends had all been involved in helping someone deal with such a major thing as an abortion and that they didn't trust her to join in had hit her hard. Her tone of voice was ice and Joyce picked up on it.

"Come on, Lill, are you going to beat me up over this forever?"

"I was seriously thinking of hanging up on you."

"Look, we decided last spring and maybe it was the wrong one. But it's done now. Now that we know how bad it made you feel, we wouldn't do it again."

That made Lillian feel somewhat better. "I'm glad to hear that. Because really, you know, I would never put my media job ahead of any request for discretion that might come from you. Or from Glenda. Or Penny. Or Rhonda. And last spring and summer, if it had come from Susan . . . well, you know, I always thought her judgement was the best of all of us."

"That's good to know, Lill. I apologize again. We just weren't sure what your opinion on this would be. I wasn't sure about your opinion on abortion . . . you're always so careful to see both sides of everything."

"I see both sides and I don't challenge anybody's right to their own views on something."

"We weren't sure how seriously you take your loyalty to the news and to your job . . . and we didn't know if your opinion would be different because it was happening to Rhonda."

Happening to Rhonda? What?

The silence between them went on for several minutes. When Lillian finally spoke, her voice sounded like it belonged to someone else.

"What happened to Rhonda?"

"Oh, cripes, Lillian, I hate all this secrecy garbage!" Joyce was almost in tears. "It was Rhonda who was in trouble. It took her quite a while to tell any of us and then it took a while to find a doctor who would do it. Time was passing, and it was getting worse and more dangerous by the day.

Finally, we found a solution, Rhonda came down to Toronto and Glenda set it up. We had to take her to this apartment in Scarborough, late at night. It was really scary. The woman who met us said barely a word, the apartment was like . . . I don't know how to describe it, but it was definitely like nobody real lived there.

We waited about an hour, then took her back to Glenda's place and stayed with her overnight. Penny went home with her on the train to New York the next day, saw her right into her apartment, and stayed with her for two days. Dr. Arnold said she should see a doctor in New York if she ran a fever or started to bleed again, but she didn't."

Lillian couldn't speak.

Rhonda?

Dr. Arnold?

Chapter 18

October 2
1964

The next morning at work, Lillian turned up the radio on her desk and blasted Top 40, trying to drown out the thoughts in her head. It irritated Chuck no end, and it didn't work.

She was still in a state of shock over Joyce's revelation. She had hung up the phone as quickly as she could, rushing to answer Joyce's questions about her reaction with some banal reply. No, she wasn't upset; yes, she would be able to keep this to herself; no, she wouldn't mention it to Rhonda until Joyce had a chance to check with her about bringing Lillian into the tent.

Once the morning news run was over, Lillian sat down at a desk, wondering how she was going to get through the rest of the day. Ever since Susan had died, she'd been busy, and she'd been absorbed in answering the questions about how and why. But today, she felt herself flagging and her energy running out. Finding out about Rhonda's abortion and about the way that all of her girlfriends had chosen to keep it from her had taken about the last ounces of self-confidence and drive she had. All she wanted to do was run back to her apartment and hide.

Chuck rushed by, a stack of reels in his arms and a pink slip in his right hand. "Phone message for you," he said, as he dropped it on the desk in front of Lillian on the way by.

From Dr. Berman, U of T. Could you stop by Mikhail Kogonov's office today

Despite herself, she felt her curiosity aroused. And she needed something to take her mind off Rhonda and something to stop her from marching over to Dr. Arnold's office, demanding more information.

It was another warm, early fall day. After the bit of cold and falling leaves they'd had, the warmth and sunshine were back. Really, it felt like summer was going to go on and on. Lillian walked north, heading for the campus. She wasn't in any rush.

When she got to the Science Building, it was packed with students hurrying from class to class. She ducked into the ladies' room to avoid the crowd and waited out the between-class hullabaloo. The door to Mikhail's office, in the grad students' area of the building, was open, so she went in and took a chair to wait for him.

She had no idea why he or Dr. Berman had called her—maybe they had ballet tickets for her, too? Lillian scolded herself for being a smart aleck; she was being too hard on these Russians. Susan had found it worthwhile to let herself date Mikhail. There must be something good about him.

After two hours of waiting, she wasn't so sure. At hour three, she gave up and went to find Dr. Berman.

"Lillian, hello!" the professor said. "What brings you over here?"

"I had a call from you to meet Mikhail Kogonov at his office, but he didn't show up," she said. "Do you have any idea where he might be?"

Dr. Berman stopped in the midst of bustling around her office. "I heard that he'd left. A couple of days ago. Returned to Moscow, and it's not clear yet whether it's a leave of absence or an actual resignation from his PhD program." She sat down and pushed her phone toward Lillian. "I don't know who used my name to leave you a message, but it wasn't me. And I don't know how he could have been the one to call you to come over if he's already flown home. But I do know who would know. Pavel Andreyevitch. Here, I have his number."

Pavel confirmed to Dr. Berman that Mikhail had returned to the USSR. Said he was depressed ever since Susan was killed. Just couldn't shake it and couldn't get any work done. Pavel didn't know when he'd be back or if he was even planning to.

Dr. Berman stared at the phone. "He said he was going to miss Mikhail, too," she said. "This is strange."

The professor looked as puzzled as Lillian felt.

A loud knocking at the door drew their attention.

"Come in," the professor said.

Norman Taylor opened the door and for a moment, Lillian was shocked at how Susan's brother had changed in just the couple of weeks since she'd seen him at Susan's memorial service. He hadn't shaved, and he was wearing clothes that looked as though he'd used them for cleaning the garage over the past ten years.

"Sorry to interrupt . . . oh, Lillian. You're here." He stopped to decide what to do next. "Anyway. Dr. Berman, I'm looking for Mikhail Kogonov."

"You've missed him," she said. "He's returned home to Moscow."

Norman slumped into the chair beside Lillian. "Home to Moscow," he repeated.

"Yes, I'm sorry, but he's gone. Did you have an appointment with him? Could someone else in his department help you?"

It was very odd, but Norman started to laugh. "Someone else help me? Help me? No, I don't think so. Nobody else can help."

He didn't say anything more and after a few minutes, simply rose and walked out of the office. Dr. Berman and Lillian exchanged mystified looks and raised eyebrows, then Lillian stood up. "Well, I think I'll be going, too. Thanks anyway, Dr. Berman."

"I'll let you know if I hear anything more about him," the professor said.

Lillian walked through the building and down to the street. She sat down on a bench at a bus stop, just to rest, and when a bus pulled over to let her on, she shook her head at the driver. She wasn't going anywhere; she just needed to take a little while to think things over.

As it pulled away, she couldn't help but notice the cigarette advertisement that covered the side of it, the model with the cowboy hat and the handlebar moustache making the habit look so cool. It reminded her again of Pavel, and his moustache, and that started her thinking of Mikhail and Susan again.

She hadn't been able to talk to Mikhail about Susan, but there was another conversation she wanted to have. She had a few things to say to Glenda about Dr. Arnold.

Lillian walked over to a nearby phone booth, went inside, and pulled the door behind her.

The phone rang only once when Glenda picked it up. "Howard?"

"It's not Howard, Glenda, it's me," Lillian said. "I have to talk to you about Rhonda. And Dr. Arnold."

Glenda was silent, so Lillian pushed on. "I won't spend any time on how bad I feel that you didn't include me in helping Rhonda when she got in trouble. But I have to know more about how Dr. Arnold got involved in it all."

"That procedure needed to be done, Lillian," Glenda said. "It was Rhonda's choice . . . and I was glad to be able to help her. It was also her decision about whom to tell. Secrets don't last long if you tell dozens of people."

"I'm not 'dozens of people'!" Lillian said.

"Well, I'm sorry your feelings got bruised, but, as I said, it was Rhonda's decision."

"What about Dr. Arnold?"

Lillian watched the traffic go by and waited until Glenda answered. "I've known for some time that Dr. Arnold was helping women in this way. You couldn't help but pick up on it, in the office, if you were paying attention. He thought he was keeping it all secret, of course. Men so often miss the information signals, don't you think?

Anyway, a few of us, over the time I was there, caught on to what he was doing. A couple of them were really judgmental, but I wasn't—I think women should have the choice about what happens with their own bodies."

Glenda took a long pause, but Lillian didn't say anything. She wondered sometimes if she spoke too often and even interrupted too much; maybe, she put people off and drove her friends to decide they couldn't talk to her.

"Then, when it came around that Rhonda needed help," Glenda continued, "I was in a position to introduce her to the right person. I was glad to be able to help her. I knew she would be discrete. It's very dangerous for Dr. Arnold and he has to be very careful not to get caught. Every woman who comes to see him for the procedure is referred by at least two people, sometimes more. He was even a bit reluctant to see Rhonda, because she wasn't from Toronto, but Susan and I convinced him."

"Susan talked with Dr. Arnold?"

"Well, you know she always was the most persuasive of all of us. I couldn't get an answer from Dr. Arnold and the clock was ticking. Rhonda was getting so upset, waiting up there in New York, and she was talking about going to one of those back alley people. So, I asked Susan to meet with him, with me. She convinced him that Rhonda needed help and that he was the only one she could turn to. It was even more complicated because last spring somebody started blackmailing him and he went ape at first, then he seemed to chill out."

"Blackmailing him!" Lillian hadn't thought she could get any more staggered by everything that had gone on—but she was. "Was he paying?"

"I don't know. I thought he was, and that was why he suddenly stopped talking about it. Got very uptight one time, when we were speaking privately and I asked him about it. Said he believed so much in providing the service that he was willing to invest his own money in it, if he had to."

"Yeah, but it's one thing to just invest your money. That's easy. It's another thing, entirely, to risk prison. "Lillian took a few minutes to try to understand all this. "All right, so you and Susan met with him to try to convince him to take care of Rhonda. How did the meeting go?"

"Okay, I guess. He made the appointment. She came up from New York, and a few days later, Penny saw her home. Susan was very convincing. But he didn't seem happy about it," Glenda said. "But then, he didn't seem happy about anything much throughout the entire summer."

"How is he now?"

"Well, I don't really know. I haven't seen him since I quit and moved up north to live with The Called."

"What did Dr. Arnold think of Howard Ronson?"

Glenda laughed. "About as much as all of you do."

"Oh, Glen, it's not that I'm that down on him—" Lillian started.

"I know, but you're not his biggest fan," Glenda said. "I get it, I see it now. I'm starting over, and I'm not going back up there. You don't have to worry about driving me into his arms because of your disapproval. You're not my mother."

Lillian joined in with her laughter. "Touché, m'dear. What *is* the situation with Howard right now?"

"Oh, you know, Lillian, he's not a bad guy. He wants to build his group, and he wants to show people the right way to live. He might be a little . . . abrupt in the way he does things, but he's not a bad guy."

Chapter 19

October 3
1964

Lillian was not so sure, and that was one of the points she made when she met with Detective Sinclair the next day.

The driver on the bus on the way there had a transistor radio, blasting Roy Orbison. Some other station, not CUBR. She was feeling groggy from insomnia the night before. She'd been restless all evening, but then turned down every invitation and rejected every idea she'd had about something to do.

She didn't like to handle Friday nights that way, but she just couldn't settle down to anything. After watching *Man from U.N.C.L.E.* and *Peyton Place* on TV, she sat through the *11 o'clock News,* with stories about speculation that Martin Luther King Jr. would win the Nobel Peace Prize and dissection of the Warren Commission Report on President Kennedy's assassination. The Queen and Prince Philip were due to land at the air force base on Prince Edward Island to begin their eight-day visit to Canada.

Lillian knew she should be excited about that, and about all the other events coming up, but she wasn't. Everything just seemed as bland and dry as ash. Through the night, she changed position in bed about a hundred times. She couldn't get comfortable and she couldn't fully wake up.

It was now almost a month since Susan's death and, as far as Lillian knew, no one was any closer to solving the crime and bringing somebody to justice. Big justice, that's what she wanted. Someone to pay for what had been done to Susan, cutting her down just as her life was barely getting started. Someone to pay for the grief all of her friends had to live with every day. The grief, and the fear. Lillian had never before had the feeling that security and safety weren't to be taken for granted. She had it now.

And someone to pay for her guilt about not saving Susan.

Detective Sinclair had called to say that he had new information about the case and wanted to meet to talk to her about it. He'd suggested Casa Loma, the immense house on Davenport Hill where hundreds, if not thousands, of Toronto's celebrations, weddings, graduations, and passings of the baton, had taken place.

"Well, this is strange," Lillian said as she sat down on a bench beside him in the public gardens.

"No inner meaning," Sinclair said. "I had to be here for a meeting and I'm at another one on Spadina in half an hour. It was convenient."

Lillian nodded. "What's happening?"

"We're closing the case on Susan Taylor."

Lillian gripped the bench under her left thigh with one hand. The hand he couldn't see. "Why?"

"We're at a dead end," Sinclair said. "The case against Raymond Chernowski evaporated, for one thing."

"How so?"

"The drugs that were in his apartment weren't his. He and his lawyer were able to establish that he's not a user, not a buyer, and we couldn't set up any kind of trail."

"Do you think they were planted there?"

"We do. But we have no idea how. Or why. No fingerprints." Sinclair stared out over the view of Toronto, out to the lake. "We gave him a polygraph test and he passed it. We had no reasonable grounds to hold him, so we let him go."

"What about Corey Lang? You thought he had major motivation, as her ex-boyfriend."

"Airtight alibi, as I told you."

Lillian had a feeling of losing hold of a rope as she slid down toward an abyss. "What about the theory that it was random, some sort of psycho killer, somebody who just stumbled on Susan alone?"

"No evidence of that. Not much evidence of anything, to be frank. And, the department has put in thousands of man-hours on it, interviewed everybody. The overtime bill was astounding. We've just run out of leads. And gas. Chief won't put any more resources into it." Sinclair didn't look at her while he spoke. The castle gardens seemed to get ninety-five percent of his attention. "I'm sorry."

"So, what then? It's closed? Susan's case is closed?"

"No case is ever really closed. There's still a file on my desk. And it's on my mind. If any new information comes up, we'll investigate it. But you know, since we've hit a wall on this, we're back to a theory that it wasn't murder. It was a self-inflicted overdose."

Lillian felt the landscape tilting in front of her. Was he just seconds away from leaving this bench and walking out of her orbit? If she let that happen, she might never get any closer to finding the answers for Susan.

"What about the other theories?"

"What other theories?" Sinclair turned to look at her. "Do you know something? Talk to me, Lillian."

"Well, there's Howard Ronson, the religious group leader. He knew Susan through our friend Glenda. You know she joined his following and Susan was critical of that. She tried to talk Glenda out of it . . . maybe Howard decided to silence her."

She could see the skepticism on his face, but she pressed on.

"You don't know if he was capable of being a killer, but you don't know much about him at all. Nobody does."

Sinclair said nothing.

"Or Kevin Arnold." Lillian felt like she was driving a car, desperate to catch up with something or somebody, and pushing the accelerator pedal to the floor with every bit of strength she had.

"The doctor? Dr. Arnold?"

"He was at the station that morning to do his on-air expert bit. He's very involved in . . ." Lillian was ready to tell Detective Sinclair the entire story of Rhonda, Glenda, and Dr. Arnold, but something stopped her. "He's got a lot of controversial opinions. And I just heard that he was being blackmailed over something he did. He and Susan didn't see eye-to-eye on things and maybe he suspected Susan of being the blackmailer! She wasn't, of course. That wasn't who she was. But maybe he didn't know that, and maybe he was desperate!"

Sinclair continued to stare at her. It was fuel on a fire.

"Maybe the new boyfriend, Mikhail. Why isn't he at the university anymore? His sister defected . . . maybe Susan helped them—maybe she helped them once, then she wouldn't help them anymore, and he got angry at her!" Lillian jumped to her feet. "Or Corey! Maybe Corey's alibi was made up! Maybe somebody paid somebody to say those things!"

Sinclair rose, then made intense eye contact with her. "You watch too much TV, Lillian. We have no evidence of any of those things. You'll drive yourself crazy if you keep on thinking that way."

He reached into his pants pocket and pulled out his keys. "Look, I thank you very much for the help you've given me, investigating this case, and I'll stay in touch with you. If anything important ever comes up, I'll let you know. But, in the meantime, I suggest you move on. Leave it behind. I know it's devastating when a close friend dies, but she's gone, Lillian, and you have to let her go. You still have a lot of life to get on with. It wasn't your fault she died and you can't do anything to bring her back. You can't find her murderer. You tried, I tried, but it just didn't happen."

But it was supposed to happen. I can solve this. I know I can.

"You know, Lillian, I learned a long time ago that I'm no hero. I don't ride in on a white horse and solve all the mysteries or prevent all the pain. You won't be any different." He separated the car key from the others and stroked it with his thumb. "I have to get going. Can I drop you somewhere?"

She shook her head. He watched her, watching the garden, for a few more minutes, then shrugged and walked away.

Lillian dropped back onto the bench. The sobs, when they came, were uncontrollable.

Chapter 20

2019
Alamos Island, Florida

Lillian could hear whistling from the hallway at almost the same moment that the doorbell rang. The man at the door looked as if he might have been a sailor who had circumnavigated the globe, picking up tattoos in every port. She couldn't help staring with fascination at his neck, with the open collar of his shirt revealing a dagger dripping blood, and at his arms, with the rolled-up sleeves of his shirt exposing more ink drawings.

She sighed as she reached out for the pen and pad to sign for her package. The popularity of tattoos was just one of the many changes in the 21st century that she still had to adjust to. Not that it mattered, anyway. Nobody was on her case to *get* a tattoo, and looking at them wasn't exactly a full-time job.

The delivery man handed over the parcel, which was in plain brown paper, addressed to Lillian Howe, with a return address in Canada. Canada, of all places! *Erica Taylor.* Not a name she recognized. Lillian turned the box over twice, then went to the kitchen to get the scissors.

Inside, a blue notebook rested in a nest of white tissue paper. An envelope addressed to Lillian lay on top.

Dear Mrs. Howe,

You don't know me, but my grandfather, Norman Taylor, gave me this notebook and asked me to get it to you. He had quite a bit of faith in the power of the internet and thought I could search you easily, but it turned out not to be quite that simple. It's taken me a year to find you, in Florida, and I hope you won't mind that it took me so long to carry out one of his last wishes.

Norman died in 2018, but even in his last months in hospital, he continued trying to find out what happened to his sister, Susan Taylor. She was a friend of yours, I believe (if I've found the right Lillian Howe, and I think I have.) Your name used to be Lillian Clarkson, right?

Lillian dropped the note and took a deep breath. Yes, Susan was a friend of hers, one of the best of her life. She hadn't seen her in fifty-five years, but she thought about her frequently. At least once a week, and more often—maybe even once a day—in these last few years.

She picked it back up and began to read the rest.

Grandpa never really got over what happened to his sister. I never met her, of course, but he's told me she was just a bright light on the planet. A bright light. Those were his words.

A bright light. She'd agree with that. Susan was the match that lit up all six of them when they'd first arrived in Toronto.

The family hadn't wanted her to stay in Toronto, Grandpa told me. She was only twenty-two and had never been to a big city. Grandpa told me some of the relatives blamed her for what hap-pened, thought she must have done something to cause it.

He seemed to blame himself.

But I can't imagine why. He was her younger brother—why would he feel responsible? I could get it if her mother or her father felt some guilt for some reason or other, but why would her younger brother? They passed long ago, of course, and didn't leave any infor-

mation about anything. Oh, there were the newspaper clippings, of course, but there was nothing, Grandpa said, that everybody didn't already know.

Lillian had once had her own box of newspaper clippings about Susan, but she'd thrown them out, along with many other boxes, when she married and stopped being Lillian Clarkson to become Lillian Howe.

It was just a horrible tragedy, as you know, Mrs. Howe. Grandpa told me that this notebook was Susan's diary from 1964. I don't know whether or not he read it. I haven't opened it. Once he started me on looking for you online, it just seemed to me that it belonged to you and that it would be wrong, somehow, to read it.

Lillian looked toward the window and out at the view of the Gulf of Mexico. Her dog, Carl, seemed to pick up the disturbance in her mood and came over to rest his muzzle on her knee. She stroked his head, then looked down at the pages and continued reading.

I hope it doesn't bother you to see this, after all these years, and I hope you won't feel some weird stranger has invaded your privacy. I'm completely normal and okay, really! I sent the package registered mail so that I could be sure it got to you. It's irreplaceable, after all.

I guess my job is done and my promise to Grandpa kept. But Mrs. Howe, I'm sorry, but I don't feel it's over, somehow. I still have so many questions, and Grandpa really didn't want to talk to me about the 60s.

Do you think you'd ever want to come back to Toronto? For a visit? Maybe to see some of the places you saw back then? I would

love to show you around, and I wonder whether you'd let me ask you some of my questions about the family.
    Yours sincerely,
    Erica Taylor

Lillian couldn't remember the last time she'd felt so—she wasn't sure what it was she felt. Surprised, certainly, but beyond that. Shocked. Confused—why had Norman Taylor sent Susan's journal to her and what did he expect her to do with it?

She also felt a little resentful. Or … maybe it was fearful. She wasn't sure she wanted to hear Susan's voice, her twenty-two-year-old voice, via pages she'd written in her diary all those years ago.

The next moment, she was ashamed of herself. How could she deny Susan a little space in her head and her heart? She'd had so many more years, so many more experiences, while Susan's life was cut so short.

Lillian opened the notebook, and at the first sight of Susan's familiar handwriting, slammed it shut. She would read the diary—but not now. She had to be in the right frame of mind, and right now, she just wasn't. She put the journal back in the box, closed it, and put it on the top shelf of the front hall closet.

If she was going to read it, she'd have to have plenty of time for it, and today she just didn't. It was her birthday and her grandson, Donovan, was expecting to celebrate with her at his home in Miami that afternoon. She had a two-hour drive ahead of her, from her condo on Alamos Island on the Gulf Coast, to the marina where she was meeting him.

Once her small suitcase was packed, Lillian loaded Carl and his gear into her car. She plugged in her phone and fiddled with her phone app, trying to find the podcast she downloaded last night. Her eyesight wasn't what it once was, but she was resisting getting the surgery, even though it seemed as though every second person in her condo building had had their cataracts removed and good-as-new lens implants put in.

Donovan and his wife, Hailey, urged her at least once a week to get on with it, and their three-year-old, Bronte, was forever climbing on her lap, book in hand. So far, she'd been able to get away with making stuff up whenever she couldn't quite read the blurry type, but in another couple of years she wouldn't be able to fool him.

Her vision for driving was still perfect, as long as the sun was up. Lillian didn't drive at night any more, but that was no great loss. Her condo building had its own movie theater, swimming pool, and dining room. She played cards in the evenings with friends, walked her dog in a small, well-lit park just behind the building, and was sleepy by nine o'clock most evenings. Why would she need to drive anywhere at night?

When she was going to visit Donovan, or take a drive up the coast to Tampa, she always timed her trip for the daylight hours. This time, the plan was to leave her car at the marina where Donovan would be finishing up his day on his boat and ride back with him in his pickup truck, a treat that Lillian always enjoyed. Donovan found it hard to believe that his grandmother liked the truck, but she did. She liked to ride high above the cars on the road, able to see everything with nothing blocking her view. True, she did find it a little more difficult these days to climb up and into it, but she thought she did pretty well for a woman of seventy-seven.

When she got there, he still had a few notes to make in his day's log and some tackle to pack, so she sat herself down on one of the boat's benches and leaned back to let the Florida sunshine bathe her face.

"Grandma, do you want something to eat? Maybe some juice?"

"I'd like coffee, Donovan."

He raised an eyebrow. She rarely drank coffee, but today was her birthday and it would be all about treats.

She gave Donovan a smile in thanks, but he didn't notice as he rushed into the galley to get her coffee. He seemed very preoccupied these days, always on the go. But Lillian thought most people were rushing around too much, so perhaps it had to do with her, rather than them.

"Alright, there you go," he announced as he put a mug in front of her.

Lillian gazed at the rows of gleaming white hulls all around. It was a busy afternoon on the dock, with groups coming and going from the tour boats and solo sailors steering their small craft back and forth among the luxury yachts. The drone of half a dozen engines filled the air with a constant hum.

When she first heard the words shouted above the background noise, she couldn't catch much more than garbled syllables at first.

"Wuchutfirthtec!"

Half a dozen people ran past Donovan's boat. They seemed to be heading toward a crowd that had gathered at the end of the dock, all shouting and waving arms at a small powerboat moving through the marina. It seemed, to Lillian, to be going too fast.

"Watch out!"

An old man stood at the wheel in the boat, shaking his fist back at them. The anger was flowing in both directions. Lillian still couldn't make out what was being said, but it was clear that the old man wasn't happy about whatever they were yelling at him and they were just about ready to have him locked up.

"Whoa, that old guy is just about to drive right over a manatee!" Donovan had come up from below-decks and was gazing at the fight unfolding in front of them. "Frickin' dangerous, to be going that fast through a marina, anyway. But when there's an animal in the water..." He shook his head.

A siren cut through the afternoon air, and Lillian involuntarily put her hands up over her ears. A police boat pulled into view and an officer on board pulled out a megaphone.

"Sir! Pull that boat over to the dock immediately!"

Lillian watched the old man hesitate, then give the wheel a spin, to turn the boat out of the waterway. He cut the engine, then stood waiting. She looked toward the water and saw the bulky, unmistakable shape of a manatee moving toward the open end of the marina.

The police boat came alongside the small powerboat. "Now, sir, let's sort this out."

"He was going to drive right over a manatee!" The onlookers had gathered on the dock right beside the police boat, and one of them was determined to be sure the police understood what was going on.

"On purpose, sir?" Law enforcement was not impressed. "They're endangered, in these waters, sir. Protected. We can't have people racing through a marina, running them down."

"I wasn't racing!" The grizzled old man was wearing a weather-beaten brown sweatshirt and old jeans. He didn't look capable of racing anywhere.

Yet Lillian and many others had seen him plowing through the water here with no regard for anything living in the depths beneath. Racing or not, it wasn't safe.

"Tell you what, sir. We're going to help you tie up here and you're going to come with us for a discussion about this."

"Am I under arrest?"

"Not at this time, no."

"Then, I'm not going anywhere."

Donovan appeared at Lillian's elbow. "Come on, Grandma, Hailey's waiting for us at home. Got dinner ready to go, complete with birthday cake."

"Donovan," she said. "Aren't you curious to see how this plays out?"

Donovan shook his head. "I'm glad the manatee is gone and there was no damage done. I really don't want to stick around to watch this little confrontation, particularly if it escalates. And the old geezer looks like he's itching for a fight."

"You're probably right," Lillian said. "None of our business, anyway. Let's go have some birthday."

Later that evening, after all the burgers had been eaten, the gifts opened, and the candles on the cake blown out, Lillian sat alone in Donovan's backyard with Carl and the setting sun for company.

And the memory of Susan.

Susan would also be seventy-seven years old today; she and Lillian were birthday twins. They'd started school together, got their driver's licenses together, and they'd graduated high school together.

But Lillian was here, still, and Susan wasn't.

She pulled her mind back into the present and tried to stay there. The day had been a sensational Florida day: robin's-egg-blue sky, soft subtropical breeze, golden-yellow sunshine. The evening was soft and fragrant, another glorious sunset just a half hour away. The sort of time and place that made you glad to be alive.

Chapter 21

The next day when she was home, Lillian pulled the box containing Susan's diary from the shelf in the closet. She had procrastinated on looking at it for long enough. Walking slowly out to the lounge chair on the balcony, she concentrated: her head was spinning, and she wanted to be careful not to fall. Carl sensed that something was up, and followed her through the sliding door, then lay down at her feet. She put her phone down on the balcony table, opening the music app and choosing her instrumental jazz playlist.

The diary was a blue journal, about two inches thick, and bound in fake leather, with 1964 embossed on the front. Lillian flipped through the pages and recognized Susan's handwriting instantly. All those notes they'd passed back and forth in math class, waiting for Mr. Ferguson to turn his back to write something on the blackboard—she'd never forget Susan's handwriting. The book was about three-quarters full, with the lined pages filled with entries, some a full page long and some just a line or two. The dates were at the top of each page.

Lillian began to read.

January 1
Resolutions: Study four hours each night. Swim at the Y every morning. Give up fan magazines
January 3
Snowed all day. At the library
January 10
Exam schedule out today

The entries were brief and repetitive. Lillian started to leaf through more quickly. She had an intuition that this journal was important and had landed in her hands for some reason. After all, Susan's brother, Norman, had held onto it for all this time, and had made sure it found its way to her, as one of his last acts on this earth. But so far, it was dull reading, frankly. During that year, Susan had been absorbed in her university life. Maybe that was why they'd drifted apart.

Then, Lillian spotted her own name.

March 31

We haven't been able to get Lillian to come out with us since St. Patrick's Day. Whenever I call her, she's just . . . remote. She doesn't have much to say and if I ask her any questions, she jumps down my throat, acts as if basically <u>everything</u> is none of my business.

I mean, she's still one of my best friends, she always will be, but it's been really hard to feel happy about that lately.

It was one of those things you wish you hadn't read. Not that it was news to Lillian, that somehow she and Susan had had a falling-out, but it had happened fifty-five years ago. She had felt the pain, lived through the shock of Susan's death, and then time had passed and she had healed. Many, many other things had happened in those fifty-five years, and Toronto 1964 wasn't something she thought of very often, if ever.

Now, it was as if it had all happened just yesterday.

Lillian felt an urge to put the journal down. What was this feeling? Reluctance, certainly; maybe even dread. But she had to keep going. Something even stronger compelled her to continue reading. The unanswered questions about Susan Taylor needed to be laid to rest.

April 8

I don't know what I'm going to do about Corey. He came over here this morning and just wouldn't believe that I couldn't just blow off a class because he'd showed up. I told him three weeks ago that we were done but for some reason he seems to think we still have things to talk about. I think he might be using drugs. And not just soft stuff like pot. I think he's shooting up.

April 10

My grad school application is accepted! Now all I have to do is come up with $1200 for tuition each year, finish my thesis, and get it turned in to Dr. Berman. I can't wait to tell Mikhail.

Lillian remembered how a thousand dollars seemed like so much, in those days. Even a hundred dollars seemed like a lot. But with inflation, that would be almost ten thousand dollars for a year's tuition now. About the same, unless you were going to a top Ivy-League school or taking a pricey business degree.

What did Susan do to come up with that money? Lillian couldn't recall.

April 15

Mikhail asked me out. We're going for dinner to George's Spaghetti House.

April 17

Just a fabulous time! It's the cutest little place, with red-checked tablecloths and candles. They were playing jazz—I don't know a lot about it, but Mikhail does! I liked it, too. We had spaghetti and wine and we talked about everything! He is so cute. And so smart. But I don't know how I'm going to have time for this, and get all my course-work and my thesis done, too.

April 17

He phoned twice!

April 18

*Lunch with Glenda. I don't like this Howard Ronson she's al-
ways talking about, but maybe that's because I just don't have much
use for religion in general. She told me all about his meetings, how
moving they are, how much she's learning. She keeps saying I'll have
to go with her one time.*

April 20

*A tour of the radio station with Lillian. I think she's getting too
fixated on this job. It's all she ever talks about—the news this, and
politics that. Even Joyce isn't as dug in—and she works for the government in Ottawa! I miss our days in the band—well, I miss what
Lill was like, in the band. (I don't miss playing in the band.) Des says
he doesn't see any change in her but I do.*

Lillian put down the journal and tried to catch her breath. It
had been fifty-five years and yet she still remembered her feelings
from those months as if they'd blown up last week. But she did not
know that Susan thought she was fixated on her radio job. Why
hadn't she said anything?

Maybe she had.

April 21

*I'm going up to Ottawa to visit Joyce for a few days. Mikhail
wanted to go with me but I said no. I just want a girlfriends kind of
weekend. He was completely cool with that. It's just one of the best
things about him. He's not possessive or demanding, just lets me be
myself.*

April 22

*Gave in and went to a meeting with Glenda. The whole thing
was creepy. The pressure that Howard is putting on Glenda is too
much. I told her but she wouldn't listen.*

Meeting Lill and Des later tonight to catch a show.

April 23

Corey crashed our evening out last night. I had to practically scream at him to leave the bar. He was drunk or maybe high on something. The way he disrupted the performance. The singer was very kind but if it was me, I would have been really ticked off.

April 24

Mikhail got into the physics program!

I've seen him every day for the past ten now. I could fall for him. There. I said it. I introduced him to Norman and they really seemed to hit it off.

April 28

Dr. Berman offered me a summer job, helping with her research on the new mainframe. Yes! Will look great on my resume plus it means I won't have to spend the summer at home in Albany, working at the ice cream store again.

April 30

Ottawa trip is canceled. Rhonda phoned, so upset. Her period's really late.

May 1

Had dinner with Glenda and Penny. We talked about Rhonda. Should we bring Lillian in on this? We took a vote, I voted no. We all decided no. Glenda is going to talk to Dr. Arnold. He can do it. He's done it for some other women.

Haven't talked to Rhonda yet about whether she wants to come all the way from New York for this but Glenda says she knows she will, if she can get the money together. We'll all throw some in the pot for her. We can come up with enough for train tickets. She can stay at Glenda's place.

May 2

Joyce is coming to T.O. too.

May 4

It's set up for next week.

Lillian tried to coax her memory into recalling what she'd been doing, and where, in the second week of May in 1964. How ridiculous—who would remember anything that far back? It was true, she could remember every line of the lyrics to almost every girl-group song and she almost never forgot a face or a name, but a memory of the exact date of an event wasn't one of her superpowers, as they said nowadays.

May 11
It's done.

After the entry about the abortion, many of the pages were blank. Had Susan become unusually busy, just unable to find a few minutes each day to keep a journal? She'd gone from being a fourth-year computer science student to a full-time employee, working for Dr. Berman. Maybe the work load was really heavy? Or maybe the experience with Rhonda had affected her in some way? Made her depressed?

No matter how much you believe in choice, it was not an easy decision and the episode would be gut-wrenching, even if it weren't happening to you, personally. Maybe Susan was really upset.

If anyone had asked Lillian, even yesterday, what she remembered most about these girls or about 1964, she would have laughed and had to really think, to come up with anything. But Susan's handwriting, her words, and the revelation of the activities that spring brought it all back, her entire twenty-two-year-old life, in dramatic detail.

She needed a drink.

Carl scrambled out of a deep sleep and got to his feet as soon as she moved. He stretched, the way dogs do, glanced at her, and then stopped, cocking his head to one side. He knew something was up.

"Come on, Carl, we're heading for the wine rack," Lillian said.

Five minutes later, she sat with a glass of red on the balcony table in front of her. The sun was just beginning its nightly slide into the Gulf of Mexico and the horizon to either side of it was a rich, glowing shade of gold. Lillian picked up the diary and continued to read.

May 23

The weather is finally changing. It was a long winter and then spring was so rainy. But today I could get out the cut-offs and the T-shirt. Mikhail and I are going for a walk at The Beaches.

May 25

Dinner at George's.

May 28

Four hours together in the library.

June 10

This has to be the best summer ever!

Lillian took a long pull on her glass of wine. She felt like crying—this beautiful young woman, her life cut short at twenty-two, just a few months after enjoying what she wrote was her best summer ever. Once, they were contemporaries, and Lillian might have written a diary just like this, herself. Now, she was seventy-seven, and she had lived a life and had experiences that Susan had never had.

The next few dozen pages were filled with short notes about all the good times that Susan and Mikhail took in together that summer. Walks on the lakeshore, dinners on Yonge Street, evenings in Yorkville.

It was a summer when the whole world seemed to be exploding with events and new ideas: civil rights, elite athletes at the Olympics, Royals on numerous tours, a World's Fair, the Beatles. Susan was just one young woman, living a life like many others, but she was breathing the air and hearing the music of a time of great change, and Lillian felt that coming through in the lines of her diary.

The notes about dates with Mikhail were mixed in with entries that Susan had made about her research and working for Dr. Berman at the U of T. Lillian flipped through them until she came to a day that had inspired Susan to write three-quarters of a page.

August 20

Mikhail has asked me for a favor. A big favor. I don't know what to do—I wish I could ask somebody but he made me promise to keep it to myself.

And I can see why!

His sister is staying with him, and nobody can know about it. She DEFECTED a week ago. I didn't even know what that was until he explained it to me. Anna is the first violinist of a very important orchestra in Russia, in the Soviet Union. She's on tour and she doesn't want to return. Ever. Life is very hard there for many people. Not for artists like her, but she thinks that is very unfair. And it's a very secretive society, Mikhail says. Everyone is monitored very carefully.

I wanted to know what he thought about life there, about his home and his city, and he said he barely notices when he is there. Of course, he is here now, studying, but when he goes back to visit, he says, it is the same as when he is in Toronto—he doesn't notice much of anything because his life and his world are completely orbiting around physics.

But then, he told me, the one other thing he notices, is me . . .

So, she ran away from the orchestra when they were in Montreal and rode the train to see him in Toronto. It's very dangerous for her right now because they want her back, so she's been hiding. Hiding at Mikhail's place, and with some of his friends. Changing places every night. Hiding in the library.

His friends are getting scared now. I told him I would have Anna at my place for a few nights. He doesn't want her in a hotel because he doesn't think it's safe enough. There is a plan for her to go to Ottawa but not for a couple of days.

August 27

Anna has been here a week.

August 30

Ten days.

September 1

Mikhail came to get Anna today. I'll miss her. She is very like Mikhail and yet somehow, very different. Tougher than he is, I think, although I'll never tell him that.

September 2

Dr. Berman really likes my work this summer. She is giving me half the credit on this research project. Says she wants to get me started in the field and help me get to a point where I can get a really good placement for my doctorate. If I get the time to do it.

Lillian put down the journal and looked out over the Gulf. Did Susan expect some other demand on her time?

September 3

The New York Times interviewed Dr. Berman about advances in computer science and her work on this hush-hush project for the government. She mentioned my name in the article!!

September 4

Glenda is talking about going to live on Howard Ronson's property up north. It's some kind of commune! She is nuts. But a good person, under it all. We couldn't have taken care of Rhonda the way we did without her.

I hope she's made Dr. Arnold aware of how much we appreciated what he did. It's very dangerous.

September 6

I've been invited to be interviewed on CUBR radio about Dr. Berman's research project! Because my name was in the Times, I think. I have to start thinking of it as my project, too. They want me there super-early tomorrow. Not sure what studio to go to. I'll ask a technician when I get there. I think Lill will be there, she's been on the early shift all the time lately. She hardly has any free time for us anymore.

I'd call her to tell her but she makes a big deal about how she has to get to bed early and it's already ten.

I miss her and I miss our days in the band.

I think Lill likes the radio station better than she ever liked the band. She certainly spends a lot of time there.

And that was Susan's last entry. Lillian put down the journal and dropped her hand down to Carl's head, stroking him and breathing deeply. So sad. So tragic. She wasn't sure whether she was appreciative that Norman had made this effort to get it to her.

At the moment, she felt very mixed-up about the way she felt, and one part of her wished she had never seen the words and had never been reminded of Susan, Rhonda, Joyce, Penny, and Glenda in such detail and so vividly. The back of her throat ached.

But an instant after she had that reaction, she put it aside. She *was* grateful. That diary had yanked her back fifty-five years, and because of it, she had a new idea about the person responsible for Susan's death.

Chapter 22

At the park the next morning, Carl raced around the lawn chasing a ball while Lillian sat on a bench, listening to the bluebirds and the warblers. After they'd both had a good dose of fresh air, she returned to her condo kitchen and sat down at the computer on the table to try to reconnect.

She spent five seconds on the search engine and she had Rhonda Sheridan on the screen. To be more exact, she had six pages of Rhonda Sheridans: a professor in Minnesota, a graphic designer in New York, the owner of a dive shop in Hawaii—the list went on and on. She couldn't figure it out by the occupations, either. It had been more than five decades; who knew what education she'd picked up and what career she'd chased?

Maybe she would have more luck with Penny Lennart. Again, Lillian watched dozens of names load on her screen. Glenda Levy? Same thing. Joyce Lansing? And once more. Come to think of it, she didn't know whether any of them had kept their original names anyway. If one of them went looking online for a Lillian Clarkson, how would they ever follow the path to Lillian Howe in Florida in 2019?

Lillian closed the computer and decided to go down to the dining room for one of the mid-morning cookies they put out with the coffee and tea. As she stood over the tray looking for one of her favorites, chocolate macadamia nut, Sam and Dwayne walked in, carrying their golf bags.

"Wow, you stop in here for cookies even before you stow the golf clubs?" Lillian teased.

"They are very good cookies," Sam teased back.

"Hey, there is something you might help me with," she said, knowing that Sam would love the challenge. Throughout the four years she'd known him, he never turned down an opportunity to help somebody. "And you, Dwayne. You're on your computer a lot. It's a computer problem I have."

"Sure," Sam said. "Is it something you need to show us on your laptop?"

"No, it's just a question. How would I go about finding somebody online? I've done a general search but there are just too many leads. It's like trying to find the right Mr. Smith in the phone book."

"In the wha-a-a-t?" Sam grinned at her.

"Alright, you're right, I'm dating myself."

"Same concept, though," Dwayne said. "To find the right Mr. Smith, you need more. You need a first name, a middle initial, an address or at least a neighborhood."

"That's a big part of the problem. I don't know anything more about this person except their name. And so much time has passed, I'm not even sure I have that right."

"Try one of the community sites or the groups," Dwayne said. "Look for connections, circles of interest. Who do you know who might have known them then or who might know somebody who knows them now?"

"We grew up together in upstate New York."

"Try that then," he said, approvingly. "Look at your town, places that have websites where names are listed, look for last names you might know who might have connections to this person you're searching for."

"We all worked in Canada for a while, too," Lillian said. "Toronto."

"Toronto. I thought you were from Vancouver, originally," Dwayne said.

"Both," Lillian said. "But thanks for the tips. I'll just take a few of these cookies back to my place and give it another try."

Lillian spent most of the day following trails across websites and down rabbit holes without finding any firm clues about anybody. She started looking at images to go with the names but didn't spot anyone who looked like she could be the oldish version of the twenty-something she had known. Of course, she knew she could try using one of the many name-searching websites, but she didn't want to spend the money.

She was about to give up when a thought struck her. She'd known their employers, back in the day . . . maybe that might help?

Dr. Rand, Glenda's boss, didn't show up in the Toronto listings. She didn't remember where Rhonda had worked in New York. The government of Canada, where Joyce got her first job after university, had a website directory with about a thousand sub-directories, cascading down the screen like the steps of a Mayan temple. She looked at the CBC Radio pages and didn't recognize any of the names; even if they'd worked there at the same time as Penny, they'd be long since retired, wouldn't they?

A light bulb went on. Would there be some sort of retired employees association? Lillian searched the term for both CBC Radio and for the government and found websites for them. She sent emails off to their info@ addresses . . . would any human being see them and reply to her?

Another light bulb—maybe friends of friends on the social media sites? She posted to the three where she had accounts and almost instantly, there were responses. Nobody actually knew Penny, Rhonda, Joyce or Glenda but they all had an abundance of ideas about where Lillian might go looking.

Lots of great ideas, but it exhausted her just to look at the posts. She would put all this aside for a while, maybe until tomorrow.

She was about to log off when the most recent comment caught her attention. *I remember Joyce Lansing from grade school and we've stayed in touch. She's Joyce Morgan now, and she lives in Florida*

Joyce Morgan? Joyce *Morgan*, like the Joyce Morgan who lives here, on the fifth floor?!

***

Lillian was walking as quickly as her legs would carry her—actually, she had to work to prevent herself from breaking into a run. When she got to Joyce's door, she forced herself to stop and take ten deep breaths. It was not an unusual name. There might be hundreds in the country.

She knocked.

When Joyce opened the door, Lillian gazed at her as if trying to memorize her face. She tried, but for the life of her, she couldn't see any resemblance between this woman, with her silver hair cut short and her generous curves, and the stick-thin girl with the long, straight, blonde hair she'd known in her twenties.

"Joyce? Joyce Lansing?"

"Hi, Lillian, what a nice surprise," Joyce said. It seemed to take her a moment to realize what Lillian had said. Then, she stepped back in the doorway as the last name registered. A huge smile came over her face. "I knew it! I knew there was something familiar about you, ever since you first moved in! You're Lill!"

"Well, I am." Lillian couldn't stop staring at Joyce. "But I didn't pick up on anything about you. Where are your glasses? You had your glasses ever since you were eight!"

"Cataract surgery," Joyce said. "Don't need the specs any more. But you're not Lill Clarkson, you're Lillian Howe."

"Married name. You have one, too, right?"

Joyce shook her head. "Such a strange custom, I wonder if it will ever go away? But yes, I married a Mr. Morgan."

"In Ottawa? What year?"

"1978. We moved to New York in the 90s." Joyce reached for Lillian's hands and drew her into the apartment. "Come in! Sit down! We have *so* much to catch up on."

Lillian smiled. "Yeah, of all the gin joints in all the world. Thank you."

Tucked into arm chairs in Joyce's living room with numerous cups of tea coming from a big pot and a radio playing classical music softly in the background, they traced each of their travels over the fifty-five years. They started in 2015, when Lillian moved into the Aragonese condo building, and worked backward. It was as if they were avoiding talking about those years in Toronto and Ottawa. But they knew they'd have to get there, eventually.

"I think I remember that you left Toronto shortly after Susan Taylor died," Joyce eventually said.

Lillian nodded. "I couldn't stand to stay there, honestly. I was just so upset that the police weren't charging anybody. Hadn't solved the crime. One of them even said to me that many of the officers thought it should have been ruled a suicide, rather than put in the cold case drawer." Lillian could feel tears starting up, as if it had all happened yesterday. Joyce was looking at her with eyes silently speaking sympathy.

"We were all shocked, I think," Joyce said. "And upset."

Lillian looked at her for a long moment. She realized that if there were ever going to be fresh air blowing into the dark, stuffy room that was her memory of Toronto in the mid 60s, it would have to start in this conversation. "If you were, none of you ever let on to me," she said. "I felt like I was all alone, in the middle of a lake or an ocean or something."

"What do you mean?"

And it came spilling out. "Susan was one of my best friends. You all were. But it all fell apart when she was killed. Even before that—I was absolutely shocked when I found out that I hadn't been told about something as important as Rhonda's trouble, that you didn't care enough about me to include me, to let me help, too."

"We cared about you, Lill. We just didn't trust you. And the consequences of letting that secret leak out were just too . . ." Joyce shook her head. She couldn't even think of the word.

"But why didn't you trust me?"

"When you took that job in the newsroom, you changed. You got so busy, for one thing. You were working all the time. When we talked about things, you were so hard-nosed, so cynical. You didn't believe in affection or romance anymore."

"You didn't want me around because I didn't want a boy-friend?" Lillian was shocked.

"It wasn't just that. And it wasn't that we didn't want you around. We invited you all the time. You just didn't come along very often, because you were working," Joyce said.

"But that spring and summer before Susan died, I came along with you to lots of things," Lillian said. "At least, that's what I re-member."

"It's all in your point of view, I guess," Joyce said. "You saw it as lots, we didn't. And I think I remember that there was an incident. Something happened. One of us told you something, and you were supposed to be discreet and keep it quiet. Something about . . ." Joyce paused for a very long time, then shook her head. "I just can't remember the details. My memory is like that, these days."

Lillian smiled at her. "I get it. Happens to all of us. But it's funny, isn't it, that now we can't remember anything about something that was a big enough deal, back then, to make you all decide to turn your backs on me."

"My mother used to say to me, 'None of this will matter, down the road' and I never thought she was right. Turns out, she was." Joyce leaned forward to pour herself another cup of tea.

"But it mattered a lot at the time," Lillian said. "Why didn't we talk about any of these things then?"

"Yeah, it would have saved everybody a lot of pain," Joyce agreed. "What I can't figure out, though, is why all of this is coming up now? We've lived in the same building for years. Why did you go searching my name online now?"

"I had a delivery," Lillian said. "Susan's diary from 1964."

Joyce almost spit out a mouthful of tea. "Who on earth sent you that?"

"Susan's brother, Norman, asked his granddaughter to send it to me after he died. He'd been given it by Mikhail Kogonov—do you remember him? Susan's boyfriend from the university?"

"After she broke up with Corey, yeah."

"I'm not sure why Mikhail had it but apparently, he had it for years. Must have carried a torch for her. Maybe he finally got over her and wanted to return it?" Lillian stood up and started to pace. She just couldn't help it; she'd been sitting still long enough. "It's full of references to me, to all of us, and it's pretty clear that I wasn't in the in crowd anymore."

Joyce's cup rattled as she put it down on the saucer, her hand shaking. "I'd like to read that, when you're through with it."

Lillian nodded. "It was quite spooky, in a way. It just sounded as if she were speaking, in the same room with me, and we were twenty again."

"Was she mostly happy that summer? And earlier, in the winter and spring?"

"She was. She really liked Mikhail a lot and her studies at the U of T were going really well."

"Nothing ever makes up for the horrible thing that happened to her," Joyce said. "But I always wanted to feel that she had a good last month and a good last year. She was just so young!"

"I feel guilty, sometimes, that I had so much more time than she had. Even though not every one of my years was all that great, at least I had so many of them."

"I know what you mean," Joyce said. "I've felt guilty about that, and about the fact that she asked me to go with her for a weekend back to Albany that summer and I turned her down."

"Regrets," Lillian said. "You can drown in them."

"One advantage of the memory lapses. Let it go."

Lillian grinned at her. "There, you see? I'd forgotten that you were funny."

"So, what are you going to do with this diary?"

"I'd still like to find out what happened that morning. One thing she mentions in there, that I never knew about, was that she was worried about getting the money for her tuition for her grad year."

They didn't speak for a few minutes, listening to the radio playing. Then, as the clock ticked over to noon, the news broadcast began.

Today in Florida news, a Miami man has been charged with public mischief, culpable negligence, animal cruelty, and reckless boating. Corey Lang, seventy-nine years old, is alleged to have driven a boat at high speed near a marina, colliding with two other boats and a manatee. Lang will make his first appearance in court on Tuesday.

Lillian stared at Joyce, as the words sank in. "Corey Lang!"

"An awful lot of northern people find their way down here, I guess," Joyce said.

"No kidding. I was at that marina with my grandson when that happened, Joyce!"

"Did you recognize him?"

Lillian shook her head. "He just looked like some grumpy old man."

"Arrogant young man, grumpy old man. I wonder whether he'd recognize either of us?"

"One way to find out," Lillian said.

"You think we should go see him?"

"Susan died from a drug overdose. Corey was using drugs. Shooting up, she wrote in her diary. And he was harassing her. The police said he had an airtight alibi but what if those people were lying, to help him? Maybe his family or one of his friends owed him a big favor, and he called it in when the police started breathing down his neck!" Lillian took a few deep breaths.

"I don't know, Lill, I don't think people agree to lie to the police in a murder investigation all that easily," Joyce said.

"I tried to confront him then, but I should have done more, I should have pushed the police detective more."

"Lillian, you were only a kid. Give yourself a break."

"Maybe so, but I'm not a kid now. I think this time I'll be able to follow through."

Chapter 23

"All rise." The voice reached the far corners of the courtroom. The rows were full when Corey's appearance finally began. Lillian and Joyce had arrived a full hour early, in order to get a seat close enough to the front to see him when he was brought in.

When Sam Gavigan from the condo heard about their plan to go to Miami to see if this man was the same one they'd known back in the day, he insisted on driving them the two hours east. Lillian was happy to have his company, as well as his suggestions about what to say and do, if she had the chance to confront Corey the way she wanted to.

Corey Lang had been a hunk when he was in his twenties but no glimpse of those good looks remained. His white hair was stringy and too long, his skin pitted and marked by too many hours in the wind and the sun. He shuffled into the room, even though there were no shackles on him.

Most of the people in the crowded courtroom were there because of their outrage about the attack on the manatee. Many carried cardboard signs that they'd brought to a demonstration organized just before Corey's appearance began, and they'd been warned to keep them out of sight once they took their seats. Lillian saw Corey's look of surprise when he saw all the people, a look immediately replaced by one of apprehension.

The proceedings were swift. Corey got a fine and a stern warning from the judge. He didn't say a word. After the appearance was over, a recess was declared and the spectators headed for the exit. Corey stood at the front of the room as if unsure about what to do next.

"I want to talk to him," Lillian said to Joyce. "Could you and Sam please wait outside? I want to talk to him alone."

"Alright. But you yell for us if anything goes wrong."

"It won't," Lillian said. "Look at him. He's no threat to anybody now."

"Don't ever let anybody fool you," Sam said. "Keep your guard up. And don't forget what I said about the phone. Keep it close."

As soon as the courtroom was cleared, Lillian approached Corey. He still stood by one of the front tables, holding a manila folder. Everyone else was gone but the fifteen-minute break declared by the judge was shrinking by the second. If she wanted to have her say with him, she had to get on with it.

"Corey? Corey Lang? I'm Lillian Howe . . . Lill Clarkson, I mean. I knew you in Toronto. In the 60s."

He didn't seem to register anything she'd said. She took a step toward him, reaching her hands behind her to try to look as unthreatening as possible.

"I want to talk to you about Susan Taylor. Do you remember? She was your girlfriend for a while. In 1964."

He'd better remember.

"I didn't get to speak." Corey turned and made full eye contact with her. His eyes were bloodshot and his voice had the rasp of a long-time smoker. "I had some research to present on the dangers of the overpopulation of manatee in these waters and I didn't get to speak."

"You're lucky the judge dealt with you as quickly as she did," Lillian said. "You could have had as much as a year or more in jail. All you got was a fine."

"I won't be able to pay that." Corey didn't seem to be upset about that. Just stating a fact. "I wasn't even going to bother to come here today, but I thought I'd get to speak and present my research. For the TV news, you know."

"I don't think you have to be in court if you want to be on TV," Lillian said. "You could get them to come to a news conference."

"Can you get them to come and listen to me?"

Lillian shook her head. This was getting weirder by the minute. "Not my job, Corey. I don't think that's anybody's job. That's not why I'm here, anyway. I came all this way to talk to you, after all these years, because I want to talk to you about our friend. Susan. Susan, who was killed."

Corey suddenly seemed to find a light through the fog that surrounded him. He stared at her. "What do you want to know, Lill?"

Behind her, her fingers found the recording key on her phone, marked by a tiny piece of tape. She was about to get Corey Lang's confession.

***

When Lillian walked out of the courtroom five minutes later, Sam and Joyce were standing so close to the door it almost hit them as it swung open.

"Well? Are you okay? Is he still in there?" Joyce's curiosity could have filled an arena.

"I'm fine. Yes, he's still there. He says he wants to wait for the judge to come back so that he can ask her to listen to his research about the manatees." Lillian felt a sudden whoosh of a loss of energy and she needed to make her way over to a bench in the hallway to sit down.

Joyce and Sam sat down on either side of her. "What happened?" Joyce asked.

"Well, it took me quite a while to get his focus off his manatee research and get him to recognize Susan's name. But as soon as he did, he got this mean, crafty look on his face and told me to go ahead and ask my questions." She turned to Sam. "I had turned on the phone, like you said, and I think I recorded the whole conversation."

"Let's see," Sam said, holding out his hand for the phone. He laid it on the bench and turned it on.

I want to know if you were anywhere near the radio station the morning Susan was killed.

How do you know she was killed? Maybe she offed herself.

She would never have done that.

Well, I wasn't there. Okay, I was near there. With some friends, just walking by. But I didn't have anything to do with it.

I don't believe you.

Who gives a damn? There's no evidence. Of anything. And besides, it happened so long ago, who would care? The police don't care. It's cold, man, completely cold.

Shut up! Shut up!

The sound of scuffling and static blocked out any more words.

"Did you hit him?" Joyce asked.

"Not actually hit. Just kind of shoved him. Pulled on his shirt sleeve, maybe. I just couldn't stand the sight of his stupid face, telling me nobody cares about Susan anymore. I don't know. I guess I got carried away."

"It's alright," Sam said. "Nobody could blame you. Maybe you were a bit disappointed with how it turned out?"

"I really thought he would tell me the truth, after all these years."

"Maybe he did," Joyce said.

Lillian shivered in the frosty, air-conditioned air. "Then we're no closer than we ever were, are we? Even with Susan's journal, and with the bizarre coincidence of seeing Corey Lang here, we still don't know who killed her."

***

That night, Lillian took her phone out onto the patio for her regular Tuesday evening chat with Chelan Montgomery and Nevada Leacock. They'd been her friends for more than ten years now, since their paths had crossed in Vancouver when Chelan was trying to find out what happened to one of her TV newsroom colleagues.

Over the past year, the calls had become shorter because Chelan was doing the busy-mom life and Nevada was slaying dragons in New York City. But they always took the time to wave in Lillian's direction once a week and she was very appreciative.

"Hi, Chelan, how are you?" Lillian said as she heard the connection made.

"Well, I'm fine, Lillian, you? And how about you, Nevada?"

"Good! We're all here, I guess," Nevada said. "What's new?"

"I have something," Lillian said. She knew a youngster needing a popsicle or Nevada's other line demanding her attention could cut the call short at any minute, so she wanted to get right to the point.

"What is it? No, sshhh, honey, Mommy's on the phone."

"You remember that long ago I lost a friend in Toronto under strange circumstances."

"Yes, I remember you telling us about it years ago," Nevada said. "Young woman died of an overdose at the radio station, and the police never made an arrest."

"And you were beating up on yourself because even though you were in the building, you weren't there early enough to prevent it," Chelan said. "I always thought . . . I told you then and I'll tell you again now . . . that it wasn't your fault."

"Thank you, Chelan. I guess I made a sort of peace with it eventually, but it rocked me for a long time." Carl was curled up beside Lillian's chair and she reached down to pat him. "So, this week two of the people from that time turned up here in Florida. Well, sort of turned up. Corey Lang, he was my friend's ex-boyfriend. She'd dumped him and found someone new. He lives in Florida now. And the new boyfriend, Mikhail, it turned out he'd taken Susan's diary . . . that was her name, Susan. . . . from her apartment and kept it, all these years. Sent it to her brother. He recently passed, but before he did, he arranged to send the diary to me."

"Wow," Chelan said. "And you've read it? What does it say? Does it say anything that might explain what happened to her?"

"It kind of reinforced some of the suspicions I had, even back then, about some of the men in her life, about her worrying about getting tuition money. But it's all circumstantial, you know? Lots of connections and possible motives, but nothing there that would be called actual evidence, I don't think."

"How many times did you read it?" Nevada asked.

"Once."

"Read it again. And again. Sometimes, you have to get past the expected, walk around in what you know you know a few times, before the new information will jump out at you."

"I'll do that," Lillian said. "I have a question, too. Would the police look into it, after all these years, if I brought them this new thing, this diary? Would they consider that evidence?"

"Probably not unless there was some direct accusation in there, or maybe details about a previous attack somebody made on her," Chelan speculated.

"My experience with cold cases was they declared them unsolved after three years," Nevada said. "But if new information or a tip is received or there's some new technological tool, some new forensics method, they'll assign an investigator."

"Well, this could be a new tip," Lillian said. But it was false optimism, she knew. She flinched at the idea of trying to make a contact at the Toronto Police Department now, fifty-five years later, as an oldish woman, to talk about a case that they'd already shelved back when it was fresh.

"I'd say a better approach would be finding something she wrote in there that gives you a lead and trying to follow that up," Chelan said. "What about the part you said where she was worrying about money? Is there any way to follow that up now? Find out how much money she had, how much she needed? Whether she was due to come into any sort of windfall? Did anybody benefit financially from her death?"

Lillian leaned back in her chair and closed her eyes. "It was all so long ago. I don't know how we'd ever answer those questions now."

"We?" Chelan said. "There's a 'we' in on this?"

"Yes, a couple of my friends from the condo building are interested," Lillian said. "Corey Lang was arrested earlier in the week for endangering animals and causing a big commotion at a marina in Miami. He had his first court appearance this morning and Sam, Dwayne, and Joyce came with me to watch."

"Did they hold him in custody?" Nevada asked.

"No, they released him."

"You know where he is?"

"We can find him, easily enough," Lillian said. "I spoke with him. He's as much of a jerk in his seventies as he was in his twenties. Joyce couldn't believe he'd survived all these years."

"Joyce?" Nevada was on it, like a hound on a scent. "One of your neighbor friends knew him back then?"

"Joyce was one of my friends in Toronto in the 60s," Lillian said. "And one of my friends growing up. We lost touch decades ago but then turned up in the same Florida town."

A long silence told her that Nevada and Chelan might be finding this a bit implausible. "What? It's not so weird," she said. "I knew a woman who had lost touch with one of her bridesmaids from thirty years previously and crossed paths with her as members at the same club years later. Neither one of them recognized the other."

"Okay," Nevada said. "So, you're in touch with this Joyce, as a neighbor now. What about the others? Do you hear from any of them now?"

"No, those friendships dried up," Lillian said. "But with the internet and email, I don't think it would be that hard to find them."

"I think you should look," Chelan said. "If you read the diary to them, or maybe scan some pages and send them, it might trigger something for one of them that you're not seeing."

"Alright, good idea," Lillian said. "Joyce will help me look."

"I can help you, too, Lillian," Chelan said. "We have, what, four girlfriends. And maybe we can also trace some of the others in her life. Her advisor at the university? Her other boyfriends? Her girlfriends' boyfriends?"

Something Chelan said prompted a memory for Lillian. Other boyfriends? That would be Mikhail Kogonov.

Whatever happened to him?

***

They would get started the next morning. Actually, Lillian started the minute she ended the conference call with Chelan and Nevada, but she hit a wall within the first half hour, if a web could be said to have walls.

She tried searching Glenda, Penny, and Rhonda, and ran into the same issue as before: different names. How was she to know whether Glenda Baker of Vermont was once Glenda Levy of New York, then Ontario? She tried peering at the images helpfully supplied by the computer for each name but recognized no one. Fifty-five years! What could she expect?

Eventually, she gave up in exhaustion and just followed the blue underlines in whatever direction they happened to go. She found herself reading about sports cars in Arizona, weather conditions in the Kalahari Desert, and a theme park in Texas before she looked at the clock and realized it was past midnight. Maybe Chelan could show her something tomorrow that would unlock the tomb of the internet for her and make it cough up the secrets she wanted to know.

Chapter 24

Lillian's phone was ringing at 8 the next morning.

"Chelan? What on earth are you doing, calling me so early?" Lillian asked. "Isn't it 5 in California?"

"It's the best time of day for me to get anything done. The kids are all still sleeping."

"I get it. Alright, let's not waste any time. We need to search Glenda Levy, Rhonda Sheridan, Penny Lennart. Let's do me, too, while we're at it. Although I guess I can look up myself any time."

"Have you ever done that?" Chelan asked.

"Well, no, I've never bothered. But I would bet that hundreds of 'Lillian Howe's' will come up."

"I have a few ideas on how to drill down on that," Chelan said. "Same with the other names of your friends. What are some of the others? Let me make a list to work away on later, in case we get interrupted by somebody wanting a juice box or something."

"Dr. Kevin Arnold. Corey Lang. Howard Ronson. Oh, and let's track down Raymond Chernowski, too. He was the technician in Master Control that morning."

"And what about the Russian boyfriend? And his sister?"

"Mikhail Kogonov? He went back to the Soviet Union in the 60s. How would we ever find him?"

"Let me try," Chelan said. "You don't suppose Susan's brother, the one who sent you the diary, would have any sort of return address, do you?"

"He's passed."

"Oh, right. Well, what about his granddaughter then?"

"Worth asking," Lillian said, thoughtfully. "Do you think Mikhail might have had something to do with it?"

"Worth speculating about. Worth suspecting anybody and everybody, I'd say. What's the worst that can happen? We hit a bunch of dead ends and you never get any closer than you are to solving the mystery. You're no worse off, right?"

Right. Except for the pain of dragging up terrible memories. Lillian had been living with her guilt for not being able to prevent Susan's death by being on the spot in that control room that morning, and most of the time, she had been able to suppress those thoughts. It got easier as the decades went by. But all of this had brought it all back, falling in around her like a ten-foot bank of fresh snow.

***

When Joyce arrived for coffee an hour later, she echoed Chelan's opinion about the possible outcome of the search.

"We've never known what happened to her and if this internet searching or bumping into Corey Lang after all this time doesn't answer the questions, we'll still never know. We'll be no worse off," Joyce said. "But there is a possibility of some ... what's the word? Closure, that's it. If we find out."

"Whatever we find out about what or who actually killed her," Lillian said, "I still won't get past knowing what I know, and have known all these years. If I'd been there, if I got to work half an hour earlier, if I'd been in the control room, she wouldn't have been killed."

Joyce looked at her in shock. "You don't know that! My God, Lillian, have you been carrying that around all these years? You don't know that you could have prevented anything. None of us does!

You're being much too hard on yourself—and giving yourself too much importance, at the same time. Who knows, but that she might have been killed a day later, in a different place, by the same person, if someone was stalking her? Or you might have saved her, yes, and then she might have been hit by a bus, six months later? For God's sake, Lillian, you have so much compassion for everyone else. Have a little for yourself!"

Lillian breathed deeply and tried to take in all the implications. Carl roused himself and walked across the kitchen to lie down at her feet. He always seemed to know when the mood in the room was emotional.

"Alright, Joyce, I hear you. I'll think about all that, I will. In the meantime, I want to try this search engine Chelan told me about and see if we can't get anywhere closer to finding Penny."

"It would be nice to be back in touch with her," Joyce agreed. "I miss her. I miss everybody."

"I do, too," Lillian said. "But do we, really? Or do we just miss being twenty-two?"

Joyce nodded. "Might be a little of that, too. Okay, what do we do?"

They were both hunched over their laptops an hour later when the phone rang. Lillian put it on speakerphone.

"Okay, quick, I've got the kids agreeing on a show and hypnotized for the next who-knows-how-long," Chelan said. "I've got your Dr. Arnold, your Howard Ronson, and your Anna Kogonov."

"What?" Lillian and Joyce spoke simultaneously.

"Anna Kogonov lives in Montreal. Her name is Anna Kogan now. She had a career as a violinist in Canada, she married and had a big family. I found mentions of her performances over the years and a school where she taught. And I have a few phone numbers to try."

"Unbelievable," Lillian said.

"Howard Ronson will be a bit more difficult to call. He died in 1992."

"In Toronto?"

"On the west coast. In prison."

"In prison!"

"Heart attack. He was in for kidnapping. Apparently, his methods of bringing people into his commune got less refined as he got older."

"Ugh," Lillian said. "I'd be interested in what Glenda has to say about him now. I wonder if she knows all this?"

Joyce shrugged. "Lots of us made mistakes in judgement in our twenties, Lill. There's no point in saying I told you so."

"You're right, of course." Lillian laughed. "It's that I was *so* right when I was in my twenties. I thought everybody should listen to me *all* the time."

"So, if this Howard Ronson had more to do with Susan's death than you knew at the time, it would be impossible to ask him about it now," Chelan said. "But there's more. Dr. Kevin Arnold. I found him through his college alumni association. You'll never guess where he is."

"Excuse me for saying, Chelan, but you're thirty-five, not twelve years old. No guessing games." Lillian smiled at Joyce as she said it, and she knew Chelan could hear it in her voice.

"Dr. Arnold retired to Florida."

"To Florida!"

"To Florida. He lives in Sarasota."

***

Lillian's means were limited, and there were many locations Chelan might have discovered that would have meant phone calls or emails only for her. But Sarasota, Florida was do-able, as a short trip—just a couple of hours, by car.

She was past marveling at the number of people she knew, or knew of, who surfaced in Florida. It seemed to be a magnet, particularly for those who were over the milestone of three-score-and-ten.

The retired physician's home leaned back from the street like a rich man with a thirty-dollar glass of brandy, pushing back from the table after a five-star meal. A glowing green lawn lined up on each side of the sidewalk, with not a weed or a blade of grass out of place. Two luxury cars in front of the garage completed the picture.

Lillian didn't hesitate as she walked up to his front door and pounded. That was the only moment when she doubted her decision to do this all alone. She could have asked Joyce to go along, even Sam and Dwayne, and no doubt they all would have thought she should have. But she trusted her own belief that she would know the right thing to do when the moment came and she didn't want the opinions of any other people, no matter how well-intentioned, to influence her.

She waited for about five minutes and then thought to reach inside her shoulder bag, pull out her phone, and turn on the recording app. A moment later, the door opened. An elderly man with a walker looked at them through eyes rimmed with the darkness that often signals extreme ill health.

"Yes? What is it?" His voice was weak.

"Dr. Arnold? Dr. Kevin Arnold?"

"Yes. Are you the new public health nurse? I've been waiting half the day for someone to get here to give me my meds."

As much as she wanted answers from this old man, there was no way Lillian was going to lie just to get in to see him.

"No, Dr. Arnold, I'm not the nurse you're waiting for," she said. "My name is Lillian Howe. I knew you long ago. When I was Lillian Clarkson."

The more time that passed, the more sure she was that she wanted to just stay here on the front step. The inside might be opulent and luxurious, like the neighborhood, and it might be three-quarters empty and threadbare like his old brown pants and tattered sweater-vest. Either way, she didn't want to know.

Dr. Arnold's eyes widened when he heard her name. For just a few seconds, Lillian thought she saw fear there; then, it was gone. Nothing was left but a man who gave off a wave of fatigue.

He pushed his walker toward her, out into the sunshine on the step. "Here, help me with this," he said, then motioned that he wanted it turned around so that he could use the built-in seat. He perched on it, crossed his arms, and started to talk.

"Well, hello, Lillian. I thought somebody would turn up here, eventually. Oh, not here, in particular. I've been expecting a visit like this, from somebody, ever since 1964. At first, I thought it might be the police. Then, Susan Taylor's family. Or one of her friends. I thought it might be in Toronto, or Boston, or Philadelphia. Then here."

"So, you moved around a lot over the years?" Lillian asked. "Did you have a family, too? Children? Grandchildren?"

"Yeah, all of that. All of them live up north and don't want to come down here to visit much. But that's all right with me. I don't know them anymore."

"What about a Mrs. Arnold?"

"Yes, Shirley. She passed in 1999."

"And you've been on your own all that time? No remarriage?"

He shrugged. "Old women are even more annoying than young ones."

There was nothing Lillian wanted to say to that. After a few moments of her silence, he picked up his story.

"Susan Taylor was an ordinary girl. That's why you're here, isn't it? To talk about how she died?" He squinted into Lillian's face. "I don't recognize you, but it's been a long time, hasn't it? I recognize your name, though. I remember all of your names and I wrote them all down, just like I wrote down my recollections of that day, in case the time came when I couldn't anymore. I've seen enough old people to know that happens."

Dr. Arnold cleared his throat. "Susan called and asked to meet me that morning to discuss something that concerned both of us. I had an appointment at the radio station for an interview, but she insisted on meeting me beforehand."

"What was it that concerned both of you? Was it Rhonda Sheridan's abortion? Was Susan ..." Lillian almost choked on the words, then reminded herself to think like a professional. "Was Susan Taylor blackmailing you?"

Dr. Arnold sniffled, then he reached into his pants pocket to pull out a handkerchief and blow his nose. "So that's what you think, is it? Shows you didn't know your friend very well. No, she wasn't blackmailing me. She wasn't the type to try to get a financial advantage like that. Even though she disapproved of what I was doing, and she let me know it. Oh, not that she disapproved of the procedure. No, she was pro-choice all the way. But she wanted me to do it openly, start a clinic, take the heat, like that Dr. Morgentaler did five years later in Montreal. Oh, yeah, ahead of her time, that Susan Taylor."

He seemed to drift off into his memories and Lillian wanted to keep him on track. "So, if she wasn't there to confront you or ask you for money she needed, what was she there for?"

Dr. Arnold stared at Lillian as if he didn't quite remember who she was or how he had found himself on his front step. "It was a holiday Monday, I remember. Everybody was babbling on about those Beatles that summer. I agreed to meet her at the station before my taping time. She had to be there that morning, too. Something about some interview about the work she was doing on computers, at the university. Oh, yes, I remember, she was developing into somebody who might be a big noise someday. It was a shame, really. Such a shame."

"What was a shame?"

"That she died so young."

"That she was killed, you mean."

Dr. Arnold fixed Lillian with a tired gaze. "It was coming anyway, you know."

"What are you talking about? Is that how you justify what you did to her?"

"What I did to her? What do you mean?" She saw his eyes show a flicker of comprehension.

Then he blew up. "She wasn't my *victim,* you stupid woman. She was my patient."

A patient? Susan was his patient? For what?

Chapter 25

Lillian shook her head to get rid of the mild dizzy spell that took hold. Then, crossing her arms and setting her chin, she decided it was time to take charge of this conversation more assertively. Either she was on the brink of finally getting a solution to the mystery or she was being misled, deliberately or by accident, because of dementia. Whichever, she knew she needed to push him a bit to get the curtain pulled all the way back.

"Your patient for what?"

He sat a little straighter on his walker seat and she thought she saw a glimpse of the medical doctor of fifty years ago, about to have an important conversation about a prognosis. "She had cancer."

Cancer! Lillian reached out for the porch railing and wished she were sitting down for this.

"The tests had all been finished mid-summer. She was still getting used to the idea and hadn't made any decisions about her treatment, but she seemed to be over the initial shock. Sometimes, I thought she was still in denial, though. I'd been pushing her to get on with it, and when she said she wanted to see me and didn't want to wait until office hours, I was glad to fit the conversation in, since we were both going to be at the station, anyway. We had chatted for a while and she seemed to be ready to make a treatment plan. I had to use the bathroom, and I left her in the green room. When I was coming back down the hall, I saw her walking down the hall twenty feet ahead of me with two men. She was relaxed, chatting with them, and I thought nothing more of it. I thought they must be employees she knew at the station, maybe somebody she'd met through you."

"What happened then?"

"I saw them go through a door and then a few minutes later, one of the men, the younger one, I think, came out. He didn't see me and neither did the older man, when he came out into the hall a minute later. They went into the stairwell, and back to work, I thought."

"Did you tell the police any of this at the time?"

"At the time, I had no wish to speak to the police or draw attention to myself in any way," he said. "It was a practical decision. Cancer at that time was a death sentence and so I thought that the outcome was going to be the same for Susan Taylor, one way or another. But for me, life was still a big question mark. I didn't want to do the abortions anymore . . . there really wasn't much money in it . . . so I figured out how I could emigrate to the States."

"And you've never talked about it since then."

"Not even with Shirley," he said. "She used to get on my case from time to time, about why I wasn't more fun, why I never seemed to be happy. But I never told her why. She wanted to go back to Canada, too, but I never took that seriously. I guess I put up some high barriers around my life and just stayed contented, living inside them. Quietly."

Lillian settled her bag over her shoulder and got ready to leave. "You weren't just a quiet man ," she said. "You were cowardly. And selfish."

***

When Lillian got home after her drive from Sarasota, a talk with Chelan was the only thing she wanted to have. She brought her up to date on the conversation with Dr. Arnold, then asked, "Okay, what have you turned up?"

"Well, I went on the dark web—"

"The what?"

"Never mind, it's complicated. It's enough to know that it's a place to get information. I found Mikhail Kogonov in Russia. Contact information."

"So, he *did* go to Russia right after that September."

"Well, it was still the Soviet Union then, but yes, that's where he went."

"How soon after?"

"I don't know."

"Did the police ever question him? Was he the man who was at the station that morning, the one Dr. Arnold saw? Who was the other man?"

"I don't know any of that, Lillian," Chelan said. "But shouldn't we also wonder whether this Dr. Arnold was even telling the truth? The kind of man who might sit on information like that for decades might also be the kind of man who would make stuff up. Constantly. He might be just a liar, through and through."

Lillian was so upset by all this information, roaring at her like a flooding river, that her usual radar wasn't working. Was Chelan speculating and imagining a terrible and very unlikely scenario? Or was it more likely that the doctor *had* lied about seeing two men at the station that morning?

"Lillian? Are you still there? Hey, sorry, but I have to go. It's chaos here," Chelan said.

"Yes, yes, of course. Thank you so much for finding this out. I'm not sure what I want to do next, but I'll keep you posted."

Dinner that evening was just a salad, and Lillian barely had the energy to throw that together. Ever since she'd talked to Dr. Arnold, it felt as if she were living in the past, fifty-five years back.

Every detail of the radio station, the events of September 1964, and even the weather that week were as vivid to her as the features and facts of her life today in Florida. Later, as she walked through the neighborhood with the dog, she went over and over her memories of that time, wishing that something would jump out at her. But nothing did.

As she sat on the edge of her bed, rubbing cream into her hands, she sensed Carl was watching her from his bed in the corner. "Well, what do you think, boy? Are you as tired as I am of not knowing the answers to the questions?" She wanted justice, and she wanted punishment for Susan's killer; she'd always wanted that. But even more, she wanted an end to the questions.

The blue diary on the edge of her dresser caught her eye. Nevada had suggested she read and reread it, staying open to any new thought about those events that might float up. Lillian reached for it, then settled back against the headboard to read it again.

Two hours later, she was still skimming and she'd found nothing. Her eyes aching from the strain, she put the book aside, then patted the place beside her, inviting Carl to jump on the bed. They each liked their own space a lot of the time, but there were other times when his warmth and his soft fur were as nice as a good cup of tea.

The chocolate Lab only needed one invitation. He lay down beside her, his ever-curious nose nuzzling her hand and then the book. His investigation went on for quite a few seconds as he pushed the book with his nose, then swiped it with his tongue.

"Carl, leave it!" Lillian grabbed for the diary. Too late; he'd already made it soggy.

She rubbed the wet upper corner with her thumb. It was so old, almost falling apart. It was a bad idea to let him anywhere near it. The binding material was wrinkled and worn, particularly near the spine. And here, up near the corner, it was practically peeling away...

There was something inside. Something between the case and the cloth covering! Lillian hurried to the kitchen to find a knife, the journal clutched in her hand and Carl close at her heels.

Working slowly and carefully, she slid the knife point in at the corner and slit the covering material along the top of the book. Something yellowish was there, but it would not come out quietly and easily. After trying to excavate it with her fingers, then with a ruler and then with the knife, she gave up and used the knife to cut another opening along the long side of the front cover.

Lillian peeled back the cloth and saw a very old, folded piece of paper. Once pale blue? Onionskin paper? She gently unfolded it. It was a letter, words filling the entire page, with the date *September 1995* in the top right corner.

The signature at the bottom gave her an actual wave of dizziness. Mikhail.

Lillian sat down at the kitchen table and began to read.

Dear Norman,

I hope this letter finds you well. I know it will surprise you to hear from me after all these many years. I do not know if you have ever thought of me again, but I have thought of you every day. And of your sister, Susan.

I am so, so very sorry.

It has tortured me, not to be able to tell you this or to change anything. It was done, and nothing will change it, but perhaps it will give you some release to have this information. I am hoping it also will help me, somehow, to tell you.

Susan died that morning, not because she just happened to be there, in the wrong place at the wrong time. There was no maniac lurking there, taking a young woman's life at random.

And it was not a jilted lover or a crazy man who couldn't find a way to speak to her, as you and I speculated when we talked, at her funeral.

It was Pavel. He had orders to find her and make her tell where my sister had gone after she was at Susan's apartment. I know you understand about sisters, Norman. I know you would have been as desperate as I. The KGB was determined to find her and I had to protect her. I was able to convince Pavel that I knew nothing about her whereabouts, that she had taken off from Susan's place and would not talk to me anymore.

I thought he was only going to see her to pressure her to make her talk. I did not go into the studio with him and when he came out, I did not know what had really happened. I thought he had just tried to pressure her and when he did not get an answer from her, decided to search her place. We went there soon after and took some things, I'm ashamed to say. Pavel took a suede coat and boots, things we cannot get in the Soviet Union. I took her diary and (I don't know what possessed me) her pearl earrings, the ones she wore so often.

I did not know what he had done to her, I swear. I was so proud of her strength and I felt she had convinced them to leave her alone.

When I heard later, that she was dead—I do not know what to say to you now, Norman. Except that I am very, very sorry.

They made me come back to Russia that autumn, and I have never returned to North America. I was questioned about Anna many times but gave them nothing, and as far as I know, she is living out her life in Canada.

I hid Susan's diary.

They did not appreciate that I could not help them get Anna back and sent me to a labor camp shortly after I returned. Twenty years.

As you probably know, we have more freedoms in Russia now. As soon as I could, I got Susan's diary ready to send to you. You are the one who should have it.

No one hunts for Anna anymore, but I will always look over my shoulder.

Goodbye, my friend,

Mikhail

Chapter 26

Lillian passed a sleepless night after that. Who wouldn't? Even someone not seventy-seven years old with a lifetime of conquering insomnia would find it hard to settle their mind after reading that letter.

She could barely wait for the sun to rise before calling Chelan. She'd tapped five of the digits before she realized it would be only 4 a.m. on the west coast. Not kind, especially if the little ones had had a busy night. Lillian called Joyce instead and told her about Mikhail's letter. There still had been no progress on locating Glenda, Penny or Rhonda—and perhaps they'd never find them.

For now, it would be enough for Lillian if she managed to make contact with Mikhail.

When her kitchen clock ticked over to 10 a.m., Lillian got on the phone to Chelan.

"Chelan, I want to follow up on the information you found about online."

"Okay, will do," Chelan said. "I have an email address for him and I can try to set up a video chat."

"Where is he?"

"I don't really know. The address I have is just email. There was nothing else."

"That's alright, email is good."

"I'll let you know when it's set up. The time zones complicate it. They have eleven there."

"I'll be ready to go whenever it is," Lillian said. There was no way she was taking a pass on this conversation, if it could happen.

***

It took Chelan three days, but Lillian logged into her computer one morning to see an email announcing that her young friend had found Mikhail and arranged a call. Lillian should be at her laptop and logged into the website Chelan had linked.

This blows my mind, Lillian thought. Tens of thousands of miles around the world, into a country as foreign to her as Mars. With the help of this keyboard and this little screen, digital blips could reach into Mikhail Kogonov's world and life, demanding that he speak to a woman he barely knew. And with this face technology, she could demand that he look her in the eye and answer her questions about that morning long ago.

She sent Chelan a reply email. *How were you ever able to find this? And him?*

Tricks of the reporter trade, Chelan typed. *Good luck.*

The time came. Lillian clicked on the link—and it was magic. There on a screen, from all those miles away, was Mikhail Kogonov. Fifty-five years older, but recognizable. He had a small, white goatee combed into a point under his chin and a head of hair still as full and wavy as when he was a young student. His skin looked as if it belonged to a person who had spent many hours and years in the sun, and his nose looked as if it belonged to a drinker.

"Hello." he said.

"Hello." It was all she could manage.

He narrowed his eyes. "Lillian? Lillian Clarkson?"

"Yes, it's me. Lillian Howe is my name now."

"You have changed."

"It's been a long time."

Mikhail stared at her image for a full minute before nodding. "Yes, I believe it is you. Maybe we should have a test. What was your band, with Des and Susan?"

Lillian thought this was a good idea. "Mountain Sky. And what was the name of Susan's advisor at the university?"

"Dr. Berman. Who did we see at the Mariposa Folk Festival that summer?"

"Buffy Sainte-Marie and Gordon Lightfoot. Who did we see at the Half Beat Club?"

"Joni Anderson." Lillian sat back in her desk chair. It was like a rapid round of *Jeopardy.* "I'd forgotten that you came to see folk music with us."

"I liked all kinds of music. I read, after I left Toronto, that the Purple Onion closed the next year. But there was another good one, The Riverboat. I always meant to return, to visit that one, but it was not possible."

"All kinds of music, you liked," Lillian said. "Susan told me. Classical music was also on your radar."

Mikhail smiled. "And now we come to it. Yes. Classical music and the violin. And my sister, Anna."

"I read about her in Susan's diary."

"She helped me save her. She promised me that she would tell no one about Anna, but I was always afraid that she would write something down. And as it turned out, she did. I found that out when we took her things."

Lillian swallowed. "You sent the diary to Susan's brother."

"Yes, and then he sent it to you?"

Lillian nodded. "And then I found your letter to Norman. I don't think he ever saw it."

"That is unfortunate."

"I still have many questions."

"Of course. I understand," Mikhail said. "Let me begin by telling you, as I told Norman in the letter, I am so, so very sorry. It began with me asking Susan to hide Anna just for a few days. I did not tell Pavel Andreyevitch, but somehow, he sensed that something was going on. They had been hunting for Anna all over Toronto and Montreal."

"They?"

"KGB. They knew all about my life, too, except about my Canadian girlfriend. They knew that Susan and I were friends, but that was all, at first. Later, she cared enough about me to help me in that way. Susan and I got Anna on the train to Ottawa, and we could breathe for a few days."

Mikhail took a drink from a glass, then went on. "Pavel followed me to Susan's office at the university one day and I had to tell him all about her. He thought it was a good contact I had made, that it might be useful, he said. He wanted to know all about Susan, what she studied, what she thought, and what she did when she wasn't with me. We followed her for a few days and he was very impressed by her interview in the newspaper and her invitation to be on a radio station."

Mikhail stopped talking, and Lillian waited him out. Don't be too afraid of dead air in an interview, Candace, the producer had once told her. Listen to people.

"I did not know what Pavel had planned," Mikhail said. "When he followed her into that studio and came out alone, I did not know. I did not know until I heard the reports that she had been found dead. To this day, I do not know exactly what happened."

"You never asked him?"

Mikhail shook his head. "We were not alone again, except for a few minutes in the airport lounge before he put me on the plane back to Moscow. I did not ask. He frightened me then."

"He doesn't frighten you now?"

"He is dead. Executed, I have heard."

"So, if there was an opportunity to find out exactly what happened . . . whether he struck her, whether she refused to tell him anything about Anna, whether he intended all along to kill her . . . that is gone." Lillian was becoming upset.

"I do not know those things and my chance to ask him, and put to rest all our curiosity, is gone forever now, yes."

"What about right after? Or when you first got back to Russia?"

A shadow passed over Mikhail's eyes and he took his time in answering. "I was sent to labor camp when I returned home. Twenty years in prison."

"For what?" Lillian asked.

Mikhail shrugged. "It does not matter. There was a charge of some kind, and I was sent east. In those days, family members of traitors were also sent away, and my father was incarcerated for seven years. They continued to question me periodically about Anna's defection, but I did not ever tell."

"She is still in Canada, you know. She's been free all these years."

"I had heard, in the years after I was released. For that, I am grateful."

"Have you ever tried to see her? Communicated with her?"

Mikhail shook his head. "Her life is elsewhere now. Why would she want to see or know me? I am not worth her time."

"You are the one who helped her get away."

"It was not enough to do. It was one small drop of rain in a desert."

"Compared to what happened to Susan?"

He nodded. "I led Pavel to her, and I did not prevent what happened. There is no looking away."

His face crumpled, and Lillian was afraid he would cry. She had the answers she needed now, but she didn't want to end the call. What else could she say or ask, to keep him on the screen?

"You said in the letter to Norman that you and Pavel had broken into her apartment. I understand why you took her earrings, but why did you take her coat and boots?"

"That was Pavel. He wanted them to send to his girlfriend back home in Kirov. You couldn't get anything like that then, in the Soviet Union. The earrings, I wanted because she wore them almost every day. Her diary I took because we thought there might be something in there that would lead the Canadian authorities to us."

Mikhail sipped at his glass of water (or perhaps, vodka) and then pulled his lips into a tight smile. "And it turned out to lead you to me, even though it was Norman to whom I was sending it."

"How do you feel about that?" Lillian asked.

"I am not unhappy that he sent it, although I do not know why he sent it to you. Do you?"

Lillian shook her head. "Maybe, because he knew that Susan and I had fallen out a bit, in those last months, and he thought I felt badly about that. And I did, for years. Maybe, he guessed I felt that I should have been able to prevent her death. Maybe, he just couldn't find any of our other friends."

"In truth, it does feel good to speak about it." Mikhail seemed drowsy, and his voice was dropping to a whisper. "I have lived with this responsibility for so many years now that it has poisoned me. I know what it is to carry my conscience like an evil creature inside. There was no one to whom I could speak of Susan. Or Anna. Even my father, I could not speak to him. He was able to endure every question and because he truly had no answers, eventually they left him alone. But they always watched him, as they always watched me."

"And what exactly happened to Pavel?"

"After my trial and his testimony, I was put on the train and I did not see anybody that I knew for many years. After I was out, I asked my father if he had ever heard, and he said that Pavel Andreyevitch had disappeared. There were whispers he had been named as a spy and executed. But we did not know for sure."

Lillian took a few deep breaths. It was a lot to take in.

"Why did you decide to send the diary to Susan's brother?"

"I knew that he still grieved. As I did. I had had the comfort of taking the journal out from its hiding place after I was released, and looking at it from time to time. I wanted to share that and so I sent it to him."

He was tiring. She could see it in his eyes and in the slump of his shoulders, and she felt that she probably wouldn't get many more minutes of his time. She was so grateful to Chelan that she'd been able to use this technology to see Mikhail and get many of her questions answered. She no longer felt the crushing weight of self-blame mixed with resentment and defensiveness that she'd felt for years whenever she thought of Susan Taylor.

But she still felt that the chapter in her life was unfinished.

"How do you live with it, Mikhail?" she asked.

His face almost seemed to move perceptibly downward, each wrinkle and jowl sinking with the effects of gravity and fatigue. "I have done my time. I will live here in Omsk, in this apartment, with no family. Old man. I did not save her, but I did not kill her either. I did not save her, it is true. But I spent twenty years in prison for that."

Lillian felt a sudden blaze of rage. "It was not long enough."

Chapter 27

The sun was just rising as Lillian took her coffee out onto the balcony, her dog strolling along behind her. Usually, Carl was the first one awake, and he looked a bit confused about why they were up so early. She patted him instead of speaking; voices carried on the open air and she didn't want to disturb any of her neighbors.

They were just back from a trip to Miami to visit her grandson. As usual, his life was busy with work on the boat, family comings and goings, and now, a new hobby. After lunch, he disappeared for a while, and Hailey sent Lillian to the garage to find him.

She'd peered around the corner of the garage door and saw Donovan's back. He sat in front of a bench, but it wasn't a work bench.

"Test, one, two, three," he said.

No sign of screwdrivers, hammers, or pliers—instead, she saw a hook holding a pair of headphones, a microphone suspended on a boom arm, and a laptop computer plugged into the mic, the headphones, and the wall. He faced three short panels, lined with some sort of fabric or foam and linked by hinges.

It was a radio studio, built right here in his own garage.

She crept in as quietly as she could, but somehow, he sensed her and turned around. "Grandma! Hey, I'm glad you came out to take a look."

"Donovan, this is amazing. I know you told me you'd set up for podcasting in your garage, but I didn't really picture this. I didn't know what to picture."

"It was the most soundproof place I could find," he said. "I tried a spot in the spare bedroom and then I tried a closet, like I read online that some people do. But this is better, and the sound seems to be fine."

"I am so impressed!"

"That means a lot, coming from you," Donovan said. "Let me show you around. I use the computer for all the recording, editing, mixing, and mastering. Microphone . . . this probably looks familiar to you. And headphones?"

He took them down from their hook and placed them over her ears. She laughed.

"Are you setting me up to do your work for you?"

He grinned. "No, I have plans to use all this gear for myself. I'm going to talk about the manatees, and any other endangered wildlife I'm concerned about. Climate change. The oceans. Pollution. I'm putting myself on the air," Donovan said. "Do you listen to podcasts?"

"I never have," Lillian said. "Tell me how to do it."

***

This morning, she set her phone on the balcony table and opened the app that Donovan had installed for her last night. The screen lit up with dozens of topics and categories. Where to start?

She typed "The 1960s" into the search bar and hundreds of shows appeared. She clicked on the category History and what must have been every era of the entire past surfaced. She entered Toronto in the search bar and saw the podcast version of dozens of radio and TV broadcasts.

The True Crime and Self-Improvement categories were brimming with stories and subjects she was eager to dive into.

But before she entered this exciting new world of podcasts, she wanted to spend one last afternoon remembering Susan. A sort of memorial service, all on her own. Then, she was going to put those days behind her, once and for all.

Lillian opened an ancient photo album. Photos of Penny on a ride at the Exhibition, of Glenda on a swing in a park, and of Rhonda at the New York World's Fair. She and Chelan had not been able to locate any of the women. So far.

Joyce's long blonde hair blew around her face on a windy day in front of the Chateau Laurier hotel. Lillian carefully took the photograph out from its corners and set it aside to show to Joyce later.

Of all the photos she had of girlfriends from her past, the most were of Susan. Lillian stared at the shots from their childhood days, in pigtails and bare feet in Albany, from their teenage years, hair combed long and as straight as they could get it, and from their twenties in Toronto, on stage with *Mountain Sky.*

Lillian brushed away a tear, then closed the album. *Goodbye, Susan.*

She picked up the diary and stared at it for a moment. What should she do with this? There was no one else left in Susan's family who might want it. Lillian decided to put it away with the album, just in case she was ever able to find Rhonda, Penny, or Glenda.

Susan had died young—very young—because she helped somebody. Did that mean it was a bad idea to ever help anyone? How much of Lillian's life had she spent, actually helping anyone? When she was working in news, at twenty-two, she thought she was important, that she was helping to save the world. But what did she do, really? Nothing, compared to Susan, who had made her home available, in service to Anna and Mikhail. And ultimately paid for it with her life.

Lillian knew, too, that she had come a long way in forgiving herself for not being there to prevent Susan's death and to save her. Now that she knew so much more about the events that morning and the kind of people that Susan had been dealing with, Lillian was even less confident that she could have made a difference.

But there was still a tiny sliver of guilt, wedged somewhere in her heart, and she knew she had more work to do, to get it out.

She had this feeling that she needed to do something to help someone else, somehow.

She needed to hear more from these podcasts about self-improvement and self-care.

Somehow, she had to bring an end to this story that began fifty-five years back. Make a change in herself.

Even at seventy-seven, she had miles to go.

***

AUTHOR'S NOTE

Thank you so much for reading *Red Herrings Radio!* I hope you enjoyed it.

I'd like to thank everyone who read portions of the book while it was in the story and early draft stages, and the numerous writers and radio professionals, past and current, whose advice, experience, and insight I absorbed while on my own journey through radio, as a listener in the 60s, and as a reporter, show host and interviewer in the 70s, 80s and 90s.

Special thanks to my husband, David. For everything.

A couple of historical notes you might find interesting:
- *Toast and Jamboree* was the name of a real CBC Radio show from the 1940s.
- The 1964 U.S. Surgeon General report was pivotal in establishing that cigarette smoking causes lung cancer, and

led to the warnings that all tobacco companies were required to put on cigarette packages.

- Many terms used in 1964 have fallen out of favor and are inappropriate today. I've used several in the novel to add to the authenticity of the novel: waitress, stewardess, ladies room.

This is the sixth book in my Media Mysteries series and I'd like to invite you to check out the others, which are set in TV, movie, community newspaper, social media, and book publishing worlds.

You can find paperback and ebook editions of the six Media Mysteries at your favorite online bookstore. If you'd like to stay in touch, please sign up for my newsletter at my website or at the WindWord Group website.

www.ingramcontent.com/pod-product-compliance
Lightning Source LLC
Chambersburg PA
CBHW072258130726
47910CB00012B/2114